Chick for a day

what would

you do if

you were one?

Fiona Giles, editor

SIMON & SCHUSTER

new york   london

sydney   singapore

SIMON & SCHUSTER
Rockefeller Center
1230 Avenue of the Americas
New York, NY 10020

Designed by Karolina Harris
Manufactured in the United States of America

10   9   8   7   6   5   4   3   2   1

Library of Congress Cataloging-in-Publication Data
Chick for day : what would you do if you were one / Fiona Giles, editor.
    p. cm.
1. Women—Sexual behavior—Literary collections. 2. Gender identity—Literary collections. 3. American literature—Men authors. 4. Erotic literature, American. I. Giles, Fiona.
PS509.W6 C48 2000
810.8'03538'082—dc21   99-057826
ISBN 0-684-85517-8

"Pig-Family Game," copyright © 1999 Robert Peters, first published in Poems: Selected and New 1967–1991, Asylum Arts Press, 1992.
"The Major Wants to Adopt the Girls," copyright © 1999 Tad Richards.
Episode 17 of Situations, an epic newsletter sent to subscribers of Old Mole Press.
"Ineluctable Modality of the Vaginal," copyright © 1999 by Rick Moody. First published in Lit, Summer 1999.
"Joe Gets Blunzed," copyright © 1999 Rudy Rucker, adapted from Master of Time and Space, Bluejay Books, 1984.
"Breast Men," copyright © 1999 Bill Bozzone, based on the play Breast Men, by Bill Bozzone and Joe DiPietro.
"The Mangina," copyright © 1999 Jonathan Ames, first published in two parts by NY Press, 1998.

Acknowledgments

his collection would have been nowhere near as rich and strange without the generosity of Janice Eidus, who freely opened her book of one thousand friends to me. Others who offered contacts, recommended contributors, and provided support and encouragement include Lyn Lifshin, Rick Peabody, Janyce Stefan-Cole, Alexander Laurence, Bruce Bauman, Michael Hathaway, William Levy, Rick Moody, Trish Warden, Robert Peters, Ginu Kamani, Fiona Inglis, Courtney Gibson, and Andy Nehl. Gretel Killeen deserves credit for suggesting the title.

I would also like to thank the many writers who contributed work that could not be included. In only a few months I received enough material to fill several volumes; inevitably many worthy contenders were left out. To those who are included, I am grateful for your wonderfully diverse stories, essays, and poems, and for your patience, encouragement, and all-round agreeability.

At Simon & Schuster in New York, David Rosenthal, Marysue Rucci, Nicole Graev, Victoria Meyer, Veronica

Jordan, Cindy Hamel, and Zoe Wolff all in their separate ways helped, encouraged, aided and abetted, and accommodated me as an editor in a far-off land. Also in New York, my agent Elaine Markson has been crucial to keeping me plugged in. At home, my partner Richard Andrews and my friend Lisa Hill have each watched out for me with love.

For Brodie and Hugo

Contents

Introduction

Fiona Giles

n*early* thirty years ago, in 1972, the editors of *Suck,* an English-language magazine published in Holland, put together a special issue called "The Virgin Sperm Dancer." Written by William Levy, whose poem "All" appears in this anthology, it is a large-format black-and-white collage of images and text which tells the story of Joopie, a young Dutchman who has the good fortune of becoming a woman for a single day.

Blessed with "the kind of body I always wanted to fuck," Joopie embarks on "an ecstatic journey" around Amsterdam. After masturbating in her bed at home, she applies too much red lipstick, wraps a long velvet maxicoat around her naked body, and laces up her knee-high boots. With a "dildo buzzing in [her] new cunt," she sets out into the world, steadying herself against a lamppost as she comes in the street, seducing a man on a bench in Vondelpark, interviewing a male prostitute about his trade, and having her photo taken in a window in the red-light district. She masturbates in various public places, has sex with a woman, seduces "a couple in white," whom she takes to her party, and is finally fucked by a man before turning back into a boy.

"The Virgin Sperm Dancer" is told not as a single, continuous story, but as a collection of accounts pieced together like a puzzle that doesn't form a coherent whole. It has several different narrators and it uses a variety of materials—photographs, maps, diaries, interviews, newspaper cuttings, quotations. Not unlike sexuality itself, the story of Joopie resists confinement to a single category. Not unlike a cunt, it has a disorderly quality that suggests layers of meaning and contradictory truths. And not unlike good sex, it combines arousal with insight based on a narrative fantasy.

Chick for a Day is also a puzzle, an anthology combining different stories into a whole that doesn't fit seamlessly together, and which exceeds its boundaries. Like its predecessor *Dick for a Day*, in which women imagined becoming men for a day, the contributors were invited to submit stories, essays, and poems about what a man might do if transformed into a woman for twenty-four hours. Unlike its predecessor, it turned out that a day just wasn't enough. Whereas many of the women welcomed their midnight release from the shackles of testosterone, many of the men are saddened by their return to maleness. Although most contributors heroically confined themselves to twenty-four orgiastic hours or less, others insisted on a looser interpretation as if to acknowledge that a woman's body doesn't fit its rhythms into this tight time frame. Bernard Cohen's character gives birth in "Go With the Flow" as does Robert Peters's pig in "Pig-Family Game"; in Kevin Downs's "The Duke and the Duchess," John Wayne has sex-change surgery over several days.

Perhaps the most obvious way in which this anthology differs from *Dick for a Day* is that the idea of men becoming women is more commonplace in our culture than that of women becoming men. In literature, there is the occasional example of a woman character disguising herself as a man to achieve her ambitions, or to avoid harassment; in real life, there are many fewer candidates for female-to-male reassignment surgery than there are male-to-female candidates. And although there is a nascent drag king culture in lesbian communities, it is still obscure compared to gay male parades and performances by drag queens. In contemporary literary fiction, John Updike has written about the metamorphosis of sex in his poem "Cunts," while Philip Roth has written a Kafkaesque novella, *The Breast,* in which a middle-aged male academic wakes up to discover he has become an enormous female breast. Hollywood has had a veritable obsession with the fantasy of male transformation, from *Some Like It Hot* to *Birdcage.* In vaudeville, the dressing up of men in women's clothing must qualify as the world's longest running gag, which still exists in Britain and Australia in the character of Barry Humphries's Dame Edna Everage. And this is not to mention the long and rich tradition of male cross-dressers, from the heterosexual rummaging through his partner's wardrobe to the fully fledged gay transvestite, of which Ru Paul is perhaps the leading contemporary example—and proof of just how acceptable the theater of cross-dressing has become.

At the same time, it has for the past few decades been considered normal, and sometimes sexy, for women to dress like men. Male attire often has the effect of making women look more serious, more businesslike, more powerful. While it has been less common for men to adopt the female uniform, those who have done so are usually onstage, knowing that it's a traditional shortcut to a good laugh. This has been the challenge for the anthology. For women to put on maleness is merely to blend in, to be accepted, to realize freedom. If the costume is exaggerated, it is to accept a carnivalesque opportunity to parody the more powerful sex. For men to put on femaleness is to stand out as comically shocking, or at least flamboyantly frivolous. If the female costume is exaggerated, this is funny not because women are powerful but because womanhood appears to be an inherently risible option within patriarchy.

Although many contributors to *Chick for a Day* took the opportunity to dress up, get down, and sashay out, the majority of writers have sought to bypass the stereotypes. They all show, in their different ways, a genuine interest in exploring what it's really like underneath the costumes and conventions. At the same time, clothes are crucial to many of the stories, and the act of dressing becomes one of the most satisfying and significant parts of the day. Alexandre Rockwell's "Spinach Dress" is about a dress as a badge of belonging to the girl club that was a family; in Rick Moody's "Ineluctable Modality of the Vaginal" it is the adolescent boy's experience of being dressed as a girl that allows the grown man to claim a female affinity; Jeremy Reed's alter ego in "Dream On" relishes the opportunity to dress in his sister's black seamed stockings and suspender belt under a tight skirt; Justin Chin's "Marianne Faithfull's Cunt" puts Victoria's Secret lingerie to good use; and nearly every writer who dresses his character knows the importance of shoes—from wobbly Gucci's to knee-high Doc Marten's. But many contributors opt for a normal outfit for their special day. Rudy Rucker's Joe initially plays out his fantasy of being a Monroe-esque vamp but he soon abandons this for a more subtle uniform that suits his wife as well as his purposes of evading the authorities. The appeal of Joe's disguise is that the female form offers endless potential for transformation, through hairdressing, makeup, and a wide variety of dress styles. In almost every case there is an avoidance of drag so that each writer dreams his character into a more-or-less real world, testing the clash between the fantasy of sexual transformation and the demands of the everyday.

If the two anthologies had been conducted as a survey in other-sex envy among heterosexuals, the large number of contributions I received for *Chick for a Day* and the positive tone of the stories would confirm that there are many more

men wanting to be women than there are women who want
to be men. My initial fear for this book was that men are already famous for denigrating women and have easy access to
superior cultural firepower, so there is surely little need to
provide them with further opportunity for satire. But I believe there is a place for satire against female pieties, feminine excesses, and feminist sacred cows. Moreover, I was
interested in exploring the diversity of male fantasies of
woman-time, from the militantly heterosexual to the wildly
gay, and the many permutations in between.

As it turned out, the contributions were almost entirely
reverential, and even where there is some satire, for example in Alfred Vitale's "So Much To Do and So Little Time,"
it is mostly at male expense. Furthermore, many of the stories indicate a desire to experience the particular forms of
suffering identified with women. In the poem "My Lady"
Bill Buege depicts the loneliness and touching decrepitude
of an aging woman. Bruce Bauman's "The Newly Born
Man" delves into the dark heart of female reproductive
calamity, while the even darker piece by Ian Kerkhof,
"Sometimes It Ain't Easy Being a Gal," confronts the grisly
reality of rape and sexual abuse in the context of South
African race wars.

There is also an endearing recurrence of the hope that
womanhood is better than the trap of maleness—even if, or
perhaps because, it is perceived to be harder. This is not just
a quaint belief that women still occupy the high moral
ground. Without giving away any endings, several stories
(and many more that I received but couldn't include) play
with the idea that lesbianism is preferable to straight sex for
both temporary and permanent women. One author has the
protagonist lose his girlfriend to another woman after she's
tasted lesbian sex.

Brian Bouldrey's reflective and autobiographical essay
"Monster" considers the way in which women live as spectacle—with being, as a matter of course, watched through-

out life—and how this might contribute to a degree of social responsibility. He argues that men need to be forced out of their uniforms of maleness, and dare to be seen. For Bouldrey, becoming a woman is to learn how to become visible, hence to be a man "at [his] best."

The idea that becoming a woman brings out the best in a man points to another crucial difference between the two anthologies. With one or two exceptions, the women in *Dick for a Day* adopted and then ultimately rejected maleness as resolutely foreign. In contrast, the men in *Chick for a Day* often use the opportunity to prove the existence of a repressed womanhood already within. At first glance this might appear as an arrogant belief that woman is a subset of man. Or it might be a confusion of having and being, as Rucker's character discovers when he risks losing his wife by becoming female. Perhaps it is a way of romanticizing what are perceived to be male inadequacies—that is, they're not male at all. Perhaps it is a form of Pygmalionism: the ideal woman as a more perfect version of its creator. Or perhaps it reveals a desire for the sexes to dissolve all difference and be joined together again like the composite third sex in Aristophanes's speech to Plato's *Symposium*. Whatever the origins of the ghostly interior female, Richard Foerster's poem "Tiresias at Evening" seems to extend an invitation on behalf of all the contributors: to "open to these words and feel/each syllable thrust inside your hidden self."

In describing the nature of difference between the sexes, two stories, Rick Moody's "Ineluctable Modality of the Vaginal" and Ron Sukenick's "Womanizer," stand like goal posts at either end of the field of possibilities. Moody's story acts as a cautionary tale to the romantic fantasy of understanding sexual difference even with the best intentions and the most sophisticated analytic tools. It suggests that the struggle to acknowledge difference, to see it clearly, is as great a challenge as the struggle to understand it. From the male point of view, the female has an ironic impenetrability, no matter how attentively he orbits. Sukenick's story gives free rein to the postmodern dream of an endless play of identities, creating a joyful erotic fantasy that combines the sensibility of Donna Haraway with Henry Miller.

In all these stories, poems, and essays, the question is asked: in what ways is it possible for a man to imagine the vagina and how does this attempt at imagining change things? Plausible or not, the effort to extrapolate meaning from sexual longing, to achieve, as Rucker writes, "A supreme merging with the object of desire," lends hope to the wish of mutual understanding.

The Duke
and the
Duchess

Kevin Downs

howdy, pilgrim, it's the Duke here. From *The Searchers* to *Sands of Iwo Jima* nobody defines macho as much as me. But it's time I 'fess up and admit that I was much more sensitive in real life. See, fact is, I've always felt more like a woman than a man inside. Now I'm no pansy, mind you, and any punk fool enough to say so is lookin' for a whuppin' they'll never forget. It's just that I prefer the smell of perfume to trail dust, and under my army fatigues I enjoy wearing nothing more than a pair of sexy lace panties.

It's the reason why I did my best work in movies directed by John Ford. I loved the man. Not like a man loves another man, but like a woman loves a man. I wanted to cook his meals, raise his young 'uns, and do whatever else it took to please him. Were my feelings unrequited? A conversation we once had when his old lady was threatenin' to file for divorce leads me to believe otherwise.

"Duke," he declared, "you ever think if a broad was more like a fella the world would be a lot better place?"

"Nope, Big John," I lied. "What in tarnation makes you say a thing like that for?"

"I mean, we'd take a bullet for each other any day, right?" he explained. "But a broad? Shit. You can't trust 'em as far as you can throw 'em."

"Then maybe we oughtta get hitched?" I answered back, trying hard not to sound too excited.

"Wouldn't that be a sight!" He guffawed. "Tell you what. Grow yourself some sweater steaks and cut off that lasso hangin' 'tween your legs and you got a deal."

Sure, we were just joshin'. But inside I knew he was right. I'd never have a shot at a man like him looking as I did. Trouble was sex-change operations were as scarce as hens' teeth in my day. So when I heard about a top-secret experiment the Pentagon was conducting I nearly jumped for joy. Its code name was Project Sheehy. And its objective was to win the arms race by building the first nonphallic weapons of mass destruction. How? By implanting a woman's sex organs on a male volunteer who would then brainstorm such ideas with a team of munitions engineers.

My sources at the Pentagon, many of whom I met as consultants on the set of *Operation Pacific*, filled me in on the details. The brass was tired of bombs that shot off their wad and were then left useless. They wanted something capable of multiple explosions. A weapon so seductive that all the Japs, Chinks, Injuns, and other Commie types might actually want to have their asses blown into oblivion by its force.

Now if I'd been running the show, I'd simply have hired some no-nonsense broad like Barbara Stanwyck to handle it all and been done with it. But the thought of a dame calling the shots was too much for those four-star generals to bear. So they came up with a line of b.s. about how a woman's motherly instinct might render their entire scheme a wash and moved forward with looking for a man.

Surprisingly, I wasn't the only one feeling a little androgynous back then. And the initial request for applicants turned into a cattle call the likes of which I hadn't seen since the old days at R.K.O. A lifetime of celebrity has its rewards, however, and when I made my interest known, the brass fell starstruck. The Secretary of Defense, who was spearheading the project with the Surgeon General, had only one concern. Did I have enough killer instinct? They weren't out to just reinvent the shotgun. They wanted something that could put a hole in the ground the size of Wyoming if need be. I reminded him that in my last three pictures I'd racked up a body count greater than the population of most small countries. From then on, all systems were go.

The operation itself was a grueling ordeal that would have killed a lesser man. But I'm one tough hombre, and it was going to take more than a bunch of city slickers to put me six feet under. Now what actually took place during surgery I have no idea. They'd given me enough anesthesia to knock out a horse, and it was almost as if I blinked and then woke up in my hospital bed.

"You came through it like a champ," the Surgeon General was boasting as he stood by my side.

"Those Russkie bastards are in for it now," the Secretary of Defense chimed in from nearby.

The two continued to gloat, but my mind was on only one thing. After a lifetime spent living a lie, the woman inside me was free at last. I could barely wait to explore the new me, so I pretended to fall asleep, and, after a few moments, they tiptoed out of the room.

My hands were trembling with excitement as I slid them down my chest. There they were, exactly as I'd ordered, two big knockers just like Jane Russell's. The temptation to caress what waited below grew too great to resist. I plunged my hands down to my crotch, but froze in horror at what I discovered. I couldn't find my vagina anywhere. Worse than that, the bastards had forgotten to cut off my six-shooter.

I started screaming bloody murder. An intern rushed in calling for help. Four others hurried to his aide. Fists began to fly. I sent one intern through a window, another through a wall. It looked as if they were about to turn tail and run, but two big orderlies joined in, and they finally managed to sedate me. I woke up hours later with the Secretary of Defense and Surgeon General standing over my bedside again.

"Violence won't solve anything, Mr. Wayne," the Secretary was saying.

"We gave you the reproductive system of a woman just like we promised," the Surgeon General added.

"We just don't think it's in the best interest of the nation to implant it in the obvious place for now," the Secretary concluded.

Where the hell did they put it then? My hand groped frantically under the sheets looking for any sign of my maidenhood. The men took pity on me, and with the help of a hand mirror, showed me the back of my head. There, barely visible under my thinning hair, was the fleshy crack of my new vagina. I could hardly believe it. What was I supposed to do? Hide it under my cowboy hat?

Crestfallen, I slumped back into bed as they tried to explain. They began by telling me their research had indicated the skull as the best location for my vagina considering the thought process Project Sheehy required.

It would remain there for a month or two at most, they continued. They would relocate it to its proper position when we entered the project's final phase.

It was all bullshit. I knew the real reason why they didn't put my love hole where it belonged. They feared the sexy broad in me, as men have feared sexy broads throughout the centuries, and I'd have been too hot for them to handle as a dame. But if the Feds wanted to pull a fast one, they'd picked the wrong girl to push around. So I threatened to go public with Project Sheehy if they didn't finish what they started. If that didn't work, I threatened to shove a grenade up their assholes and blast 'em both to kingdom come.

You never saw a pair of varmints turn yellow so fast in your life. They swore they'd complete my sex change immediately after I finished working with their design team. They'd put it on the fast track. It would take no more than a couple of weeks, they insisted.

A couple of weeks? I could last that long I figured. Hell, what else could I do? Walk around with my snatch in my head for the rest of my life?

I closed my eyes and imagined John Ford and me walking down a beach in Malibu. There was nothing abnormal about us being together like that. It was just a man and his woman out for a leisurely stroll.

"Girl," he was saying, "ever since you got your parts fixed, I've been wonderin' what I should call you. Duke just don't seem to fit anymore."

"Shucks," I casually answered back. "How's Mrs. John Ford sound to you?"

"That's a given," he stated matter-of-factly. "But I was thinkin' of something less formal. I was thinkin' of calling you my Duchess for now."

As the sun set over the Pacific behind us, he took me in his arms, and we kissed. It was just like the big dramatic moment in one of those romantic tearjerkers I've always loved.

I turned my attention back to the two men standing in my hospital room. In the end, I knew the Feds'd be too chicken-shit to jerk me around again. So for the sake of Big John and me, I agreed to play along for a few more weeks.

The days that followed were far less excitin'. You know the score. Bland grub, uppity nurses, kinfolk you can't stand droppin' by to visit. I almost went loco. Up until the day I found my clitoris, that is. See, much as I hated the way that hole in my head looked, I sure liked the way it felt. It was kind of like breakin' in a skittish filly. Only a filly that never gives out on you. And once she cuts loose into a gallop, if you let her cool off for a spell, she's ready to start buckin' all over again.

From that day on I was happy just to lie in bed and fondle myself for hours on end. But my contentment didn't last long, and I soon became haunted by a hellish fantasy that tormented me both night and day.

The time was the eighteenth century, and I was attending a costume ball at a magnificent palace in England. My dress was cut low to reveal my cleavage, and I disguised myself by holding a small mask over my face. Countless virile men wearing similar masks filled the room. A string quartet was playing. One by one each man would ask me to dance, and then whisk me away to an adjoining chamber where he would begin to seduce me. Then, just as I was about to scream for help, he'd reveal himself. And no matter how different they appeared at first, under their masks they were all the same. They were each John Ford.

Now had this been the end of it I would have had no complaints. But then this fantasy would repeat itself, and its images grew more disturbing. It all began when I made my grand entrance into the palace not knowing my powdered wig was askew and my makeup smeared. Thankfully, no one noticed, and the ball continued as always. But in the next version, I was even harder-looking. And in the version after that one, I was dressed as a cheap saloon girl and everyone was pointing at me.

But what's worse, it wasn't just John Ford revealing himself in the end. First it was Howard Hawks, which wasn't so bad. But then it was Alfred Hitchcock. And then it was Orson Welles. And then it was every two-bit hack you could ever imagine.

Usually I'd come back to my senses about then feelin' somethin' awful. I wasn't even out of the hospital yet, and already I was actin' as if I'd been born in a Tijuana whorehouse. So I took a solemn vow. A vow to be more than some cheap floozy when I got out of that place. I vowed instead to be a true-blue, God-fearin', school-marm type of gal. The kind that would keep the home fires burnin' if a guy had to go overseas and blow away a few hundred gooks or so.

But almost in spite of my promise, that same fantasy continued to plague me. I tried thinkin' about baseball. I tried countin' backwards from a hundred. Nothing would keep that darn thing out of my mind. I'd be more ladylike once I got rid of the old one-eyed rattler I kept sayin' to myself. Until then there was nothing I could do but hang tough.

A few days later it looked as if my wait was over when the Secretary of Defense and Surgeon General entered followed by a flock of young whippersnappers dressed in white lab coats. This I was told would be my design team, and they introduced me to their chief engineer, a puny-looking, milk-fed mama's boy who seemed barely old enough to drive. I was far from impressed, but I shook hands with the runt all the same. And to my surprise, when his hand touched mine, I felt my pillowcase grow a little moist and wet. He seemed so sweet. We even locked eyes, but the moment quickly passed when I sized him up next to John Ford. One was the greatest director of all time; the other a mere half-pint who didn't own a pot to piss in or window to throw it out of. Naturally, I wrote the whole thing off as just a passing fancy.

The very next morning they wheeled me down to a conference room where the kid and design team were waiting for me. Sure, I caught the little shit making goo-goo eyes again, but I ignored him and went straight to work. For hours on end I brainstormed pussy-inspired weapons of mass destruction the likes of which the world has never seen.

I began with *The Flying Lips*, a fighter jet with a huge envelope on its nose that could swallow an entire division of enemy soldiers. Next came *The Pink Cloud,* a gigantic atomizer that sprayed a deadly, sweet-smelling nerve gas over a hundred-square-mile radius. Last was my greatest creation, *The Black Iris,* a massive satellite that looked like a flower, but this flower could engulf and destroy any atomic device directed at the United States from outer space.

The design team and I then called it quits for the day and made plans to meet again in the morning. If I kept going at this rate my pocket rocket would be floating in alcohol in no time, I thought to myself. But as I watched the last of those white lab coats exit the room, I felt someone begin to massage my shoulders, and I knew I wasn't home-free yet. The shifty-eyed chief engineer had gotten the drop on me when I wasn't looking.

"Your ass has been driving me wild ever since they wheeled you in today," he purred.

"Hold on, punk," I objected. "I already got me a man, a good one I don't plan on runnin' around on."

"I'm not askin' for your hand in marriage," he cooed, "just a little something to tide me over for now."

I nearly coldcocked the son-of-a-bitch, but that massage was feelin' pretty good so I let him slide. Then he started sweet-talkin' me. He told me how turned on he got when he saw me in *Stagecoach.* Then he told me how intelligent I was, and how he loved me for more than just my body.

Now I'd always planned to give myself to no one but Big John. Was I going to throw it all away on some two-timing Romeo I'd only known since yesterday? My mouth said no, but my body said yes, and the next thing I knew that boy and I were goin' at it like a couple of jackrabbits. And it wasn't just a one time thing. We gave new meaning to the expression *giving head* every night that week.

My work on Project Sheehy wasn't worth a plugged nickel after that. Word started to spread that I was easy, and I lost all self-respect. Not just because of my affair with the kid; more shameful to me was the fact that I'd also started cheatin' on him whenever I got the chance. No one was safe from my charms. Not even the janitor who mopped up the hallway at night.

In the past, when I used to picture myself as a woman, I'd always see John Ford and me living on the outskirts of some small midwestern town. Every evening, there I'd be, standing on our porch wearing a plain gingham dress, waiting for him to return from a hard day spent in the cornfields. First, I'd serve him a big plate of vittles. Then, we'd read from the Bible until it grew too dark to see. Later, as we lay sleeping, he'd rest his calloused hands on my back, and I'd feel safe and secure. Our world was good and pure, just as I always dreamed it would be.

But picturin's one thing, and bein's another, and if there'd been any justice at that hospital, they'd have ridden me out the door on a rail. So when the Pentagon pulled the plug on Project Sheehy and offered to complete my sex change, I started beggin' and bawlin' like some hog-tied steer to be turned back into a man. See, all my philoso-phizin' aside, I could handle a five-hundred-pound grizzly better'n I could that little pussy. So the next time you find yourself thinkin' how nice and easy life would be just sittin' around lookin' purty all day, I hope you keep this one thing in mind. It takes balls to be a good woman, pilgrim. More balls than I ever had.

Breast Men

Bill Bozzone

*Y*ou would not like my friend Lloyd. He's a bigmouth. A bully. The last guy in the world you would trust with a woman. Still, he is my friend. He got me my position with the City of Trenton Fire Department back in '86. When I have a problem, I turn to Lloyd.

Lloyd, were he here, would clarify something. "Before you continue," Lloyd would say, "we should get one thing straight. I'm a fireman. I'm the guy in the slicker who breaks down the door and carries people to safety. It's my picture you see on the cover of the *Daily News*. You, Stuart, are a dispatcher. You talk on the radio and make coffee. You do not ride on the truck."

This demeanor is nothing new to me. It goes back to high school. Lloyd was the obnoxious athlete everybody despised. I was the squirrelly nebbish they never noticed. Within that silence, we somehow connected. Lloyd liked to tell me my place, and I liked knowing I had one.

Anyway, Lloyd calls me a couple of days ago wanting to know would I be interested in going to the Poconos. The two of us. A guys' weekend. Lloyd's wife, Sarah, recently walked out on him, so it doesn't take me long to put the pieces together. Lloyd's probably had this place reserved for a year. From when Sarah and him were still together. Non-refundable deposit. If he drags me along, he can at least recover half his outlay.

And I have to admit, his timing is good. I needed somebody to talk to, somebody to borrow a substantial sum of money from, and like I mentioned, my realm of friends is not what any dictionary would define as "vast."

"Gynecomastia," the doctor called it the day before Lloyd phoned. "A not uncommon, usually benign condition resulting in enlargement of the male breast." To me, it was boobs. Two small but not unnoticeable lumps, which, for over a month, had been forcing me to make some rather strange clothing choices. Like here it is July and look at me in a cable-knit sweater.

The name of the place is Love Acres. Before we even pull into the reception area, Lloyd admits what I already suspect. That he's stuck with this prepaid weekend package deal, that he'd pictured driving up here with his beloved Sarah, that today is—or would have been—his thirteenth wedding anniversary. "Not that a bitch like Sarah could ever appreciate a place like this," he says with what appears to be a tear running down his cheek.

Behind the desk in the main lodge, a guy with a name-plate identifying himself as "Desmond" gives us a map, a set of keys, and that *look*. You know the one. Can't-you-go-do-this-in-some-homo-bathhouse? That look. He finally directs us to a cottage called "The Cupid II."

"Can you grab the bags?" Lloyd asks me. "I got hand cramps from driving."

Let me say that the word "tacky" does not even begin to describe what we come upon once we're inside. The pink and purple motif, the furry rugs, the tub shaped like a huge champagne glass. Stereo speakers in the headboard of the bed. Not five minutes there, we notice the air-conditioning unit is out. Lloyd calls maintenance and they promise to send somebody over.

"We can hang out at the pool," Lloyd tells me. "Show off our bods."

Time, in other words, is not something I have an ample amount of. So I say to him right off. As soon as we're settled. I go, "Lloyd, I need an operation." He's squeezing into a Speedo, a bathing suit not much bigger than your average coffee filter.

"An operation?" he asks.

"It's going to run about six grand."

"Good thing you got medical insurance. You seen the sunblock?"

"Our medical insurance doesn't cover this," I tell him. "It's considered cosmetic."

"Like a nose job?"

"It's what's called a suction-assisted lipectomy."

"Why are you still wearing a sweater? It's ninety degrees in here."

Finally, I have to come right out and spill it. I say, "I've grown breasts." To which Lloyd goes, "Yeah, right. What's the punch line?"

"I'll show you."

I should perhaps mention at this point that Lloyd, although he can be a crumb, is still totally in love with his wife. His ex-wife. He treated her horribly, but I suppose that's the way certain guys show emotion. I don't know, I'm not an expert in the field. I only bring this up as a possible reason for Lloyd's behavior. Here he is in a place designed for romance, couples walking hand in hand, his Sarah in Baltimore with a guy who cleans roof gutters for a living, and—hey—who knows what passes as acceptable behavior these days?

"Jesus Christ, you've got tits," Lloyd says the second I lift my sweater.

I tell him to please not use that word. That it's considered offensive in some circles.

Lloyd gets real quiet after this. Has a look on his face. Kind of like a dog gets when you hide a biscuit behind your back. Confused, yet hopeful. "Not to worry," he assures me as he zips into a one-piece warm-up suit. "We're going to sit down, we're going to talk this out, we'll have the whole thing ironed out in no time."

I tell him all I need is money, a comment Lloyd chooses not to hear. Instead, he's on his way out the door, out to find beer somewhere. "There's no problem so big it can't be solved over a twelve-pack," he announces just as the screen door slams shut behind him.

The guy from maintenance has the smallest head I'd ever seen. I mean here he is, a normal-sized man who looks to wear like maybe a size 2 hat. I should mention perhaps that he comes upon me in a somewhat embarrassing position. After Lloyd leaves I'm dying from the heat, so I take my sweater off. The maintenance guy walks in without knocking, which gives me just enough time to grab a throw pillow and hold it in front of my chest. He apologizes for the intrusion, claims that when he saw a car pull out he figured the cabin was empty.

"You put me in mind of my wife," he says as he goes to work on the air-conditioning unit. "She does that same kind of thing whenever I walk into a room and catch her without a top on."

"Just a natural reaction."

"I don't know what she's trying to hide," he tells me. "I just wish she'd try and be more like LaToya."

"LaToya?"

"Jackson. She was on the pay-per-view a few nights ago.

'Breast-a-Thon '99.'" I admit to him that I missed that one.
"Too bad," he says. "For forty bucks you got ninety-nine
women—very classy at first, they're all wearing feathers—
then five minutes later they're all topless and it's raining."
He bangs the air-conditioning unit with a wrench, calls it a
piece of shit, keeps right on talking.

Unfortunately for me, there's no way I can get to my
sweater without this guy catching on. So I take a shot. I go,
"Would it possible for you to go out to the machine and
bring me back a Coke?"

"Who are you? Christopher Reeve?" he asks.

"It's just that—"

"You know why guys like breasts so much?" he interrupts.
I shake my head. "Our mothers."

"Now what are you talking about?"

"Think about it," he says. "The woman you'll always love
most. For like two years she provides you with the milk of life.
Then bango. They're gone. Which is okay, because you've got
other interests. Toys, school, baseball—things like that. Then
all of a sudden you hit maybe fourteen and you say, 'Hey, wait
a minute. What happened to those breasts?' And you think,
'Well, I ain't going after my mother's again. That's sick. So I'll
go after every other pair I see.'"

He hits a button and the unit kicks on.

"You here with your wife?" he asks.

"Yeah," I lie.

"Well, enjoy your beautiful lady and her beautiful breasts
in the cool comfort of The Cupid II."

Lloyd comes back about a half-hour later, but he doesn't
seem like himself. Instead of beer, he's got a bottle of white
wine. He's also brought some candles—in case of a power
failure, he says—and some Brie. I tell him about the maintenance guy, figure the story's good for a laugh, but Lloyd
finds little humor.

"What else did you two do while I was gone?" he asks suspiciously.

I go, "Are you serious?"

"I'm sorry," he says. "I'm just a little stressed-out. Open the wine." Lloyd dims the lights, fires up the candles, goes to the stereo. Sinatra music fills the room. "Now then," Lloyd says as he takes a seat next to me on the sofa, "about your 'problem.'"

"I can hardly see my hand in front of me," I tell him. "Maybe we should switch the lights back on."

"Not conducive to serious thought," Lloyd informs me.

"If you could just lend me the six grand, I'd be happy to sign a note saying—"

"Money and friendship do not mix well," Lloyd tells me. "We're buddies," he says, slipping an arm around my shoulders in an effort to prove the point. "Buddies take care of one another far beyond simple monetary matters." He pauses. "Now about these quote/unquote breasts . . ." His hand, I notice, is creeping closer and closer to the source of the problem. "You suppose I could take another gander?"

"This is too weird," I say as I get up and flip the lights on. "If I didn't know any better, I'd think you were trying to . . . you know."

Lloyd is on his feet. Red-faced. Maybe from embarrassment, maybe from something else. He digs a sheet of paper from the pocket of his warm-up suit and he holds it out to me. "Read it," he says.

It's a poem. A bad poem. About love and longing and desire. I notice he's actually tried to rhyme "fondness" with "magic wandness."

"I wrote that while I was out," Lloyd admits. "You can even sing it to the theme song from *Gilligan's Island*. I'd like you to have it."

Okay. At this juncture I must make somewhat of a confession. My heart melted. Nobody has ever really noticed me before, no less written a poem. Had Lloyd at this moment asked me to jump from a building—to stick my head in a fire until my eyes popped—I would have been power-less to refuse.

He continues on to tell me something I never would have expected to hear. That he thinks my breasts are beautiful. That he thinks I should keep them. That if I give up my job at the fire department, he'll be only too happy to provide me with an apartment of my own. That he'll look out for my needs. That he might not be able to see me every night, but Tuesdays and Saturdays seem doable.

"Isn't this kind of sick?" I ask him.

"Just because it's sick," Lloyd answers, "doesn't mean it's wrong."

I honestly don't know what might have happened if the phone hadn't rang at this exact moment. All I can tell you is that Lloyd answers it, takes it into the bathroom, closes the door. "That was Sarah," he announces when he comes out a couple of minutes later. "She tracked me down."

"What does she want?" I ask.

Lloyd goes to his suitcase, jams it shut. "Believe it or not." He smiles. "She wants me back."

"So you're leaving?"

Lloyd finds his car keys next to the Brie. "Good thing, huh? I was so depressed I might have wound up touching those things on your chest."

I remind him. "A minute ago you told me they were beautiful."

He grabs the poem from my hand. "A minute or two ago," he says, "they were."

I'm not even sure when the realization hits me. I do know I'm three-quarters through the wine, I'm stuck up here without a ride back, Nat King Cole is singing "Unforget-table" on the stereo. I turn out the lights, relight the can-dles. I think about what I'll say to Lloyd, how I'll really let him have it this time, once I get back. I think about how unfair life is, giving him everything, giving me nothing.

Except breasts. Two of them.

I take off my sweater, lie across the bed, stare at myself in the overhead mirror. Nobody has ever bought me a bottle of wine before, nobody has ever bought me cheese of any variety. I continue to gape at myself. Lloyd, I suddenly realize, was correct. They *are* beautiful. Small, well-rounded, pouty. My best feature. Maybe the best thing that's ever happened to me.

I get off the bed and go over to the stereo. I start looking for something—anything—by Helen Reddy.

"And I'm going to use them," I say out loud. "I'm going to use them on every weak-kneed, lily-livered, flat-chested man who stands in my way! I'm going to use them to convince Captain Flynn to make me a real fireman! One quick flash of these babies and I'll be riding on that truck!"

I throw open the front door, hold my arms up, and announce bare-chested to the world: "I have breasts, goddamnit! Either love 'em or get the hell out of my way!"

Which is when I notice the maintenance guy standing not three feet in front of me. Agog, as they say. He mumbles something about leaving his wrench inside the cottage, and then he goes, "Look at you. You got titties."

"Breasts," I tell him.

"This is the sickest thing I've ever seen," he says. "You're a freak. You should be in a sideshow somewhere."

I say, "Get me a Coke."

In less than two minutes he's back. A Coke, a glass of ice, a lemon wedge, and two straws.

Tiresias at Evening

Richard Foerster

how can I say it plainly: such knowledge
at first is never wisdom, but waking

as if in a strange, troughed bed to a shock of
sunlight that almost blinds, to the frantic

trill of a warbler that makes no seeming
sense: What I found missing suddenly

was something found, a fumbling
after the memory of what I was, but

was not now. A rare sensation:
I'd become the cave of my own unknowing,

and cried for the lost, hard half I
thought had kept me whole. In the mirror

my razor still crafted the usual face, my
voice still echoed with the familiar

registers of work, but I could not stand
(you laugh!) in the arena of men,

nor boast of what they'd see as shame.
Accursed, blood-driven vessels—both. Was I

doubly less or more for this (now that I can speak
as a man) this gift? They can never know—

nor you—except you open to these words and feel
each syllable thrust inside your hidden self.

Ineluctable Modality of the Vaginal

Rick Moody

arguing about Lacan's late seminars, about the *petit objet a*, or about the theory of the *two lips*, about the expulsion of Irigary, I think that's what it was, though I'm willing to bet most couples don't argue about such things, at least not after two or three margaritas, probably not under any circumstances at all, but then again we weren't really arguing about that, not about French psychoanalysis, not about the *petit objet a*, not about Irigary and that *sex which is not one*, but about some other subject altogether, it's always something else, that's what was making me so sad, how it was always some other subject, a subject that was bumped aside, some isolate, hermeneutical matter that I couldn't pin down in an Upper West Side bar while he was assuming his particularly vehement boy expression, a kind of a *phallocratic* face, or a *carnophallogocentric* face, a *politics of face simulation*, a phallic politics of facial deformation, it should have been about *finances*, this argument, or about the economic politics of sexuality, or about his inability to allow into debate the discussion of matrimony, which he always said was *a social construction of commitment, rather than a commitment itself*, and if I could agree with the liberating theory of contingency, *the contingency of committed relationships*, then I would see that this social construction of commitment was irrelevant, just something that magazines and television programming tried to hard sell me, and it's not that I disagreed, at all, I understood that marriage had feudal origins and *was thus about bourgeois power and patrimony*, but I took issue with the fact that we could never even discuss the nuptial commitment, because if we did he said that I was assuming a *fascist totalizing language, a feminine language in the becoming of male totalitarian language*, and then he would start to drink to excess and his face would flush and we couldn't touch each other for a week or more, well, maybe it was on this occasion that I did say it out loud as I too had drunk or was just plain fed up, maybe I *raised my voice a little*, observed that he was a *phallocrat*, that despite his seminars in Marxist aesthetics, or whatever, Walter Benjamin, women disgusted him, that the way he required the first and last word, the alpha and omega, was an oppressive thing, always the last word, always a dead stop, which was when he got going on some nonsense, on algorithms of the unconscious, on *Borromean knots, those psychosexual and linguistic constructs that are essential to the conjunction of language and consciousness, the gossamer moment of ontology, the knot that binds, the erotic, the feminine*, couldn't be untangled, couldn't be separated and formulated outside of feminine consciousness, these knots, a *girl thing, Borromean knots*, I don't know, up until then we might have found the spot where we agreed that we didn't disagree, and we might have listed the things we agreed on, a history that swept backward behind us, we agreed on being in that certain bar on the Upper West Side and, prior to that, we agreed on certain jukebox selections, Tom Waits or Leonard Cohen or Joni Mitchell if available, and, prior to that, we agreed on a sequence of semesters and vacations, ebbing and flowing, and, prior to that, we agreed on moving in together, cohabiting, and, prior to that, we agreed on a certain narrative of our meeting, a narrative that spun out its thread in this way: both of us trapped on the subway one night when it rumbled to a stop between Ninety-sixth Street and Seventy-second Street, both of us reading, coincidentally, *The Lover* by Marguerite Duras, straphanging, talking and giggling during the quarter hour that the Number 2 was hobbled in the express tunnel, the injustice of collapsed trains, it was sweet, and I asked for his number, because he was too shy to do the asking, or so we agreed later, and, in my black tights with the *provocative stylized tear*, he said, which was actually an accidental tear on the thigh, and in my gray miniskirt, which was only slightly racier than office garb, I was the one who was *ready to move*, ready to yield to some *subliminal discourse of romantic love*, we agreed on this narrative and recounted it periodically, refining and improving, *concretizing or reifying its artifice*, and he occasionally included actual passages from the Duras, blunt short sentences, claimed to have read these to me, to have read them aloud in the subway tunnel, as we hung on those straps, though there were no actual straps (it was a train that had only poles and transverses), and though I was actually reading Djuna Barnes, and later anyhow he always said that *the romantic was a destructive force*, responsible for all the worst poetry of the nineteenth century, responsible even *for the theory of Total War, because by extrapolation, there would be no war without the romance of the Empire, the romance of nationalism, the romance of purity doctrines*, he even said that he no longer liked Duras, whose idea of upheaval was *decadent, alcoholic*, still we wrote this story together, shared the quill,

about a time when we had been irresistible, when we used
to burst into each other's apartments eager to fling off *layers
of fashion*, when we used to cry out, making use of that
philosopher's stone of romantic mythology, *jouissance*, I admit it, that time was lost, and when in the singular precincts
of our separate offices we tried to locate that time, that fab-
ulous unity, it was as part of our intimate folklore of abun-
dance, rather than a part of *actual experience*, and that was
maybe the real argument, the one we didn't have in the Upper West Side bar, that was the *stiff breeze*, and our relationship was a Mylar balloon slipping out of a toddler's moist
fist, helixing around and around up into the elsewhere of
the musky New York City skies, landing distantly back in
time, during the Sandinistas, during El Salvador, during
Iran-Contra, fogbound in the dim past, we had loosed our
balloon, even if all this simply made him furious because he
always said that *I would not stay on a particular subject*, that
was the problem, the culture of femininity asserted as its
moral right a fuzziness with respect to meaning, *You're a
sloppy thinker!*, I arrived at a point, he said, through a kind
of labial circulation, *a vicus recirculation*, as Joyce said,
meaning probably both *vicious* and having to do with Vico,
but maybe *viscous*, too, as in labial, viscous, heavy with a
heavy menstrual fluidity, *You won't stay on the point, you ex-
ceed and overflow*, he said, in the bar on the Upper West
Side, in the seventh year of our entanglement, our Borromean knot, but I insisted that staying on the point was his
way of dictating the terms of the discussion like arguing
about whether *oval table* or *rectangular table* as preliminary to
détente, and if he was willing to let the point vacillate, then
maybe he would know *what it was like to be on my side of the
negotiating table*, to be me as I was perceiving him, *overcoming in a flutter of jubilant activity obstructions of support in order
to hold him in my gaze*, perceiving that he didn't care for me
any longer, perceiving that we had come to the time in
which it was probably right for me to engage the services of

a good Realtor, *No*, he said we were existing in *segmentarity*, but I said if he would let go of the point, and *wear my skirt*, feel the constriction of tights for the purposes of being professional without being provocative, being an adjunct without being a *castrating cunt*, as one guy in the department said of a colleague who didn't try to be a little bit sexy, if he could wear my skirt, he would understand how sad this was all making me, and this is why I was *on the verge of tears*, in the wood-paneled bar on the Upper West Side, though I refused to allow him to touch me as I cried, as I also refused to use tears strategically, they were just how I felt and I would not conceal it, they were *a condensation and displacement*, sure, but they required no action, and I was, it's true, a woman with a doctoral degree who *believed against all reasonable evidence that there was some justifiability to the Western tradition of marriage*, and who happened now to be crying, and who happened to be sad more often than not, who happened to have a striping of mascara on her cheeks, okay, but this only made him madder still, and there was the whole elegant spray of his logic about how *feminine language undoes the proper meaning of words, of nouns*, and that's when I said that *he had no idea what it was like, would never know what it was like, that all of his bright, politically engaged, advanced-degreed tenure-track friends would never know what it was like to be a woman, the fact of hips, cervical dilation, labia major and minor, childbirth, breast-feeding, hot flashes, premenstrual rage, an outside that is an inside, circularity, collapse of opposites, it was something that he would never know about,* and basically, I went on in my tirade, he secretly really liked it when I cooked, the percussive clanging of pots and pans, the poring over ancient texts like *The Joy of Cooking*, or Julia Child, he liked to see me doing these things, and after I cooked there was always this stunning moment when the meal was done and the dirty plates and cups and saucers were teetering in a stack around us, in our tiny roach-infested kitchenette, there was this moment of arrest when he would feign a distracted expression, a scholarly absence, as if the life of the scholar were so profound that practicalities didn't enter into it, and it was then that I understood that I was supposed to do the dishes myself, the dishes were my responsibility, even though I had done the cooking, the same was true on the days when he climbed down from his *Olympian, woman-hating aerie* and deigned to broil a tasteless piece of fish, some bland fillet that he always overcooked, and I was still the one who had to do everything else and had to sponge down the table afterward, and I was the one who ended up making the bed, and doing the laundry most of the time, washing his fecund jogging clothes that I had to carry, reeking, to the laundromat, and his streaked BVDs, and I was the one who ended up buying the toilet paper, and I was the one who remembered to call his mom on her birthday, and I was the one who wrote the checks that paid the bills that placated the utilities that ensured that the electricity flowed into his word processor and printer and modem, and, I told him, I had done this in the past because I loved him, but that I was thinking maybe that I didn't love him that much anymore, because I didn't know how anyone could be so cruel as he was, cruel enough to cause me to feel that I didn't know what my point was, or that it was inappropriate of me to even attempt to have a point, and yet as Irigary said, *The "elsewhere" of the feminine can only be found by crossing back through the threshold of the mirror,* so, I observed again, *the Dark Continent of the social order, you'll never know it, you'll never know the possible world of the possible universe of womanhood, this Oriental city-state that exists parallel to your own stupid, unreachable, masculine world, you want to tame it somehow and never will and you'll die never having tamed it, femininity,* and the barmaid came around, and she was wearing very tight jeans and a T-shirt that was too short, purchased, I observed, at Baby Gap, so that her pierced belly button saluted us provocatively, she was like some teenaged toy girl, Hasbro waitress, she was the past of female sexual slavery, and in a moment of calculated witlessness he *gave her the once-over,* paused dramatically to look at her breasts and her middle and the curve of her hips, *Another round, please,* and, of course, this was the thrust of his argument, as his argument always had a thrust to it, a veiled entelechy, namely, that he was above domestication, couldn't be bothered, still I had my teeth into him, and there could be no distraction, as I would complete the argument, and would be through with him or else have some other kind of resolve even if fluctuating, *Okay, then prove to me in any substantial way that you know what it's like to be a woman and what our experience is like here where the legislature insists on control over how we use our bodies, prove for one second that you have an idea about what I'm talking about because we are at an impasse here where you either have to be intimate with me or lose me, the way I'm feeling about it, prove that I haven't wasted years trying to have a conversation with a total stranger,* at which point in a stunning delivery of high affect, *a prepersonal intensity corresponding to the passage from one experiential state of the body to another,* on short notice, his own eyes began to brim with tears, as the next round of drinks came, even as he began to weep he checked out the barmaid's rear as she retreated from our booth, beginning with a theatrical sigh his story, *There's something I haven't told you about myself,* and I said, *You're kidding, right, because we have lived together for a long time and I have read your IRS returns and I have typed portions of your dissertation because you were too lazy to type them yourself and I have listened to you puking and cleaned the bathroom after you puked and if there's something more intimate than all that, some preserve of intimacy that I have not managed to permeate yet I'm going to be a little upset about it,* with an expression of dreadful but stylized seriousness, his crew-cut scalp furrowing slightly, from the brow upward, he admitted that it was true, that there *was* something he hadn't told me, a certain charcoal secret, a lost cat in the fringed outback of his psychology, and he said, *Think of human sexuality as a*

*continuum with inertia at one end of it and satiety at the other,
two ends that meet somewhere we can't see,* please not the language of the department office right now, could we try to
keep this in the Vulgate, he ignored me: he was just a kid,
scrawny, homely, no good at ball games of any kind, last to
be chosen when choosing up sides, happened to be friends
with this one girl, the beauty of the middle school, theirs
was the profane friendship destined to be crushed in the im-
position of social order, something like that, when the mists
of childhood receded once and for all she would have nothing to do with him, but in the meantime the two of them
ate Twinkies in the lunchroom, traded secrets, as all these
athletes and student counselors came by to talk to her, ignoring him, unless to inquire about aspects of algebra or
geometry likely to turn up on an examination or pop quiz,
would it be all right if they copied from him, they were ambling
by in order to impress Sapphira with the fruits of their boy-
ish masculinity, they would perhaps say hello to him then,
and then later in the halls it was as if he were masked or
cloaked or otherwise concealed, outside of the radiating
force of Sapphira, no longer her satellite, moon to her great
Jovian significance, her efflorescent girlhood, she would
telephone him for forty-five minutes after the bus ride
home and speak of how Kevin or Tom or Lenny had tried to
get her to agree to this or that *home breast exam,* or the like,
and then one afternoon when her parents were vacationing
or on business, in autumn, leaves the colors of unrestored
frescoes, Sapphira invited him over, arranged in hushed
tones to meet and once inside the door, *I have an idea for
you, you are so wonderful, you are my best girlfriend, you are
my one and only, and I want you to be just like me, come with
me, girlfriend, sister of mine,* and next he knew they were in
her room, and she was helping him off with his jeans, helping him off with his T-shirt, and helping him *on* with her
white underpants, and then her trainer bra, and then her
plaid, pleated field hockey skirt, her eyelet camisole, and

then they were in her parents' bathroom, with the vanity mirror, turning him, as on a lazy Susan, to appreciate all angles, scattering widely upon the glass table the pencils and brushes of her trade, and, God, *here is the difficult part, I was so aroused, I have never felt so passive and so aroused, as she ringed my eyes with her lavender eyeliner, as she brushed on the mascara, as she rouged me, covered my actual physical blushing with her Kabuki cultural blushing, as her hands danced all around me with delicate embraces, it was as though she had a hundred arms, like she was Hindu statuary, I had never been so loved as I was loved now that I was a girl, I had never been so esteemed,* and she even had a wig, which was sort of a bow-headed thing that a cheerleader might want to wear, with short bangs, and Sapphira herself had been a cheerleader so she ought to have known, even if she was only wearing chinos and sandals and a sweatshirt that afternoon, *And she even painted my toenails in a red umber, the color of menstrual efflux, and it was true, as I lay upon her bed with the fringe skirt, and she hugged me and called me her rag doll, that I had never felt so scorched as I felt then, and I knew, I knew, I knew, I knew what it was, so outrageous in my elevated state that I had to run into the bathroom to gaze on myself all over again, feeling a racing in myself that I had never felt before, the teleology of desire, the bound and cauterized site of the feminine, that's how it was, and I was so ashamed, and so ashamed that she knew, and she knew that I knew, and she visited upon me a knowing smile, and it was the smile that did it, that toppled the carefully erected façade, and I began demanding, Get this stuff off me, Get this stuff off me, even as I knew now what she was to those guys, to Kevin or Tom or Lenny, she was no different from what I was then, I could have provided for their needs as well as she, could have provided the trophy, the object, the ravishment, the rape they desired, I had become America's delightful exotic doll;* this was a heartfelt display to be sure, and obviously it would not have been polite for me to turn away this difficult and generous admission, but I was still *upset*, you know, I was still

deterritorialized, and if he tried to explain that this assump-
tion of the clothes of *the slut from up the street* gave him access to femininity, I was going to have to get shrill, I was
going to swallow a hunk of him, with my vagina, if necessary, some hunk of bicep or quadricep, *Who, then, is this
other to whom I am more attached than to myself, since at the
heart of my assent to my own identity it is still he who agitates
me?,* I told him we needed to *leave now,* we needed to pay
the check, goddamnit, for once in our lives we would
pay the check without arguing about whose turn it was to
pay, because we needed to leave now, and there was a flurry
of settling up and tip-leaving, his hands trembled at the as-
tronomical sum, his *essential tremor,* and the bottled blonde
with the decorated navel didn't even give him a second
look as she swept the six ones and change into her apron
and carried the two twenties back to the register, and we
eased between the empty conversations in the Upper West
Side bar, the discussions of cars and shares in the Hamptons
and mutual funds, and I, in my *impervious tempest,* insisted
on a cab, though we had in the past argued about whether
taxis were an expense that fitted into the extremely narrow
budget that we were trying to observe, and, if truth were a
thing that could be revealed by argument, if truth were
some system of layers that you could husk when your relationship had assumed its permanent shape, then it was true
that our pennilessness, our academic poverty, surrounded by
this Rube Goldberg contraption of cosmopolitan New York,
by the limousines, by the price-gouging restaurants, by the
dwindling number of our classmates who practiced the *life
of the mind,* by our undergraduate classmates who were now
psychiatrists, or lawyers, or boutique money managers—this
academic penury was wearing us away, sanding us down,
burnishing us until like the professors of our own youth, we
were hollow mouths, reciting things we no longer felt or
cared at all about, we were the culmination of a genealogy
of ghosts, Marx, Freud, Derrida, Lacan, Nietzsche, Reich,

syphilitics and cocaine addicts and income tax evaders, and I asked where in this arrangement was there room for what I had once loved with an enthusiasm dynamic, dialectical, rhizomatic, interstitial, metalinguistic, defiant, the possibility that *thinking* could save lives, as at the moment when I first heard him lecture, back when he was the assistant for *Intro to Film Analysis*, when he paced the proscenium by the blackboard in that room off 116th, back when he smoked, chain-smoked, barely made eye contact with those restive kids, how I loved him, back when he said, *Anorexia, the scurvy on the raft in which I embark with the thin virgins*, misquoting it turned out, in order to make a point about Audrey Hepburn in *Breakfast at Tiffany's*, he wanted to make a difference and I wanted to make a difference, or a *différance*, a deferral, a deferment, a defacement, I recognized my own image in the eyes of that boy who was recognizing his own image in me, a flickering in candlelight, candles about to be blown out in the hushed, sudden interior of a bedroom, *flickering in the pink night of youthful graces*, all that was gone and now we had opened the windows of the taxi because the air was thick as bread, and we said nothing, and the taxi idled in traffic on Broadway, my stubbly legs crossed one over the other, I needed a shower, and I felt cross and shameful, unemployable, old, I felt he would leave me for a younger woman, like the barmaid, a trickle of blood at the corner of her perfect lips, as I pronounced these assessments, these solemn truths about us, *facteur de la verité*, as the taxi with its geometrically increasing fare expelled us on 120th and we paid the cabby a month's salary and we walked past Grant's Tomb, cromlech, dolmen, barrow, in our necropolis, what it was to be a woman in this afterlife, giving an extra bit of effort in the going hence of what you once loved, he said nothing, the key turned in the lock, it tumbled the bolts, as if the idea of the key were the perfection of an ancient ethics, I couldn't believe that I would have to lose what it seemed like I was about to lose, what it once seemed like I might *always have*, all the lights in our apartment had burned out in our absence, he always left the lights on and the bulbs were always blown, *Let's compromise*, he said, running his hands nervously across his Velcro crew cut, adjusting his eyeglasses, *I'm so tired of fighting*, and I didn't know what I was going to do until I did it, though there was a certain inevitability to these next moments, and I slammed the door, and I pulled the metal folding chair from under the kitchen table, situated it at the end of the table, situated it for spectatorship, *I have a vagina*, I said, *I have a uterus, I have a cervix*, he nodded wearily, and I said, *Man's feminine is not woman's feminine*, and he nodded wearily, and I told him to quit nodding, and I asked him if he happened to know where his *shoehorn* was, and he shook his head, no, and I said, *Of course, it's a trick question, but I know where your shoehorn is, because I keep it with mine, as with so many other things you couldn't be bothered to think about*, so I walked into the interior of the apartment, which was not so far that he couldn't hear the emanations of my breath, *Look*, he said, *I don't know what I've done to cause so much difficulty, but I apologize, I honestly do, let's let it drop, I love you*, and I could feel my steep decline coming on, as when the low-pressure system moves in and drives off summer filth, yet having made the decision, I couldn't let go of it, or maybe it's more credible to say that it was obvious that I could feel like subjecting him to this painful scrutiny and at the same not feel like doing it at all: *I demand that you deny me that which I offer you*, that sort of thing, a Saturday, a poststructuralist Saturday, the night on which I urged my lover to give me a pelvic examination on the kitchen table, which he refused, of course, *Oh, the old biology is destiny argument, it doesn't suit you at all, and don't you think you're acting childishly?*, was and wasn't, in my view, and the torrents of my argument were and were not forceful, and this *was and was not* erotic this argument, like the arguments that produced that old sweet thing so much gone from us now, and the resolution, it seemed to me, would be ephemeral, would never be what I suspected it would be, and so I went on with the display nonetheless, climbing up on the kitchen table now, holding, among other props, the two shoehorns, the one from a Florsheim on Eighth Street, imitation cordovan, and the other a shiny metallic stainless steel shoehorn of my own given to me *gratis* when I had bought, on Madison Avenue, this pair of sandals I was wearing, peeling off the ivory sandals, yanking down my beige nylons and then also my lingerie, satin and from Victoria's Secret, and then I hiked up my skirt, a thin rayon, slightly clingy wrap in a floral print, cream with navy blue blossoms thereupon, and I shoved a throw pillow from the sofa under my lumbar region, and I leaned back such that I was facing him, if facing him is the right term, since actually *my face* wasn't facing him, since, now, he was facing away, having apprehended what was happening, at last, and I readied my shoehorns, greased slightly, *They're cold, they're always cold, when they come for you with the stirrups it is always cold*, with a splenetic passivity, he mumbled, *Don't I need a light of some kind*, but I offered him one of these, a penlight that he himself used when grading papers late at night in our tiny apartment, when he did not want to wake me, and I embarked on my tour, *Look, look, look, spread wide the external petals at either side*, and I helped him along, as he seemed a little unwilling to commit, *never mind that first trompe l'oeil for now, that little nub, move indoors, where the walls are pink and ridged like when the sand upon the beach is blown by successive waves, which means that estrogen is present, because when menopause strikes the rugae will vanish, straight ahead, if you please, the cervix has a different texture, sort of a pearly pink like gums, dense, fibrous, thick, rigid, averages four centimeters across, and the hole is a tiny dark spot, the os, like the hole in a bagel that swells to threaten its cavity, in a nulliparous woman it's a hole, if you've had children it's more like the creases in an old balled feather pillow, then up through there is the uterus, of course, you*

*can't see, up there, endometrium, now lined with blood and
sludge, the color of ugly seventies wall-to-wall carpeting, my
sludge, after which we head north up into the pear, because it's
shaped like a pear with a sleeve around it, and at ten and two
o'clock in the pear, little holes, oviducts, and these go around
each ovary, like treble clefs, they wrap cursively around each
ovary, each end fimbriated, and in midcycle during ovulation,
one egg gets primed to be released on one side, sucked into the
tube from the corpus luteum, and then there's the hydatid of
Morgagni, and the mesosalpinx, and the epoöphoron, and the
Fundus of the Uterus, and the external abdominal opening, basically open all the way up there, all the way up, unprotected,
vulnerable to the approach of the fleet of chromosomes, the little
Navy Seals coming up the canal here, although you have to wonder at the fact of it from an evolutionary point of view how a perfect vulnerability makes for the reproduction of a species unless
that ends up being the locution of our biology, of our position in
things, or, to put it another way, the victim,* in your construct,
*the penitent, always has the upper hand, always has control, hid-
den from you, present and absent, sacred and profane;* yes, an
uncomfortable position, holding the shoehorns in this way,
arched over myself, while he took command of the penlight, while he tried to neglect his responsibility, and I mean
uncomfortable in a lot of ways, I mean that I didn't want to
watch his expressions of remorse, I didn't want to think
about what I was doing, I was better off looking at the stuc-
coed ceiling, an interior style that always made me feel really claustrophobic, the simulated remodeling ease of
stucco, and if at this point the penlight didn't do the job,
didn't illuminate, what did I care, now, alone or married,
fertile or infertile, pregnant or barren, what did I care that
he had gone now and left me on the kitchen table, had
gone to the bedroom, I could hear him now padding away,
the door only partly ajar, I could see the dim clamp light on
his bedside table illumined, I could see him brushing his
teeth with that furious inconsolable way he had, he sawed

at his gums, and now he was reading, of course, reading in volumes that no longer comforted, reading to repair the differences, what was all this talk, all these pages, all this prose, all these sentences, what was it all for, I thought, on the kitchen table, holding two shoehorns in this way so that I was open to the world, its first citizen, its first woman, its original woman, naked on the kitchen table, like a repast, I left off talking, my outrage lapsed, what had we been arguing about, what was the source of the argument and where did it take us, *don't leave me here like this, to refuse translation is to refuse life*, all your broken bindings, your printing presses, your history of histories, I climbed down off the table and began straightening things up.

Doug Rice

i would take myself out to dinner and a movie. Halfway to the movie theater, I would realize that I did not have to take myself out at all and would rush home to bed. I would stay at home all day and play. The next day, I would become terribly bored with my own singularity.

A True
Story from
New
Orleans

Andrei Codrescu

Of course, there were many times when I didn't know whose was whose, and there were times when mine was hers and hers was mine and I knew exactly what it was like to have it in—but those times were always in the act. I never had a cunt in the state of not being fucked (which, by the way, I think it's Iowa), so it was quite interesting to go about—the night after Halloween—with a cunt between my legs, still burning from abuse by Felicity, Lynnette, and Nurse Susan.

I was probably the only creature without a mask at Molly's Bar on Halloween night, though many people there were so scantily dressed some of them looked as though all they had on was a face mask. I was there with my girlfriend Felicity, who had on a cat head with green feathers spouting from the ears and a body stocking with holes in it with her nipples way out and her black pubic hair shooting out like seltzer. Another cat, lithe and blonde, came up to Felicity and licked her ear. A lioness with a real mane of red hair was in hot pursuit of the blonde cat and she pounced just as Felicity shrieked. The lioness slapped the blonde cat on the butt so loud it resounded right through the usual screaming plus the strains of Johnny Cash's "I Hear a Train A'comin." Some queen shouted: "Bitch fight!" and for a minute I thought that this might be the case, but the lioness subsided, content to grab the cat by her crotch, turn her around, and kiss her on the mouth hard.

Now, Felicity and I are conservative people. You have to know this because, although we weren't terribly shocked, we usually like some conversation before we go up or down on somebody. Still, it was Halloween, you couldn't hear anything, so I was almost ready to accept the situation, when the slim cat leaned into my ear, but, as it turned out, not to lick it.

"Do you want to hear the name of my band?" she whispered.

No, not that, not the name of your band. Please. You don't know how young peoples' bands annoy me. I grinned because the lioness still had a full hold of her pussy, so I nodded, and the cat said: "Our Sister Sophia She Who Is a Whore."

All my hair stood on my arms and on my head and I thought that I was going to black out. I actually went slack. It wasn't possible. Less than three hours before I had been writing in my new novel and at one point, stuck for direction, I opened *The Gnostic Gospels*, a fat book containing the gospels left out of the Bible, and I came upon this passage: "Our Sister Sophia, she who is a whore, draws her light from the Pneuma." I found the sentence intriguing enough to quote in my novel. I typed it up and stopped for the day because I couldn't figure out what to do with it.

I grabbed the blonde cat's head and brought her ear to my lips. "Do you know where that's from?"

"Yeah," she shouted back. "The Gnostic Gospels. I've been reading them since I was fourteen years old."

Three scenarios entered my brain. One, the page I was writing on floated out the window and this cat found it and named her band. Two, my house was bugged and this was the operative who bugged me, and three, the Universe Works in Mysterious Ways. One was obviously wrong because I had typed on my laptop and there were no pages, and two was too absurd to even consider.

So the Universe does indeed Work in Mysterious Ways, and an hour later all four of us, Lynnette the blond cat, Felicity my girlfriend, and Nurse Susan, were on the bed in my small apartment doing some lines of coke, smoking joints, drinking bourbon, and casually stroking our respectives and those of the nearest. Only, throughout all this, Lynnette, even with Nurse Susan's able finger massaging her dewy pinto bean, kept up a mystico-Gnostic patter the likes of which I have never heard before or since.

"Pneuma, plethora, paradise, cathar, croema, poledra . . ." On and on like a Gregorian chant coming out of that pretty little mouth and I had this intense hard-on and the strangest feeling. This went on like a church service a little too long, by which time Felicity and Nurse Susan consummated each other's bonbons and bit each other's tits. I was torn between listening religiously with my head bent or parting those well-lubricated nether lips prepped by Nurse Susan and planting all of me in there, a dilemma from which I was saved by Nurse Susan's lips, which engulfed most of me, and by Felicity's probing my anus with a long and slender finger.

The Gnostic entity that possessed Lynnette faded only

when Nurse Susan threw her flat down on the bed, mounted her as if she were going to rip her into chunks, stuck her tongue into her blabbering mouth, spread her legs, and fucked her like a guy, with about four fingers up her cunt.

I believe that at this point, the entity, left without a blabbing channel, entered me. Instead of fingers, Nurse Susan was fucking Lynnette with an honest-to-goodness dick that looked awfully familiar. I know that to an outsider everybody's dick looks the same, but trust me, this was mine. And it wasn't no hallucination neither. I, for one—and Felicity I'm sure—had had no hallucinogens, no X, no nothing. I looked at Felicity, who was lying sprawled on the bed with her body stocking torn and a big grin on her, and I poked her hard. She snapped out of her postcoital-bliss mode and looked to where I pointed. It took a second before this baffled look spread all over her face and then, slowly, her hair stood up all over her just like mine had earlier.

There was no doubt about it. Nurse Susan had a fucking dick and it looked like no dildo either one of us had ever seen, and we are Dildo Scholars. There was only one thing to do, and Felicity, a real trouper, did it. She reached out and grabbed a hold just as it came out of little Lynnette and she held it just long enough to ascertain that, sure enough, it was all flesh, blood, and hard-on, and then she let go. Nurse Susan, turned on by the grab, fucked Lynnette a little harder. Felicity started rubbing Lynnette's clit and feeling Nurse Susan's dick some more, which turned me on enough to want to fuck Felicity. I grabbed a hold of myself to point the way, but there was no holding. Inside the handful of pubic hair two cunt lips were gleaming greedily. I had a burning sensation and an unaccustomed hunger.

For the second time that evening, I had a dizzy spell of sheer weirdness, but I was too insane to consider it for long. I picked Nurse Susan up by her tits and pulled her off Lynnette. I spread myself under Nurse Susan and put her on top of me right where she'd been before and, like a good girl, she kept up the rhythm and fucked me silly.

Everything would have been all right if the mystiko-dicko-weirdness had stopped in the morning, like most reasonable things. It didn't. For twenty-four lousy hungover hours I kept looking for my dick and finding my cunt. Felicity cooked a huge pot of noodles with raw garlic with Parmesan and fed the hangovers of our two guests, who turned out by daylight to be real nice people. No talk of Gnostic anything, just shit about bands and the weather and stuff. Everybody kind of covered themselves with bed sheets and pillows and made friendly chatter and ate noodles. I stared at them like they were all insane. I kept feeling my cunt under the bedsheet, and there it was, moist and fucked and sore, clit hard, and no hint whatsoever that it had been anything but a cunt all along. Only I knew better. Finally, I couldn't stand it anymore, and I reached over to Nurse Susan and there it was, my dick, and hard.

Still talking about the weather or something, I maneuvered myself over and sat on her lap and there it went, sliding in nicely like it knew exactly where, and I moved up and down until I felt it bow up and I was flooded inside by hot stickiness. I sat there until it dribbled down my thighs and dried there. Lynnette and Felicity just watched like they were a little tired of the whole thing.

I slept ten hours. When I got up, Felicity was opening all the windows to let in some air. The guests were gone. Dear God, I prayed, let it be there. I couldn't feel anything. I let my hand slide down very slowly, very casually, and right at the top where the slit should have been, was a nice, rounded wedge of sleepy dick.

Stay away from Molly's at Halloween. Unless you like this sort of thing.

All

William Levy

*t*he vibrator was greased
with a gooey suntan oil
a pillow placed
under my hips
Lying on my back
I hooked my hands
inside my knees
lifted my legs.
Beautiful
redheaded
and from New Zealand
Ever so slowly
she slipped the hard shaft
into my anus
which I contracted
rhythmically
for its whole length
She turned on the juice
I closed my eyes
just for a moment

shuddered
melted really
this this this
transcendental oceanic
come that came
before completion
was what it was like
to be penetrated
No need to force
blood into the penis
to make it erect
just just just
move my pelvis
Thrusting herself into me
into me in to me
she fondled
an erection
while looking meaningfully
into my eyes.
It seemed like
(if you will)
being well-fucked
while having one's
clitoris massaged
When finally having
a delicious orgasm
my first thought was
This is what it feels like
to read
Henry James.

So having a vagina
for one day only
my demands would be
not merely more
I would want

ALL
that is to say
the mysteries of menstruation
I would do the things
done by myself
women seemed to enjoy

The day would begin
with waking up
to the tickling
rasping sensation
of someone
pulling out my tampon
with their teeth
slowly

I would smear
my body with blood
I would smear the walls
with blood
Blood on my sheets again
this time mine

I would kiss the lips
of someone whose
sticky moustache
had the rusty smell
of my blood

I would lick my blood
from their body parts

I would make love
wearing a mask
of Teletubby Po

I would abandon
tampons
go out in the street
with a coffee filter
in my twat
I would call it
"Cookie"

Here is the blood of a poet.

Dream On

Jeremy Reed

*a*ll that night, Billie had dreamed of the change. In his dream the metamorphosis had evolved as a slow, and elaborately ritualized process.

Billie had gone to bed feeling his customary presleep erection trigger at contact with his erotic fantasies. As the gravitation to an unconscious underworld had taken over, he had, in his repertoire of fantasy encounters, been watching a ringleted Italian girl step out of spray-canned jeans into transparent panties. He was negotiating fitting his hands to her buttocks, when he had blacked out into sleep.

At some stage in the night, he had experienced the panic of the dreamer who enters a precinct over which he is powerless to assert control. As a confused spectator to his sex change, he had watched his gender identity undergo transformation to a woman. The group who had performed it had the wraparound eyes and identity-less features that he had come to associate with alien intelligence. His severed genitalia were placed in an icebox, and the operating group, all of them dressed uniformly in metallic blue, appeared to have gained an organ vital to biological research. He remembered too how they had looked on their re-creation with the indifferent scrutiny of a species detached from emotional vocabulary.

When Billie awoke, a lazy September sun was placing blond highlights in the room. He was lying facedown in bed, and was concerned to note the absence of the characteristically indomitable erection that always companioned his awaking. When his mind push-buttoned a fantasy, it was that of a man cradling an overalert erection. Billie tried to reverse the image, but it remained freeze-framed in consciousness.

He told himself that he had never to his knowledge been attracted to men, nor had he ever entertained same-sex fantasies. When he tried to locate the familiar image of the Italian girl in black panties, his libido failed to respond. Worried by his apparent shift in sexual orientation, Billie ran a tentative hand along his groin. He struggled with terror, as he encountered the absence of taut balls and the cock that for the past twenty years had been his unfailing instrument of pleasure.

In its place, his fingers outlined the mollusk-like grotto of a sensitive vulva. He was so curious about his sexual transformation that he sat up in the bed and checked his defined male torso. He was still a man from the waist up, and Billie felt disappointed at the absence of breasts to complement his vagina.

Billie got out of bed and checked himself in the mirror. His buttocks had been enhanced, and aerosoled across one wall in Day-Glo blue letters, he read the message: "You're a woman for a day. Have fun. Tonight in your dream, you'll be reinstated as a man."

Billie instantly recollected last night's dream, and remembered in detail how he had observed himself undergoing a transsexual op. He went back to bed and began coaxing pleasure from his clitoris, touching himself with the same fingertips that he had so often applied to women. He

teased himself with agonizingly slow movements, and with
the dexterity of an inveterate onanist, quickly made himself
come. He knew now the clitoral stimulus and the ascending
scale to pleasure that were so often the prelude to a woman's
passionate lovemaking.

It occurred to Billie, quite suddenly, how he should spend
the day. His sister, Sandra, with whom he shared an apartment, was away on two-weeks vacation in Venice. He
would wear her clothes for the day and make a killing.

Billie found himself excitedly riffling through Sandra's
lingerie drawer. He fished out her tiniest pair of black
panties, snapped on a frothy suspender belt, and with con-
summate facility had black seamed nylons breathe along his
legs. It was fortunate that Sandra had a fetish wardrobe, and
Billie molded a tight skirt to his curved bottom. He then set
about the process of making up, and with intuitive artistry
applied eyeliner, porcelain foundation, and red lipstick. To
maximize on his newly adopted femininity, Billie styled a
floppy beret over his short blond hair, and stood back to admiringly view his androgynous creation. He remembered
having been told often over the years, that he looked remarkably feminine for a man, and now he delighted in making this discovery in the mirror for himself.

After having practiced walking in a pair of Sandra's black
court shoes, and having perfected a catwalk swing of the
hips, Billie grew excited to present himself on the street.
Already, his initial scheme of being unmitigatingly promis-
cuous for the day in order to savor to the full a woman's capacity for orgasm was in the process of being modified. Far
from his original intentions of cutting the figure of a loose
woman, he decided on the contrary to cultivate the mystique of an unapproachable diva.

Billie's subsequent appearance in the city provoked rapa-
cious attention from men sitting outside cafés and from those
driving through the streets with the car windows down. He
was hassled by libidinous comments, and defended himself by

retaining a dignified silence. He sat on his anger rather than risk responding to raw suggestions. His desire to have a man explore his vagina was rapidly diminishing. As his hostility toward men increased, so the desire to provoke them grew to be his dominant mood. He walked from his hips, so as to tantalize onlookers with the movement of his bottom. Up on heels, he knew he looked the perfect woman.

Billie went in and out of large department stores, touched up his makeup at beauty counters, sprayed on a little Shalimar to heighten feminine mystique, and delighted in the admiring comments he received from consultants. He began to seriously question how he had approved of being a man over the years and how he had accepted his evident misidentity with such unprotesting conviction. He was starting to realize the limitations of the gender to which he would be forced to revert tomorrow.

He had lunch in a small café, and sat staring admiringly at his reflection in the mirror. He noticed the expertise with which he had shaped his lips into a red Cupid's bow. A number of obtuse male clients were coming on to him with their eyes. Billie could feel them exploring his body with their intense, prospecting scrutiny. They were visibly undressing him in their fantasies, and each seemed individually confident that he would be the one to win his favors. Billie eye-flirted with each of them in turn, warming to the power he asserted over their uncavalier body language.

Suddenly the charged airwaves were broken by a vampish butch girl entering the café and sitting down with an air of masculine authority. Her head was shaved and her ears studded with rings, but her one concession to femininity was a mouth bruised by black lipstick. Billie found himself compelled to stare at the newcomer, his fascination with the girl having him punch eyeholes in the space separating their tables. The feeling was evidently reciprocated, for the girl stared back with dykish insolence, before her mouth broke into a conspiratorial smile.

Billie was still being persistently head-gamed by the male clientele. The one nearest to him, a suave, middle-aged businessman with a lubricious sneer twisted into his smile, was busy sizing up the sheer-nyloned legs that Billie kept crossing and recrossing under the table.

Billie found himself reconsidering the prospect of having a man, or a number of men make love to him through the afternoon and night, as part of his experience of being a woman. But instead, he decided to settle for vengeance on his own sex. He decided he would refute all male advances and confer the pleasure to be derived from his vagina on a woman. Something of the perverse in him delighted in the prospect of denying his own sex another gratifying conquest. Billie resolved to enforce this rejection in a big way.

While deepening his complicitous eye contact with the girl for whom he felt a deepening curiosity, he correspondingly began to flirt outrageously with the businessman closest to him. He angled his stockinged legs directly toward the man and pouted his red lips as an encouraging signal. It amused Billie to think that he who was really a man, and simply acting out the role of a woman for the day, was intent on granting his favors to another woman.

Billie was now showing his legs right to the stocking tops, and the businessman flushed with sexual expectation. Billie could empathize with the man to the point of feeling his painful arousal, but he was enjoying the pleasure of making somebody suffer false expectations.

The man leaned over and introduced himself as David, a consultant in real estate. Billie froze in anticipation of the usual repetitive stream of clichés likely to issue from a conventional suit. He could see that the man lacked all imaginative flair and was unlikely to place a rainbow in his individual day. Billie wanted to explore the sensual geography that he knew would never be his again after today, and to do this he needed a more adventurous partner than a straight male. He had decided finally to place his trust in a woman's oral expertise to orchestrate his vagina.

Billie stood up abruptly, knowing that every male eye in the room had settled on his legs and bottom like tetchy insects. Billie didn't hesitate. He went straight over to his assumed lover, and kissed her deeply, their respective lipstick colors mixing like red and black paints. Billie knew nothing of the girl, but they went out of the café hand in hand, into the muted amber light of a September afternoon, and kept on walking.

Spelunking

Alexander Theroux

he question is asked, how would it feel to have a vagina for a day? What would I *have* there, first of all? I mean, back in the late sixties when I read with utter shock that more than half the female population did not know whether they ever had an orgasm, never mind knowing exactly what took place or how—I am not making this up—I seriously began to wonder whether, like the ocean, space, and the human brain, the vagina was not the fourth great mystery. It seemed less an absence in adventure, at least in epistemological terms, than an aspect of stupidity, a lack of cognition. What primordial ceremony in which clearing of this "rubyfruit jungle," as Rita Mae Brown called it, burned the hot fire consuming its victim in passionate flames? In short, was the orgasm clitoral or vaginal? Women could only surmise and not tell, knew but refused to say, would be willing to divulge if it were not so vulgar or rude. Sex therapists William Hartman and Marilyn Fithian, basing their judgments on various measurements such as women's heart rates, pelvic contractions, breathing, and other physiologi-

cal indicators, determined that women were having orgasms and didn't even *realize* it!

Apparently, the situation is even graver than that, unless
things have changed drastically. "A survey conducted in
Victorian England found that almost 75 percent of women
did not know they had a clitoris or what it was for," writes
K. S. Daly in *Sex, An Encyclopedia for the Bewildered*, "despite the fact that the word had first appeared in English as
early as 1615 when Helkkiah Crooke argued that while it
resembled the yard (penis), it was not the same thing."

How Stella Got Her Groove Back, forget the film title,
seems to be a true metaphor, chilling in concept, of the
twammy's enigma, its protean nature, something that even
if it can disappear, it can return, as if, I don't know, by some
kind of preternatural filmflammery. What could be the reason—the vagina's amorphousness? Its relative lack of con-
tour? Its heart of darkness? The arrow has no single target,
correct? Thrumming causes orgasm. Irritation. *Frottage*.
General rubbing. Not one bulletlike tracer to a point. It is
all of it an enigma. Venus de Milo did not have a vagina,
while, curiously, the Venus of Willendorf had nothing but!
It is a dilemma. In Roman mythology Venus was the goddess of love, and yet it was from her that we derive the term
"venereal disease." Men, nevertheless, are deeply involved
in the cunt as the concept, for their origins, their outlook,
their onus, their onliness.

Folds are its first feature, shape its shadow. Because there
is an immediate problem of cognition, if I had a vagina for a
day—and let us say that as of this moment (a wand flourish
by Tinkerbelle) I do—I shall proceed with a quick investi-
gation of its essential landscape, its geometry. Hand me my
speculum! It is not a hole, I notice. Neither is it open, but
wonderfully, like a cabinet or an umbrella, has the potency
of openness about it, range, as it were, and can accommodate a penis in a perfect 360-degree hoop. (Do you remember The Smiths' LP, *Hatful of Hollow*? That is a phrase more

or less suited to this oxymoron.) It is not and never was a circle, which is an adolescent howler commonly rendered in hairy pictographs with black markers on the walls of men's rooms and high school toilets by disturbed little herberts, perverts, and prepubescent droolies like pranksters in the *Beavis and Butthead* cartoon. "Hole" is of course misogynistic in spite of Courtney Love's grunge group. (I once caught the fittingly coincident concert of Hole and Bush on the same bill in Denver, Colorado.) "Gash" is brutal and impossibly crude, suggesting accidents and gaping wounds and a kind of unmerciful post-Edenic unfinishedness, even if it is still used in popular parlance by semi-coherent slackers and postfeminist psychosexual punks. Dismissing it as negligible, failing to acknowledge it as "creative space," Sigmund Freud himself described the vagina as "an asylum for the penis."

Vagina. The passage leading from the vulva to the womb. From the Latin word *vagina*, which means sheath or scabbard, we get the word "vanilla." (The Aztecs called vanilla "the black flower," for, remember, the bean, which has the shape of a woman's private parts, is dark.) I begin my exploration with prodding finger and easeful eye. I notice that it is rubiously sentient, quite soft, amazingly rolling and ambulant, almost audible like water-lily pads in the flappable, slappable labia. It has a slippered beauty, volupt and wild, and the lie of its smelling like fish is a calumny broadcast by fools. Its smell at best is frangipanid, attar of roses mingling with the acrid bite of leek and scallion and the musk of perspiration.

I want to know does it go up or down? Can it widen, stretch, completely close like one of those plastic palm-sized 1960s coin purses? Does it feel a need of being filled and only at certain times? But look! It is an ellipse, a compressed circle, all of whose parallel half-chords perpendicular to a diameter have been shortened in the same ratio, that of the conjugate to the transverse axis! Isn't it rather unfortunate but typical, paralleling the arrogant male concept of women

being "deprived" of a rib, that the word "ellipse" is derived
from the Greek word *elleipsis*, meaning defect?

"Slit" is another dicey word. I *feel* split, cracked in two, at
least conceptually, divided is too strong. ("And on the way
out, hey, don't let the door smack your crack," I heard a red-
neck shop owner in Virginia once snap at a female cus-
tomer.) It is noticeably bigger than what I felt when, say,
constantly amazed, I was watching beautiful female triathletes (to me, all triathletes are beautiful), whose vaginas,
snug within their shorts, became actually, firmly, uninhibit-
edly visible. It is in the modern girl, the new woman, surely
a boast. Remarkably, many women pop groups nowadays
seem proudly to name themselves for their vulvas. The Slits
were a rock band, not the first, who did so. One of the first
all-women rock bands, Fanny, a like-named quartet, took a
more sanitized monicker than slits, which is of course a vulgar homonym in Britain for the "amber-furred dear mouth,"
to use of one of John Updike's endearing terms for that delicate commodity. Sweet Fanny Adams! "The name was
tough, slightly ironic, slightly self-derisory, features it shares
with the punk names of a few years later," Sue Steward and
Sheryl Garratt tell us in *Signed, Sealed, and Delivered: True
Life Stories of Women in Pop*. They list a number of more bla-
tant and distinctly unambiguous "riot grrl" groups who followed in their wake, most of them rough trade with spidery
tats, dark eyeliner, death-row haircuts, and black leather—
the Bloods, PMT, Snatch, IUDs, Penetration, the Castra-
tors.

Vaginal imagery might also include the aptly named The
Delta 5, art students from Leeds whose avant-funk LP *See
the Whirl* (1981) is as steamy as Ivy Rorschach of The
Cramps. Has a new Yeatsian circle come round? Is a new period aborning among the young, a bolder generation—
women, say, who have perhaps found their clitorises—that
gives grace, even if it may be only self-assertive and unself-
conscious, to the delta of Venus? I have become woman

even if only for a day, O altitudo! And can now feel like those late-seventies supergroupies, Cherry Vanilla and Clara Clit and Vinnie Vibrator.

How horrible suddenly in the light of this are all those obscene street terms used to define the vagina: "taco," "clambox," "Pringle," "pussy," "cunt," "twat." *Cono* in Italian, *con* in French. Ugh. "Snatch," "gravy-boat," "beaver," "hair pie," and "cooter" are other memorable terms. *Puts* in Estonian is not only hideous but not even meant to be intentionally derisive. The same with *pikhta* in Russian. Barbara Kligman, editor of *Plotz*, writes that a lot of the women she grew up with referred to the vulva as a "knish." Even more Yiddishisms for women's private parts are helpfully offered by Albert Stern in the *Ecstatic Moment*, most of which, at least to me, are revolting when not farcical and reductive, although you may insist they are cute: *loch, pirgeh, shmoonke, shmushka, shtalt*. A dark fear of women and their mysteries apparently forces the Yiddish language to seek out various superstitious (and puritanical) euphemisms for it, such as *oysemokem* ("that place") and *dos vayberifher* ("that female part") and *die mayse* ("the story"). They echo the Old Testament disdain for the female body.

Such expletives explode. They sound like punches. Why do sexual monosyllables always sound so vulgar? I believe for the same reason that, say, "Bud" and "Coke," to name but two, are respectively the best-selling beer and soft drink in the United States—men like to be able to fire off an order quickly. It's macho, it's cool, it's tough, it's dudeworthy. A dissertation could be written on the brand efficacy of one word. Americans love monosyllables. "Gimme a hot dog!" "Want a sub?" "He's cool." "That's hot." "She's a fox." "Hey man." "Say dude!" Wasn't it his polysyllabic speeches, as much as anything, that cost Adlai Stevenson the 1952 presidential election? Face it, a rhetorician in this country is Professor Frink.

What is unobservable and mysterious as the human back

is unfairly, cruelly, so easy to mock, to deride, to scorn, even
pretend to despise. Valerie Solanas in her self-published
Scum Manifesto (1967) was convinced that what men do
not begin to comprehend or relate to or grasp emotionally
fills them with envy. The angry author of *Up Your Ass*, a
savage play about a man-hating panhandler and hustler,
wrote, "The male, in fact, wants desperately to be led by females, wants Mama in charge, wants to abandon himself to
her care." Solanas, whom Andy Warhol called "a hot water
bottle with tits," went so far as to insist that men, weak and
insecure, living in a world "corroded by maleness," desire to
be female. What made females dominant? She found it to
be a woman's sex.

I am amazed at the presence of absence in the vagina, the
discordia concors. What is it? What is it *not*? It is an oven, a
fountain, an autoclave, a valve, a gate, a faucet, a hallway,
an entrance, a cave—"Hello, mother," W. H. Auden would
always mutter in a car when entering a tunnel—quondam
bed and bassinet, and of course a sex organ. Anaïs Nin's
Delta of Venus. Thomas Pynchon's *V.* The single "monosyl-
lable" (but unwritten) that is the last word of Laurence
Sterne's peripatetic novel, *A Sentimental Journey*. It is
"queynt," in Shakespearian punnery, and quirky as to the
proximity of orifices. (Didn't God nod here? Didn't he care
about infections? Didn't he for all his exquisite manufacture
make a construction mistake?) It is also a riverbed. In the
lurid movie *Showgirls* (1995), tall, blond, sex-dancer, green-
eyed Elizabeth Berkely kisses her entranced dance instructor, Glen Plummer, as she intermittently writhes nakedly
around, moaning, in his lap, and confides to him when he
slides his hand into her crotch, "I've got my period." He
pulls his fingers out and licks them. The *drageoir* is the essential wellspring of sexuality. "Male and sexuality, then, returning to this primal source, drinks at the spring of being
and enters the murky region, where up is down and death is
life," observes John Updike in "The Female Body." In Up-

dike's notorious 1973 essay, "Cunts," which appeared in the
New York Quarterly, he apostrophizes that particular organ:

> sweet T-bones of hair, lips lurid as slices of salmon whirlpooly
> whisps more ticklish than skin, black brooms a witch could
> ride cackling through the spatter of stars.

With my new vagina, I'm experiencing new and not always happy realities. As a newly made woman I feel suddenly anxious, even guilty, and feel bound to offer a generic
apology, first of all, for mocking men's small penises. And
why? I just found out that *only the first two inches of the
vagina have nerve endings!* Secondly, have you ever heard of
a xerocolp? It is the condition of a woman with a constantly
dry vagina. I realize indisposition-wise, a woman cannot be
blamed for such a thing, but it cannot be easy for her partner. And talk about refrigerants! I was once acquainted
with a particularly homely woman named Laura, a grim and
lying leptosome thinner than a ski pole who had the
hideous combination of ice-cold fingers and a chiva dryer
than a Sudanese handclap! I have always wondered if her
neurotic and unkind behavior was connected to this problem. I am equally astonished to learn by the strangely transfigurative act of suddenly possessing one that the tiny
clitoris, our magic bauble, has no less than 8,000 nerve
fibers, a higher concentration of fibers, according to Natalie
Angier in *Woman: An Intimate Geography*, "than is found
anywhere else on the body, including the fingertips, lips,
tongue, and penis." Is it any wonder that Angier refers to it
as a "woman's little brain" or "a trick birthday candle, the
one that keeps popping back no matter how hard you
blow"? It is not only supercharged and demanding but bigger, per square centimeter, than a man's penis, and serves for
pleasure alone — the only organ in the human anatomy designed purely for pleasure! Angier tells us that "the clitoris
operates at peak performance when a woman feels athunder

with life and strength, when she is bellowing on top, figura-
tively if not literally." Why are women so ignorant of its
power? Isn't it rather like someone having a bass drum in
her room that she never beats?

Now when I come across the assertion in *The New Our
Bodies, Our Selves* (1992) that "until the mid-1960s, most
women didn't know how crucial the clitoris was," I'm beginning to wonder, terribly filled with anxiety in my brief
female morph, whether we women, practicing youth but
serving to liquidate it, are not in fact betraying ourselves by
grotesquely placing sex at loggerheads with breeding. Could
Witold Gombrowicz have possibly been right in declaring
that a woman, in feeling her beauty less than a man, em-
bodies anti-poetry by selling the sensuality of the body for
the mode of motherhood? "She is your speedy destroyer!"
exclaims Gombrowicz, accusing womankind of betraying
the nature of her own beauty. "Look! That girl is young and
beautiful only with the aim of becoming a mother!
Shouldn't beauty or youth be something gratuitous? Yet in
women this charm serves to breed; it is allied to pregnancy,
diapers; its highest manifestation creates a child, and that
marks the end of the poem." Was this why the Kinsey report
on sexuality found in the 1950s that fully 23 percent of
women at age 25 were anorgasmic, a full fourth of "us," if I
may, even if momentarily, appropriate the pronoun? And so
what does that say regarding a woman's personal cognition
in choosing a husband? Was that why that foul traductress
Cathy Linton, treating love like a stock market investment,
chose dopey Edgar Linton over Heathcliff?

So you see some of my problems, physical and psycholog-
ical, of having a "silk igloo", a "tookie," a "cloche," a "vas,"
a "hot piñata," a "camel toe." On the other hand there are
distinct pluses.

As an honorary woman for a day—how easy suddenly to
cross one's legs, how uncomplicated now my running stride,
how refreshingly unburdened I feel, yet how vulnerable the

feeling of fronting wind!—I can defend the theory that our organs embody productive space and not penis-envying absence. But hasn't that been both the most constant and ongoing libel against it down through history? "It loves," Updike writes, "because its emptiness knows nothing else to do." Madame de Stael, dismissing the lack of refinement in women, said that the best thing about being a woman was that she didn't have to marry one. Simone de Beauvoir in *The Second Sex,* explaining how man is "transcendence," woman "immanence," seemed to harbor ambivalent feeling toward the very sex she advances to defend. In a recent essay on Beauvoir, Joan Acocella points out that while the late French feminist admits that women have been indeed "socialized into inferiority," she spent far fewer words in her watershed book on that process "than on the manifestations of women's inferiority—their weakness, muddleheadedness, fatuity, vanity, envy, parasitism, resentment, frigidity, neuroticism, on and on—which, as the force of her portrayal gathers, seem to unmoor themselves from their social cause and become absolute." More specifically, Beauvoir seemed to reduce what Frenchmen I know affectionately refer to as "*le nit chaud*" into something ugly:

> The sex organ of a man is simple and neat as a finger . . . but the feminine sex organ is mysterious even to the woman herself, concealed, mucous, and humid, as it is; it bleeds each month, it is often sullied with bodily fluids . . . a horrid decomposition. . . . Man drives upon his prey like the eagle and the hawk; woman lies in wait like the carnivorous plant, the bog, in which insects and children are swallowed up. She is absorption, suction, humus, pitch and glue, a passive influx, insinuating and viscous. (Tr. By H.M. Parshley)

Beauvoir sees a woman's genitals as a trap. A sort of poisonous flower. It appears like the blob or some jelly monster out of a sci-fi creature feature. And what about Henry

Miller, who in *Tropic of Cancer* manages to portray Llona, a woman I suspect he thinks he's praising, as an insatiable mandrill, a mink, a lustmonger, a bottomless pit? It is as if in the portrait of some sort of a *vagina cunicula*— a tunnel— that one can actually find a home, like a pup tent! And yet, invariably, there is always that threat of castration:

> The trouble with Irene is that she has a valise instead of a cunt. She wants fat letters to shove in her valise. Immense, *avec des choses inouies*. Llona now, she had a cunt . . . she lay in Tottenham Court Road with her dress pulled up and fingered herself. She used candles, Roman candles, and doorknobs. Not a prick in the land big enough for her . . . *not one*. Men went inside her and curled up. She wanted extension pricks, self-exploding rockets, hot boiling oil made of wax and creosote. She would cut off your prick and keep it inside forever, if you gave her permission. One cunt out of a million, Llona! A laboratory cunt and no litmus paper that could take her color. One cunt out of a million, Llona.

I loathe the devaluating word, considered to be the most offensive word in the English language, yet which derives from the Old English word *cwithe* meaning simply womb, that Updike uses with insouciance and Miller in the above paragraph uses as often as five times. It seems originally not to have aroused such disgust or loathing.

It is of course overcoming the coarseness that we project about our "naughty bits," as the British say, that allows for a better understanding. And I see the day is getting short with the genitals I've been lent. What more indeed should I do? I suppose I will try peeing. Retromingency, I have noticed, seems fairly awkward among sheep, but men have to squat when peeing outside in Saudi Arabia, so what's new? As a woman for a day, I'll clearly give a go to masturbation with a variety of things: candles, handles, and sandals, no doubt, hard soap, I believe all the sloping vegetables are popular, who knows, a meat tenderizer, I don't know, and some big, aluminum, electrically humming bullet-shaped thing or other that women seem to favor, just to see what that is all about. And, I promise you, I intend to be aesthetically alert (and passionately committed) at the moment of *crise*, whatever form it takes or gestalt it assumes, lest I fall into the brainless category of "Aren't Sure"! I want to feel that wetness, that itch, maybe even that eye-rolling lust, although it seems queer to say it. (Let me add that I have prayed to the merciful heavens that in the originality and suddenness of my explorative sex-transformation for a day that, please God, I look more like Garbo's Camille than Camille Paglia!)

Before midnight, finally, I suppose I will ultimately have to have sex with a man, if for no other reason than to see if Tiresias, the old blind seer of ancient Greece, was correct in pronouncing that, between the two, women enjoyed the sexual act far more than men did. It is a legitimate quest. John the Scot, Duns Scotus, a philosopher murdered at the Abbey of Malmesbury by his students with their pens, supposedly once remarked how close, in the end, a cunt was to a concept—we enter both with joy. And now I can say at last I have learned, happily, from the inside.

Pig Family Game

Robert Peters

I was the sow, she was the boar.
Six kitchen chairs for a pen.
We put on winter coats and grunted.
I lay on my side, coat open
and birthed six pigs.
Only one was a runt. Six squirts
minimal pain, minimal swelling.
I peeled the after-births,
then nudged the piglets into standing.
Boar was in a corner plowing up edible roots.
Sow ate the placentas.
The piglets yanked and nuzzled her teats.
Sow milk ran, her ovaries tingled.
There was froth on her mouth,
in the black juicy loam of the pen.

Marianne Faithfull's Cunt

Justin Chin

being a mondo faggot, I am horrified. The difference between gay men and straight men is that gay men honestly love and pamper their dicks like family pets, while straight men tend to take their dicks for granted like the beat-up beer-and-nacho-cheese-stained sofa in front of the telly. Then I read the attached tag, which I discovered I was not supposed to remove until after I tore it off, that this minor switcheroonie would only be effective for a day, twenty-four hours, clock ticking.

First off, I log on to www.our.bodies_our.selves.com to figure this thing out. Again, being a mondo faggot, I never thought about female genitalia all that much, much less seen one this close up and in full-on Technicolor. I explore, poke around. It's certainly not like what you in see in artsy photos at the art gallery, or even the shaved, primed, and oiled ones in porno-wank magazines. They look nothing like the Lite-A-Vulva candles sold at street fairs, and foreign films with full frontals are no help at all. And in spite of what I was told, it *does not* look like an overripe persimmon. The website too is no help. All it shows is cross sections and line drawings. Nothing on the diagrams 1.1 through 36.4a seems to match what I have. Maybe it's me, maybe mine is somewhat wrong. The website suggests naming my vagina to help me be comfortable with it. But what do I call my newfound friend? Certainly not a proper name, I had a hard enough time trying to name the cat. Maybe they mean something friendly to call it, something like pee-pee or woo-woo or ding-dong or man-poker for the dick. I run through my vocabulary of nouns. Vagina sounds so clinical, so Webster's. I try "pussy" but my cat is sitting across the room with a feline disdain. Twat sounds too much like a sound effect from the '60s Batman television series (Pow! Boff! Wham! Twat!). I consult the thesaurus: princess (eek! too My Little Pony), pearl (just doesn't make sense), fanny (a little girl in the enchanted forest, too nursery-rhymey, and wasn't there a musical?), bearded clam (something roasted on a bed of rock salt and served with linguine in a wine sauce), gash (eugh! no, no, too *Boy Scout First Aid Handbook*), lettuce (I keep thinking iceberg, iceberg), muff (too Detroit auto industry), minge (evil character in comic book), minnie moo (tropical drink, possibly made with rum, coconut juice, 7Up and something citric, served in hollowed-out fruit), beaver (cute furry mammal who chews trees and builds dams in faraway lakes in Canada). What a dilemma. I think to myself as I have in so many messy situations, Hmmmm, what would Marianne Faithfull do? What would she call it? She would most certainly call it cunt. It sounds so rude, yet so fashionable, so wicked, yet so alluring; so Marianne. In fact, as I wake this morning with Marianne Faithfull's cunt, I'm counting on the fact that she has record promotions to do and won't notice it missing for a day.

I have Marianne Faithfull's cunt. Mick! (those lips!),
Keith! (those jowls!), Keith (Moon!), and best of all, the
sabine tickle of The Fur Rug (luxurious! pelterific!).

That deed done, I dash to the Victoria's Secret store to
buy some snazzy underwear for Marianne Faithfull's cunt.
Victoria's Secret is way overpriced but so soft and silky and
those constant advertisements make them so irresistible. I
want Marianne Faithfull's cunt to feel like a slutty super-
model's crotch, projected on the Jumbotron in Times
Square, but angelic at the same time. I put the sheer silk
French-cut lacey panties on, but alas, the effect is ruined by
the spider legs poking out the sides. I never noticed how
bushy it was, and just because I have it for only a day, it
doesn't mean that I have to eschew good grooming.

Armed with a small pair of scissors, a pair of tweezers, a
squirt bottle of water, and a Norelco X-47B hairdryer, I trim
and shape until it is a manageable mound, not too pointy. I
considered shaving it all off for that proper Victoria's Secret
look, but I remember my friend Beth, who shaved and later
described it as looking like a poppy-seed bagel, which terrified me no end and till this day, I will only eat onion, whole
wheat, egg, and occasionally, a good old plain bagel with
just a light schmear of lox spread.

Marianne Faithfull's cunt looks so great, Mick would've
wanted sloppy seconds. With Marianne Faithfull's cunt perfectly groomed and clad, I decide that I simply must test it
out.

I drag Marianne Faithfull's cunt to one of the city's premier
sex clubs. Marianne Faithfull's cunt protests, it/she/me just
wants to stay at home and read magazines and watch reruns
of *Intimate Portrait: Iman* on Lifetime: The Women's Channel. When the guys find out about the goods, they go potty.
They're used to Chicks with Dicks in this jaded sexual Fer-
ris wheel of a town, but here's a Guy with a Cunt. Whoo-
hoo, and soon, they're all clamoring to try it out. Marianne

Faithfull's cunt is pleased it/she/me didn't stay home after all; it/she/me likes attention.

The first guy wants to eat me like a seven-course dinner. He starts with the hors d'oeuvres, and by the time he gets to soup, he's made a mess in his Y-fronts and loses interest. The bastard runs off leaving Marianne Faithfull's cunt unfulfilled and rather pissed off. The second guy straps a huge dildo mounted on a leather harness onto Marianne Faithfull's cunt and wants it/she/me to fuck his mucky poo-hole. All I have to say is, if you're going to go to the sex club and want someone to fuck your pooper, you should at least wash a little first. Now it's my turn to protest, but Marianne Faithfull's cunt wants to try something new, so we go for it. He is leaning over the platform moaning like a goat in heat, while Marianne Faithfull's penis-wielding cunt is poking his butt in firm, hard, mean strokes. "Oh Momma! Beat my ass! I'm a bad poopy-boy!" he whines. Marianne Faithfull's cunt is amused. I, on the other hand, look down at that mean shit-smeared dildo and get all teary-eyed and nostalgic. Marianne Faithfull's cunt quickly gets tired of the shenanigans, and refuses to play Mommy anymore. Shoving the dirty dildo in the poor boy's mouth and ignoring his cries and sobs for more, more, more (how d'you like it!), Marianne Faithfull's cunt goes in search of more boys. Guy #3 walked with big-dick swagger. I am impressed but Marianne Faithfull's cunt looks on with disinterest. "Oh please, can't we try this one out?" I plead. After much cajoling, arguing, and negotiating, and that one unfortunate incident when I snapped the panty band pretty hard, Marianne Faithfull's cunt reluctantly agrees. Guy #3 has a big dick and proceeds to stick it in without much foreplay or lube or anything. Hey, I'm an easy guy (with Marianne Faithfull's cunt, no less). I'm sort of enjoying how the hetero-testero guy is so into the fucking, like we were on some bad porno shoot, but Marianne Faithfull's cunt is bored. Oh no, it can't be, it better not be . . . Oh shit, Marianne Faithfull's cunt is humming "Broken English" while #3 is grunting his hefty man-thing in and out. I am so embarrassed, I hope he doesn't hear it/she/me going into the key-shift and segueing into its/her/my rather vast repertoire of Kurt Weil classics. Thankfully, he pops his load and is strangely embarrassed and grateful. Marianne Faithfull's cunt is now getting demanding; it/she/me wants to choose the next one.

"Okay, fair's fair," I say. And it/she/me chooses this weird-looking twiglike accountant-looking guy.

"You're determined to repulse me," I scold Marianne Faithfull's cunt.

"I have a feeling about this one," it/she/me replies. "Now shut the fuck up and get those panties down!" Guy #4 turns out to be talker. While fucking, he insists on reliving his exploits with a bevy of hookers in Southeast Asia.

"I've been looking at you ever since you came in," he says. "I had a girl in Thailand who looked just like you, she looked just like a little boy, little titties and big wide pussy. I like little boys too. She liked me to do this." He tried to poke really hard but Marianne Faithfull's cunt is tough and nonchalant about his efforts to show how he hurt the sad little hooker with no tits. Why is he even telling me all this? Does he tell this to every woman he has paid to screw? And when was the last time he even had a real date? Does his mother know what he's up to?

"You like me to spank you? and beat you?" he asks. "I'll even pay you?"

"Not only will I kick your ass, I will hack your dick off and shove it into your left asshole," I tell him. Marianne Faithfull's cunt is snickering. He continues to fuck in a pouty, mopey silence. Marianne Faithfull's cunt suddenly decides to do some strange contracting thing and darn near snaps the poor guy's dick off. "Owwww! My cock!" he whines. "You're too much." He limps off with his injured dick in his hand.

"What the hell was that?" I ask. "That wasn't one of those famous female orgasms was it?"

"Fuck, no, you'll know when I get an orgasm," Marianne

Faithfull's cunt says. "I just wanted to see if I could bend his dick, twist it while he was in the midst of his fun, that's all." Marianne Faithfull's cunt is evil, that's why I love it/her/me so. But the night is certainly not as I had planned.

"That's it, we're going home," I tell Marianne Faithfull's cunt.

"Wait, wait," it/she/me protests. "There's someone in the corner over there. . . ." But the lacy panty muffles its/her/my protests.

At home, Marianne Faithfull's cunt decides that it is time it/she/me gets taken care off. "Where's your vibrator?" it/she/me demands.

"What? I don't have one . . ."

"Oh never mind, just stick your fingers in there and play around," she commands.

"Should I wash my hands first?" I ask.

"Just do it. Now."

"Yes, ma'am." I am playing with myself in a way I have never played with myself before. It's not like massaging one's own prostate; it feels different, strange, titillating. Like five hundred years of guilt poking out of crotchless panties.

"A little more to the left, a little right. Now more force, more direction, more purple!" Marianne Faithfull's cunt directs my efforts. Suddenly, without warning, my legs quiver and I'm in these muscular contractions as if I were being plugged into a wall socket.

"God, I needed that," Marianne Faithfull's cunt says in her husky sexy growl. I'm too gob-smacked to speak. "We'll try for the female ejaculate next time, see you next year!" it/she/I says, waving good-bye.

A new Victoria's Secret catalog has popped in the mail, there's something on page 18 on Tyra that I want; and I know there's an old Good Vibrations catalog around here somewhere. I can't wait.

Horseback

Bayard Johnson

*t*he one passing off the love just looks for a clear path going in. You don't think about whether the other person has to reach through a wall of fire.

Four-wall a theater, invite all the fags who fell in love with me and lied about it, make them stand in the back where they can't see shit.

Invite the President, puppeteered by his own fantasies.

They'll be inside, waiting. I'll be out back, in the moonlight, riding a horse naked, cantering all night out in the country. Girls have told me that's how they had their first orgasm.

Spinach

Dress

Alexandre

Rockwell

ittle pee pee had nothing to do with it. In fact it meant no more than an armpit; like a little finger. There was no mind of its own kind of thing going on then. It did warm things up a bit or make me look twice at the sight of the mini butts my sisters had up front. It's about the same when I see a baby niece or nephew now, nothing more than a soft little pink area. The fact that they grew beards and wrinkles, and filled up with blood and juice, and dominated the biological polls later in life had little to do with my four-year-old world. As far as I knew I was a girl, if being a girl was what my three older sisters were. But being different was what it all came down to that day.

We were all living in a blender of emotional hysteria. There was a lot of alcohol and violence, crying and yelling in the adult world around us. Once in a while a grown-up would poke their head in to assure themselves that things would get better, or to maybe strike us with a blow or some other abuse. They were on the "outside" and us kids were on the "inside." The safest place to be was in a big dusty bed slowly dying of an asthma attack, watching Boris Karloff scare the shit out of me on black-and-white TV, with my sisters surrounding me. Being wedged in the middle of them was what made it safe. You couldn't tell where one arm began and another leg ended, we melted into one. The only way to attack us was one-on-one, never in numbers. Together we couldn't be touched.

That Christmas a big box arrived from my grandmother's house. There were presents inside for all of us. My sisters pulled out these green dresses with white lace sewn around the arms and necks. I waited for mine, but nothing came. My sisters had these three identical dresses and I was given what looked like baby blue lederhosen. What was up? I didn't understand why I didn't get a spinach dress like my sisters. I didn't care about the butt up front, it was the same as my little upfront finger. I wanted a spinach dress!

My stepmother, Tizzy, grabbed me after she sent my sisters down to try to coax my father out from under the oil burner so he could see what they had gotten from his mother for Christmas. She caught my arm so I couldn't follow them down and gave me a whack that sent me flying.

I remember lying on the floor, looking up at the strange, distant, hungry eyes of Tizzy, and wondering why she had caught me. The answer came to me clear as day: you catch what's different. I had no spinach dress; I stuck way out.

What I Always Wanted

Hugh Fox

What I always wanted, so
hard (but never enough for
the last 20 years) to come
across the Sierras into
home, until I got it so
small and concentrated and
nothing to prove, but just
receive, and never the
insistent galloping, hippity
hippity, hippity,
hop (you hope)
but opening the legs of
the universe to receive
whatever you choose
to put into it,
if anything at all.

Monster

Brian Bouldrey

Their uniform feels rough to them and mean:
Cold iron and sour leather and poor cloth
Though sometimes there's the softness of a feather.
They feel unloved and they feel raw, uncouth.
Only he bears as if it were a woman
Their standard in its brightly-colored dress—
The heavy silk whose touch like a caress
Brushes his hands and softly strokes his skin . . .

RAINER MARIA RILKE, "THE STANDARD-BEARER"

n the dentist's waiting room, the choices are *Highlights for Children* or a fashion magazine. Since I lost interest in *Highlights* when it stopped running the delightfully grotesque comic about the lumberjack Timbertoes family (oh!, those half-human, half-wooden cousins of Pinocchio! They scared and interested me at once), I flipped through a section of beauty tips in *Vogue*.

"Most women," reads an offhand factoid, "look at themselves in a mirror an average of eleven times a day."

I do not claim to be anything remotely close to a typical man, but I think I can safely say that, if this little nugget is even slightly truthful, there are some huge differences between me and women.

I hate to look at myself in the mirror. Call it low self-esteem if you want, but really, *really*, there is very little of interest for me to look back at from a reflective surface. I have lived with that mug all my life, and there are very few surprises left. I have even perfected the art of shaving in the shower, mirrorless; in fact, I find on those rare occasions when I do shave with a mirror, I cut myself.

It is the summer before I am to be in the third grade and it's swim period at day camp. I love Clark Lake, the big dock, the sandy bottom, the tall yellow lifeguard chair, the line of buoys that may as well demarcate the end of the earth.

I love to swim and would later become a lifeguard, a swim instructor, despite or perhaps because of one thing: I have to wear a bathing cap.

The year before, the mastoid process in my right ear (that's the anvil of the hammer and anvil) got so infected that they had to surgically remove it. The surgeon sliced through my eardrum in order to get at the rotten thing in me, diminishing my hearing in that ear by a third (and despite or perhaps because of this, I came to be a music lover) and forcing me to swim, for the rest of my life, with extensive protection against wetness in my inner ear. Today, I have clever shape-molding malleable earplugs, necessary, since the surgery also widened the opening in my ear into an irregular, huge size (roughly the shape of Australia flipped on its side; over many childhood years I studied that shape with a combination of bathroom mirror and my mother's handheld mirror). But back then, I had to make do with a jerry-rigged combination of cotton, tape, and, oh horrible of horribles, a bathing cap.

Not a slick groovy Speedo Olympic number, no. This was 1971 and all I had available to me was one of my grand-mother's fancy caps with layers and layers of latex fringe. It looked like a cannibalized fetishistic flapper's dress. It was either that or the one that made me look like a hydrangea.

I was treading water and three kids swam up. One of them, dared, said, "We were wondering, are you a boy or are you a girl?"

The new edition of the *Boy Scout Handbook* had a whole section on puberty. The magic of adolescence. There was a series of diagrams showing two or three different body types growing, developing, enlarging. There was an Endomorph, an Ectomorph, and Something In-Between. Even at that age I must have known they were throwing me a bone, try-ing to make me believe there was no such thing as abnormal when in fact they were reinforcing—dictating—the tenets of abnormality.

I prayed to be the example called Something In-Be-tween, in every way the physical equivalent of invisible. Stripped, I held the page of the *Scout Handbook* at arm's length, and the mirror was facing me, my reflection right beside the picture. If I adjusted my arm just right, I was just as big as the Something In-Between boy in the book. We were both thirteen. Surrounding his outline, however, were the onion layers of his future, a boy at fourteen, at fifteen, and so on, which made him seem to be vibrating, sending out secret waves. In any case, he had a trajectory, an ulti-mate goal, and his body was expanding in the right direc-tion. Did I match him? Were my shoulders as broad? My waist as slim? My penis as big?

"A woman is almost continually accompanied by her own image of herself. Whilst she is walking across a room, she can scarcely avoid envisaging herself walking." That's what John Berger—a man—observes in *Ways of Seeing.*

I, on the other hand, walk across the room and feel perfectly nonexistent. Being neither beautiful nor ugly, fat nor skinny, short nor tall, I am Something In-Between, I blend in. At least, that's what I like to believe: that I can be anonymous, the invisible man.

To what purpose? To spy, to collect information, to observe others—women, men, dogs, decor. It's an artist's job, I tell myself, but what about all those other invisible men who are not artists?

For I believe that many men think they, too, are invisible. Imagine a legion of little boys covering up their eyes with their fat little fingers and hollering to Mommy, "You can't see me!"—and believing it sincerely.

The invisible-man fingers-before-the-eyes syndrome may be one of the big reasons why so many men have such big, particular problems with ethics, I figure. The banker dips his hands into the till, he's unseen. The lawyer puts a pubic hair on a soda can and shows it to a coworker, who'll know the difference? A covert war is started by the CIA. If they thought they were being watched, they'd take the fingers from their eyes.

And girls, do not think this ethical problem is limited to the obvious crimes of embezzlement, harassment, and war. When in that pivotal third-grade year Joe Dalton lorded over me a hefty piece of pyrite he found in his driveway gravel, he bragged, "This is fool's gold." As if the first word had nothing to do with it, or was in fact something that made it even more valuable. Gold was gold. And Joe impressed upon me that its value was as such, because he wouldn't even trade a whole bag of marbles for it, because are you crazy, it's Fool's Gold— gold that once belonged to a man named Fuhl, or mined from a forty-niner camp near a town called Fulz.

Grown-up versions of Joe Dalton are hard at work, advertising cigarettes with cancer warnings built right in and pushing prescription drugs that are required to list their own terrible side effects. Somehow, those admen have made the stuff invisible or part of their power.

Thinking that it might enhance my ethics, I decided to start looking at myself in the mirror as often as *Vogue* said women do—my way of taking my fingers from in front of my eyes. Is my hair sticking up? Is my belt too shiny? Did I miss that spot under my chin while shaving? Are there Crow's-feet near my eyes? Frown lines around my mouth?

I'm thirty-five, time to start taking care of my skin. Time to become vain, I guess, when it's a little too late. Frankly, I'm thrilled to grow older. Watching gray hair fall onto the barber's smock, discerning the slow recession of my hairline through a sequence of photographs, seeing the wrinkles, the emergence of cragginess that, well, looks good on men— character, they call it.

These I don't hate to observe in the mirror. It's the other imperfections of myself I see there that I wish I didn't. Imperfections for which others wouldn't have a clue where to look.

My chin is my mother's, and bless her heart, I wish it weren't. The slump in my shoulders comes from my father's side of the family.

I can also see that my right eye is closed more than the left. It's lazy—I spent that same traumatic third-grade year with a patch over the left eye and big dorky glasses to strengthen it, though it was too late.

Nowadays I have to wear glasses that correct nearsightedness in one eye and farsightedness in the other. The lens in my right eye is demonstrably thicker than the left, and while the eye sleeps, sags, and lazes, its shiftlessness is emphasized by the magnifying lens over it. It is huge, and I can frighten infants with it.

My tongue is also lazy. I can't roll it, or "R"s, so that I'm shy about learning foreign languages.

It's as if the whole right side of me is a monstrous mutant, the Mr. Hyde to Dr. Jekyll. The diminished sense in my absurdly large-yet-deaf ear, enlarged-yet-blind eye must have something to do with my being left-handed—left-handed, at least, in the dexterous activities like writing, handling chopsticks, and cutting out paper dolls. I still do some things with my right hand, but they are more brutal activities, like batting a baseball, bowling, masturbating. My right shoulder muscles are more solid, overdeveloped. You can't immediately see it in me, but when I look into a mirror, I see a cyclopean, elephant-eared, hunchbacked freak at war with my more gentle, acute, and human aspects. All of those secret things I see in the mirror, and I don't like to be reminded of them.

But it's the handicapping of my senses that have also made me want to be a lifeguard, buy opera tickets, read in dim light on trains. That has become part of my character—if I am forbidden to do something, it is only a challenge.

So as I began to check myself the requisite eleven times daily in the mirror, I began to betray myself: I wasn't looking at myself in the mirror—I was looking at the mirror itself.

Pretty mirrors! Vanity of vanities! This one has a beveled edge, that one has a flaw in the upper corner, like a healed flesh wound. This one needs resilvering, that one is wreathed by a hand-carved ornamental design of acorns and oak leaves. Georgian, Gothic, bathroom, handheld. The one over a bar, the wall-sized one at the gym or in a ballet conservatory, the one in a small cramped restaurant installed to make the place look bigger, spacier. It's these restaurant ones that always throw me—I'm eating and I look across the room to see somebody vaguely familiar. Who is that man with the stooped shoulders and receding hairline? Wait! It's me!

I have come to prefer the mirrors that distort—not just the obvious funhouse waves that make me a midget or give me a gut, but mirrors hung at a severe angle so that I can see the top of my head or put in an odd light source so that I seem green, or tan, or to have more hair.

We exaggerate and distort a story in order for it to be believed. The grotesque reveal truths.

When she was in third grade, my friend Libby wanted to be a boy. She had her mother take her to the beauty parlor to get her hair cut off. Her mother said, give her a pixie, the fashion of the early seventies when Olympic star Dorothy Hamill made short hair on girls, *comme des garçons*, all the rage.

Her mother was surprised to find at the dinner table that her short-haired daughter, in overalls, was joined by a brother with a towel wrapped over his head and draped at the shoulder like a Pharaoh's headdress. "What are you doing at the dinner table with a towel on your head?" his mom wanted to know.

"If Libby is going to be a boy, then I'm going to be a girl," he said, biting daintily into his bread, a moment just barely imaginable to me, the notions a small boy might have as to how girls were different from boys.

Libby's brother was told—quite fiercely, by Father—to take that towel off your head at the dinner table and behave like a boy. Mother was more gentle with Libby and her sex change:

"You can't be a boy."

"Why not? I have a boy's haircut."

Libby doesn't recall the key phrases that convinced her that she could not be a boy, but she understood as much.

"Then I want to be something else, if I can't be a boy."

"What would you like to be?" asked her mother, probably feeling indulgent.

"A monster," said Libby.

There are monsters that scare me. The Timbertoes from *Highlights*, half-human, half-wood. The Borg from *Star Trek*, half-human, half-machine. The Creature from the Black Lagoon, half-human, half-fish. Neither fish nor fowl, these beings are impure, freakish, one-of-a-kind.

There are other, less-frightening monsters, too. Mary Shelley's creature in *Frankenstein*, standing on the ship among the ice floes, alone. Virginia Woolf's *Orlando*, a woman-man who flops from sex to sex like a fish out of water, on through the ages. Jeanette Winterson's web-footed gondolier in *The Passion*, Katherine Dunn's narrator in *Geek Love*, an albino dwarf.

These are monsters I have loved. Women writers are able to create the best of these monsters, though some men have had their successes: William Goyen's Arcadio is a circus freak show's half-man, half-woman; the Baron Corvo had his own sexually mysterious gondolier named Zildo/Zilda in *The Desire and Pursuit of the Whole*—and what about Proust, who reportedly switched the sexes of real-life friends and lovers to create the characters of his novels, as easy as flipping burgers on a broiler?

These are monsters who tell stories, who have been simultaneously in the margins, invisible, and at the center of attention too. They are object and subject of their own tales, their sight is more sensitive, their bodies more sensual. They are what we mean when we say *androgynous*.

When I was in the ninth grade, I began to grow a breast. It wasn't surprising to find that it grew under my right nipple. It wasn't what guys in gym class called hermans, ta-tas, winnebagos, but to me, it was huge. It was a lump that compounded my misery: I suspected breast cancer, among the list of other things: hermaphroditism, genetic mutation, homosexuality. Probably few people noticed it, but I couldn't keep my eye off it. I studied it in the mirror, poked it, prodded it, squeezed it hoping it would burst like a pimple, but it seemed to be growing larger. Under the soft skin of my nipple, I could feel a buildup of tissue, fibrous, muscular. It seemed some unfinished thing, an incubus, the outer space spore they let develop in a test tube in science-fiction movies to see what it will become, until it's too late and it has eaten the lab assistant.

I wasn't going to let it get that far. I called a doctor out of the phone book—not the family doctor, an unknown doctor, to get it taken care of. I had an after-school job, and I was willing to pay for all medical expenses myself.

It's a hazy memory for me now, except perhaps the exam, the questions. I don't remember what that doctor looked like, though I can remember the location of his office downtown, in an area I considered nondescript, invisible. How did I arrive at this doctor? Did I seek out a breast specialist? Somebody who was good at what I then considered "sex things"? I told him how it had been there for at least a year, and it was getting larger. He said it was rather small, did it bother me, physically? No, I said, but it had begun to secrete a little something, oh God, was it milk? When I wore a T-shirt in gym class, I could see it press against the cotton, and playing shirts against skins in basketball was the most miserable experience imaginable.

I thought of the Amazons, that tribe of women who burned off one breast so that they could shoot arrows more accurately. Such a race of beings must have freaked men out throughout history—a self-sufficient breed who were half-men, half-women. No men necessary, just drop your sperm at the door, thank you very much, we'll pick it up later. I was an Amazon, a monster, half-man, half-woman.

The removal of the growth was handled very discreetly. It was as if we were all embarrassed by this aberration. My parents were notified by this doctor—he must have coaxed their names out of me—and they did not chastise me or discuss it at any length. They were sympathetic and swift, and I was carted off to the local hospital as an outpatient, where I went under briefly and woke up to find an ACE bandage wrapped several times around my chest, the mummy, unbound.

It was my father who drove me to and from the hospital. He was kind to me, but only asked me if I was in pain, those sorts of questions. And only after the anesthetic wore out did I hurt, that very particular hurt of flesh when it has been cut—it is the sympathy pain I feel when I am told a person has had a sex change, for I know that the dull insistent throb of separated meat on our bodies doesn't abate for a long time.

The incision healed nicely, and now it is almost invisible. If I took the time to study it closely in a mirror, I might see the scar, but you would never see it, not knowing where to look. A modest slice that traced the underside of the aureole of my nipple, needlessly cosmetic since my chest has since grown over with hair. The growth never returned, but I wonder what happened to the original missing piece—did they keep it in a jar to study in a lab? Did they ever discover what it was that made this decidedly feminine thing form on me? Did it have anything to do with my monstrous right side, did I sit wrong in my mother's womb, did I fall into a heap of radioactive debris on that side? Or am I simply a monster?

Rainer Maria Rilke was obsessed with these monstrous things: transformation, watching, being watched. If I only had a nickel for every appearance of the word "mirror" in his poems. "Learn, inner man, to look on your inner woman," he writes in "Turning-Point," "the one attained from a thousand natures, the merely attained but not yet beloved form." There is another Rilke poem in which Rilke (invisible, the observer, male) watches children play with a ball. The ball is bounced about, tossed, adored. It is the object of the children's affection. Their pleasure depends upon it. The ball goes high into the air and Rilke is thrilled to note the situation magically change, if only momentarily: the children, awaiting the ball to reach its apex on the launch, rearrange themselves around the ball, trying to anticipate its return trajectory. Suddenly, the subjects become objects—it is the ball objectifying the children.

There are times when I too have turned from subject to object, watcher becoming watched. Certainly, if I do not check myself in the mirror properly, I might go out with a misbuttoned shirt, a tie with a stain, a booger hanging from my nose.

That's one reason why I have a True Love. I need somebody outside of me to observe me, and if not to adore me, then to objectify me, to say, subtly, "Are you going out in *that?*"

But there is just so much scrutiny I can bear, before I flee. Under the watcher's eye, I feel like a fourteen-year-old, and it is at that age—when my phantom breast grew—that I wished myself the most invisible. Love is scrutiny, but what will my True Love think when he discovers that I am secretly a damaged monster?

And who else watches me? The ones who desire me, I suppose, although they mostly spy, like me. The homeless watch me. On the street, some ask for money, but others say, "Just give me a smile." When I don't smile—because a false, silly smile is called a simper and I don't want to give a simper—I am immediately called an asshole. Women friends say this is what they get from men who say, "Hey baby doll, give us a smile," as if this were a harmless, unsexual request; they are infuriated when such a tiny gift is denied. "I have gone from 'Little Darling' to 'Bitch' in ten seconds flat," my friend Stephanie tells me.

Some watchers don't understand that the watched are not public property. They don't understand that complete strangers are not to be aggressively insinuated upon, nor touched, as in the case of pregnant women I have seen fondled in supermarkets—even by other women. A watcher must only watch—not insinuate a power over the watched. This is what I fear: the power.

And this anecdote, which reveals a character both salacious and sagacious:

A friend has taken me for a drink at the Motherlode. This is where the real Fuhlz Gold is mined—it's a bar in San Francisco's Tenderloin neighborhood where drag queens, transvestites, male-to-female transsexuals, and their admirers go to see and be seen. For a seedy neighborhood, the Motherlode has a cheerful, old-world charm to it. The men who love these ersatz ladies are gentle-men. They pull out a seat for a girl. They buy her a drink. They stand when one enters or exits a room. This is the fantasy: that the women are real and the men are heterosexual. But it's a very campy fantasy, theatrical, and can't exist without the stage where the queens lip-synch pop songs, and the special lighting that hides as much as it reveals.

And when push comes to shove, these ladies take advantage of their gender fence-sitting: there's a long line for both the women's and men's bathrooms, and a sweet little Thai girl drags a hand down my shoulder. "Do you mind if I go ahead of you?" Ladies first. Even for a urinal.

Craig, the friend who has brought me here, is an expert, and is happy to explain the hermetic details, the way somebody might show the proper way to eat sushi, or judge the quality of a matador. "What I like to do," he says, "is nod and smile a little if one of the trannies has momentarily fooled me. That makes them feel good, that they've done really nice work with their makeup and their outfit." There's one now, a slight white thing in a cobalt blue dress. She really could pass, at least in this calculatedly flattering light.

I decide to try it myself. There is a Latina in a smart Marimekko number at the bar. She's pretty, petite, not gaudy. Ringlets of hair frame her face. I prefer the company of men to women, so my admiration is aesthetic. As such, I nod: "Good job."

But she misunderstands my compliment—she stares back

at me as if I were her next pickup, one of the men who love
the theatrical story of boy meets girl with a surprise twist at
the end. Craig says, "Oh, she likes you. You should buy her
a drink."

I slug him in the arm, which probably looks very manly
to She Who Holds Court at the bar. For twenty minutes I
stare at my beer, and whenever I look up, I see her eyes are
locked on me like a laser beam. She wants me. She longs for
our acquaintance.

"Buy her a drink," teases Craig.

"Shutup, shutup, shutup," I return, all lips-over-
clenched-teeth. But she does not take a hint. A half hour
goes by, and the beers have run through me. I need to pee
very badly. But to go to the confusing rest rooms means running The Gauntlet of Her.

Finally, she gives up with a sigh and a slap on the bar. I
watch her get up and mix into the crowd, and I think she
has made her exit onto the Tenderloin streets. My bladder
won't wait any longer, and I excuse myself for the men's
room.

Halfway there, I feel the hand on my shoulder. "Hello,
Brian, you don't remember me, do you?"

I turn at my name. It is my girlfriend, all smiles, nails,
long, long lashes. "Remember you?"

"I'm Monica, but you know me as Eduardo."

I keen my eyes, the way I would when seeing myself reflected in an estranged way in a restaurant mirror across the
room—odd yet familiar. "Eduardo?" Seven years before, I had
dated for a few months a man who swam in my lane at the
YMCA. He was strong and bony, with a bow and arrow tattoo
next to his left nipple. He worked in a bookstore, was well-
read and on each date, lavished upon me gift books. I dragged
around a little sack of guilt for breaking off the relationship
the day he brought me Saul Bellow's *More Die of Heartbreak*.

"Eduardo?"

He told me how he was pre-op but mostly ready for the
complete change (did I momentarily grab my right nipple,

responding to the ghostly twinge of scalpeled flesh?). He had breasts and estrogen and a pearly little clutch purse. "And are you still working at the bookstore?"

"Oh no," said Monica. "I'm a maid at the Hyatt."

She had taken the whole fantasy package, disappeared into the woodwork, evaporated into thin air. She had all the accessories for being a woman, except the last thing, which was, for me anyway, merely academic. But Eduardo/Monica's way of seeing was entirely male.

No, for me, fence-sitting between genders is not androgyny. Drag queens are not of the breed I call monsters. Men who climb into the confinement of women's clothing usually do so to respond to the way they see women—they objectify women in a different way, picking up the most obvious and salient aspects. But make no mistake, they are still objectifying women, same as any hard-hatted worksite catcaller checkin' out the babes. They exaggerate, magnify, and distort the image of a woman with their big hair, big breasts, big mouths, big purses.

A uniform is a uniform. Drag queens get into their disguise, like snipers in camouflage, in order to ensure their invisibility—can there be any act more male? The most successful drag queen is not clocked—not seen. They want to hear "Good job," as if they've just performed a magic trick. And poof! Eduardo becomes Monica.

Who are the emerging monsters of androgyny, the males who yearn for female qualities? Who are the ones who are as brave as women, who do not think they are invisible?

I think they are the vain men, the debonair peacocks, the macho guy with twenty gold rings and a fast flashy car that grabs your attention, the ones who aren't afraid to say "Look at me! I'm Baberaham Lincoln!" or, "Look at me, I am one ugly motherfucker!"

There is hope in the new generation that comes up behind me. I see fifteen-year-old boys on the beach who are so full of their own beauty, they can hardly find time to be looking out at others. They strut, they let drop an occasional benevolent smile, butter wouldn't melt in their mouths. I have no doubt that they look in the mirror eleven times a day. I see handsome straight men smiling when gay men wolf whistle, comfortable with their own beauty. Unlike me, they don't mind being scrutinized. They check themselves in the mirror at least eleven times a day.

How could I redeem vanity?

Vanity is more pure than much of what is called vanity. I am mildly puzzled by contact lenses that change your eye color, nose jobs, skin peels. These are called acts of vanity but are in fact subtle forms of self-hatred. These things do not highlight one's physical aspects, they hide them, as if they were something to be ashamed of. Since when are blue eyes better than brown eyes?

With real vanity comes a self-sufficiency that is momentarily threatening but also magical. When you remove the object of desire, when the self is both watcher and watched, desire itself transforms into something like longing, or nostalgia, maybe, what the Portuguese call "*saudade*." The one who observes and is observed is also at a standstill—Narcissus gazing into the pool—somebody waiting, unmoving, full of a potential, uncontrollable energy, like the airborne ball in Rilke's poem.

Rilke, again, and finally: "And the rumor that there was someone who knew how to look, stirred those less visible creatures: stirred the women." As I grow older, it becomes more important that I not only learn how to become visible, but must also see the world through different eyes. Men are at their best when they are uncomfortable—alone, out of the company of other men, out of uniform, forced to be self-sufficient, and perhaps a little frightening, like any good monster. In other words, men are at their best when they rise to the level of women.

The

Missionary

Paul Agostino

woke up and went into the
bathroom and looked in the mirror and noticed I had
turned into a woman during the night. I wondered what
happened. Then I wondered why there were pubic hairs on
the sides of the sink and on the back of the toilet bowl and
in the soap dish and on the ledge and all around the drain of
the shower and in the corners of the floor and in the middle
of the floor and on the walls. And I wondered why the inside of the toilet was yellow and why the shower curtain was
full of mold and why there was fungus in every corner of the
floor and spiders in the corners of the ceiling and dirt clog-
ging the screen in the window and I wondered what the
original color of the wall could've possibly been. One brave,
dirty lightbulb above the mirror semi-illuminated this disas-
ter. I wondered how so much damage could've been done to
a 6-by-6 bathroom and left unaddressed. The place was not
abandoned—there were signs of someone still living there:

a still-damp towel served as a bath mat; new beard stubble was stuck to the sink, glued there by layers of soap scum and hardened shaving cream. Someone still lived here, I thought, but who? Who could possibly have so little respect for themselves to live in such squalor?

Horrified, I left the bathroom. I went to the refrigerator. The outside of the refrigerator was completely bare except for a number of unidentifiable smudges: no smiling pictures of relatives, no baby pictures of any kind, no forget-me-not magnets to hold notes, no quaint sayings to muse on.

I couldn't bear to look inside the refrigerator. I decided to get to work and, with a feeling of mixed disgust, anger, and horrible curiosity, wait for the dweller of this habitation to get home. Someone would have to inform him that living in this manner, in a civilized society, is simply not tolerable. If anyone ever needed me, it had to be this creature.

Sometimes It Ain't Easy Being a Gal

Ian Kerkhof

At the moment of my moisture the rapist smiles. This is his victory. His dry passage was my resistance. Now there is only flood and somewhere in me I am relieved. Let it come, let him be gone, let there be a tomorrow. I would keep my eyes closed but his massive cruel fingers contort me as if I were Sunday bread and his surprisingly high-pitched voice demands open. He wants to see me seeing him see me as my moisture confirms for him his firm conviction that I am enjoying this. He always knew I would. His journey here into my tunnel was predicated on that tunnel vision. He even said so. "It's only rape until you start enjoying it." His knife smiled at me and I was afraid. To let it happen was surely better than to confront scars and perhaps even the devil. But now the devil stares out from his eyes and I realize his second victory is this intimacy. The revelation of my moisture is an intimate moment. I choose carefully with whom I share this moment. He forces me to look into his eyes because he knows and he wants me to know that he knows. Violation follows violation. His eyes rape mine, surely they do. When my cunt stops hurting because of my precious moisture he transfers the place of violation to my eyes. I was not expecting this. My preconception of rape had not trained me to deal with such refined torture. Is it because they are dry and hurting that my eyes fill with salty moisture? Do I hear a sob trying so desperately to prevent the moisture from coalescing into the most vulgar of tears? This is his third victory. His relish at seeing my tears and hearing my sobs is tangible in the place where my moisture functions in a natural way to enhance his joy. I feel his hardness now nearly complete. His moment has arrived. He spits on me when he comes. There are many moistures and all of them are intimate. Today I wish I were dry. He forces my head into his underarm. He demands that I clean him with my tongue. He addresses me in words I refuse to understand. I will not lash him with my moist and bleeding tongue. He withdraws his now enfeebled rape thing out of my cunt and scuttles across my torso. He holds the knife at my face, I suppose to prevent me from struggling although god knows by now I've not the moisture for it. He calls me a toilet. His yellow moisture is greasy and not even vile enough for me to vomit. I am enraged that I cannot puke. I want him to be sullied by at least the sour shower of my bile. It is not forthcoming. He punctuates this all with a moist fart. He sits directly on my face and through his thighs I hear my orders. I am to become his toilet paper. My function is to absorb his moisture. I am not quite sure if all of this is a victory for him. Right now I am so dissociated from my own body that he appears somewhat ridiculous, a not very attractive middle-aged man holding a bread knife squatting on a naked woman's face, wiping his arse on her tongue. Did he fantasize about this moment when he was a girl? I did when I was a boy.

I have set up my video camera on the expensive new Manfrotto tripod that I purchased yesterday. I have carefully perused the manual and am confident about how to deal with the remote control. While recording my menstruation I am able to watch myself on the monitor that I set up across the way from the couch. I peel back my lips that are, if I am to be perfectly honest, truly grotesque. Before the blood seeps out I smell it. I am aroused by my own smell. Sickened as well. I am altogether and entirely confused by this prehistoric swelling of crepuscules and whorling bits. When it runs out my blood is so rich in texture on the monitor that my breath is literally taken away. If I recall correctly this is the color called CRIMSON LAKE. At first I am hesitant, but after the first ginger fingertip I smear my left hand in the trickling of crimson lake and carefully taste myself. With my right hand I operate the camera and am now zoomed into myself to the point of abstraction. How altogether odd this is, this pornography. I am suddenly aware of how ridiculous men are. Their unbridled obsession with looking into me, into what is after all, nothing more than ME. Now that I am me, woman, and have this at the bottom of me, these images seem redundant. I arise, switch off the monitor, and walk to the shower. Underneath the hot stream I realize that those close-ups aren't me, they're just ten centimeters of me.

I'd like to sleep and him suddenly to come into the room.

He wakes me up though I want to sleep, still not knowing what he's planned to do.

He comes into my bed, under the blankets, starts to explain what he wants.

I'm afraid. Don't want. I scream and he covers my mouth.

I'm afraid, fighting all the time, but he's much stronger, gets angry and starts to really hurt me by beating, hitting me, forcing me to be quiet.

I can't do anything so then just let it happen.

He keeps my mouth covered.

He comes into me hard and deep, after opening my tensed legs.

He fucks her and fucks her.

She doesn't enjoy it at all.

Every time he lets go of his hand to let her breathe she wants to scream but he's too quick.

And then, she hears him making that sound she always heard from her sister's room.

My body is not a part of me at all. I want to say that again. "My body is not a part of me at all." I want that sentence tattooed diagonally across my torso as if it were the slogan on a sash. MY BODY IS NOT A PART OF ME AT ALL is the slogan on my sash. My black sash. I am otherwise naked. It is the Miss South Africa contest. I have infused my lips with silicone. The racists in the audience howl at me. They howl derision. They howl "Kaffir lips." The organizer of the event pinches my bum. He whispers into my ear that I have the most gorgeous set of blow-job lips he's ever seen and that he's an expert and that I should take his opinion as a compliment. He mumbles that if I do something for him he could do more than a little for me. He mentions that he has a lot of "pull" with the jury. Before I am allowed to swallow his "cum" he demands that I look up at him with my mouth open. He wants to see the evidence of his spending. He is a big spender. He is the last of his kind. An old-time big spender. His spend is amazingly dense in constitution. It is the thick, undiluted spend of a bull man. He grins idiotically at me while I look up at him with my mouth open as wide as he wants it to be. I must remind him of a blow-up doll. I remind myself of a blow-up doll. Indeed, my silicone lips are nothing more than an attempt to replicate those ever-ready blow-up suckers that I know Daddy likes best. When the gray-haired Miss South Africa organizer nods his head to me I know that he means it is time for me to swallow. I swallow his spend. Hey big spender. I am Shirley Bassey and he is Goldfinger. I am Monica Lewinsky and he is Wild Bill Bigcock. Wild Bill turns me around so that my cellulite-ridden buttocks face him. He orders me to peel back my panties. He insults my buttocks and points out to me that my cellulite makes him feel ill. He points his Goldfinger at my Brownhole and demands from me that I beg him to insert it. When I do not respond quickly enough he kicks me very hard on my disgusting cellulite-ridden bum with his pointy handmade Italian leather shoe. He shouts hoarsely at me that I must beg for him to insert his Goldfinger into my "shitter." He punches the back of my head with his other hand and tells me that I am nothing more than a "shitter." A piece of shit. His finger lodged firmly deeply inside my arse I realize that this is the only part of my new body that Mr. Spender can really relate to. It is all we have in common. I am perversely delighted by this realization and fart onto his spiky finger. Mr. Spender is outraged, withdraws his digit and mutters to me that I never stood a chance anyway with my "Kaffir lips" and "baggy arse." The jury's decision is final and I am not even mentioned as a runner-up. To hide my shame and mortification I pretend that I am Tracey Emmin and drink too many piña coladas during the after-party. I am sloshed. Mr. Spender brushes past me after midnight and whispers to the back of my head that I was the worst blow job he ever had and that if I don't leave immediately he will have me arrested for being a "conduit of illicit behavior." A young man called Barber offers to take me home in his Porsche. I cannot help but burst into tears as he slips into fourth gear, whereupon he punches me very hard in the face. He drives faster and faster, all the time screaming at me that I am a "worthless sac of puss," a "cunt rag," and a "blood pudding." He drives to lower Houghton although I live in Blairgowrie. He forces me out of his Porsche and onto the hard gravel road. My knees begin to bleed while he invades my rectum with his "pecker" all the time screaming at me that I was "asking for it" because I had my lips blown up like a Kaffir's. My body is not a part of me at all so I do not feel it when he pisses inside my arse, only knowing that he is doing so because he tells me so and I trust him; he would never lie to me, not such an outstanding young man with a Porsche and a nice name like Barber. When he drives away I am sad and empty out his spend from my shamed and lacerated "shitter" and then fall asleep on the hard shoulder of the last highway in Houghton.

When I awoke and after applying my mascara I decided what I wanted most was to pick up a man. It would be as easy as I imagined because now with my décolleté and high heels I was what I always used to imagine I wanted. I went into a bar of a four-star hotel and ordered a peach margarita. A short Asian man walked up to me after a while and offered me some yen. He smiled unctuously but when I demurred and told him that I was not into yen buddhism he hit me hard across the mouth with a lamp shade. I was frightened by the headwaiter who threatened to call the cops. In the park I lost a shoe and was soon taking part in vulgar singalong music. An Hasidic man came up to me and said in the huskiest of tones, "Come back to my place, I have bread, vodka, and a fish." His "place" was a temple. He forced me to suck his feet between the toes but still couldn't get an erection. Then he beat me and called me "hoor" and threatened to call the cops if I didn't beat it out of there. I longed for a steady boyfriend. One that would just fuck me with a simple hard-on and be nice to me. His name was Jerry. He had become a cab driver after years of being something else. In his cab all sorts of things happened but at least he was kind to me and gave me that good hard fucking that I needed. Sometimes it ain't easy being a gal.

Jerry never hits me without good reason. That's what he says. He says, "I never hit you without good reason." And I trust him on this one. He's not mean. He's not cheap. He even bought me a Singer sewing machine. I do find it unfair that he hits me because my cunt stinks. He thinks I'm fucking someone else but I keep telling him that the infection is because he always sticks his thing in my cunt just after he's been in my arse. I used to beg him to wash it first but he just told me that he liked to do that and that what's good for him is better for me. He likes to stick it in my arse dry and hard. He shouts at me when he does so and calls me a "bunghole." Sometimes he pulls out of my arse and then goes into my cunt but more often he sticks it in my mouth just before he comes. He likes me to lick his cock clean. He says I ought to because it's my shit that makes him so dirty. He says I'm the dirtiest stinkiest shitgirl he ever met. Once I vomited when I tasted my shit on his cock and he punched me so hard that my lip split and my front tooth cracked. Since then I always swallow the vomit. I love Jerry. We have our problems but essentially he's a good man. We're saving up to move to Plettenberg Bay. Meanwhile, JoBurg is the place to be. One day I hope Jerry will marry me and I will give him lots of daughters. He says he wants at least four daughters. Jerry is my man. Since he's come into my life I feel complete. He saved me from spinsterhood. I was a vinegar virgin until I met Jerry. I will always be grateful to him for the opportunity he has given me to show the world that I am a real woman. God is my witness.

in my dream Jerry sauntered over to my place
i let him in
he demanded to know where i'd been
i started to tell him then bit my tongue and said i couldn't
he got enraged
he hit my lip
my lip began to cry
he liked that
he kissed it again with his fist
until i liked it too
he said it so loud and so often
with his fist in my coffin
that eventually i said it too
he liked that
then i hid under the gas heater while he waged
war with my interior designer
plaguing all his aesthetic commitments
the fact is he didn't believe me
he thought it was rude that i wouldn't tell him
where i'd been
then he ran down the stairs taking my front-door key
with him so he could easily
come back to repossess his car
and my scars
and make sure that i wouldn't
forget him or even think of not telling him
whatever it was that he wanted to know
"capisce?"

What horrified me most about my cunt was knowing that
my mother had one too. And every month it bled. And
every day it stank. And every day she wiped it from front to
back so as not to spread those bunghole germans. And every
day she pissed a slimy yellow stream and farted good and
solid. Now I was just as yucky as she. I spread my lips and

lowered my body to the floor. It was cold. My pussy lips are the most sensitive pussy lips on earth. That's why I never call them Labia Minora and Majora. I call them Sally Big Twins and Susy Teeny Twins. I do not have a sphincter. I have little Lola Di Poopie. And contrary to what anatomists have thought up to the present day my little clit button is not so small or envious after all; indeed, it is a fucking iceberg and under my skin extends all the way round to my badly dented cellulite buttocks and is so fucking sharp it's gonna do a *Titanic* on all the little boy's weiners on the beach. I am going to go to the rodeo and sit on the bucking bronco Billy with my extended clit family and I am going to have one big great big fucking orgasm, John, so just you better watch out, boy, you're expendable.

Tribadism, troilism, fanny-rubbing whatever. Now that I've got one I can see why none of the girls that I used to ask to do this wanted to. What a schlepp! Here we go, one two three, slurpy slurpy slurpy.

By the end of my first day with a cunt it became clear to me that true love would not be forthcoming in a world populated by dicks. So I became a ho instead of a good girl and decided to cash in on some tricks. Now I'm a Yemenite yenta in my fishnet stockings and padded bra, blowing you kisses from crimson lipstick and doing my best to avoid the devil's scars. So what did you expect me to become—a psychiatrist?

Lawrence Chua

everybody's got a pussy.
We just don't all know how to make it purr.

Cunt Talk

Paul Skiff

hi, my name is "Paula?" At birth this was actually supposed to be the name given me as my parents, having first a boy, planned for me, the second child, to be a girl. My father and mother had wanted me to enter the world as a biological female. I doubt, however, that they would feel any satisfaction from my having a vulva for one day. Especially since the cunt I had so recently acquired was purely an effect of culture. I will explain this.

A letter arrived for me from the continent of Australia asking that I imagine life for one day as a person with a vagina. As a social practice and habit this exercise was the kind of indulgent behavior culture has promoted since time immemorial. And as since time immemorial, the catch was my cunt would be culturally explored. Appropriate, per-haps, since the only cunt I had was a cultural cunt.

"Yep," announced the examining physician, "that's a vagina. I don't know how it got there, but it will have to be removed."

"Look," I countered, as sober as possible, "I'll just stop imagining it for the story. No need for radical surgery. I can un-believe it away."

I pulled up my trousers and left while the doc pitched, "Hey, if you're worried about cost I won't charge. You're an unusual case. This is important for medical science."

"Let's not get 'Make Believe' mixed up with 'Career Boost.'"

Now I had collaboration on my cunt's actual existence. I launched wholeheartedly into total physical-emotional relations with my newly bestowed feature that would not only devastate the sensibilities of the major commercial interest group seeking to invade my creative capacity, but relations that would also affirm my connection to higher powers of the Universe. In me the presence of life would be so intense that the vicious banalities of culture that direct me to sacrifice myself would simply be rendered ineffective. My cunt would be where I destroyed things, the center of my house.

Let me provide more of myself.

Hi, my name is Paula. I live in one room on the fifth floor of a building that stands where three streets come together. I get by on little money, am forty-one years old, quite trim and healthy. This is all true. And imaginary. Thanks goes to my cunt.

But in a way everyone who opens this book grasps my cunt.

In part, that is what makes a rather rare opportunity for me. For I am in many "places" at once here. The list is extensive and complicated. The proliferation of my multiple localities is due, mostly, to culture.

Listen. In my culture, the local culture where I am, not where you are, there is a very high commercial value placed on a cunt. Cunts are among the most highly prized natural resources. Even higher value is placed on an imagined cunt. Where I am we are surrounded with imagined cunt. So whether warm and fleshly or as a veritable ocean of imaginary inferences, a cunt is held out to be one of the most singularly great places to be. For this reason I decided not to have my valuable prize figure in the dialogue about cunts that makes every cunt a kind of pawn in the severely controlled personal happiness sphere. Instead I decided it would be important that my cunt cause a nervous breakdown, an event close with the imaginary. Because if you imagine me imagining my cunt, then the cunt you imagine will not be my real cunt. So my imagined cunt will really be my own, one I made myself. Culture would have a hard time locating and getting at this cunt.

With a cunt not subjected to debased treatment I was going to live who I was, bring myself into the unfolding of the cosmos. I was going to feel the movements of the earth, face the cycles of life. I was going to recall who I was becoming, make myself into the people who have loved me. I could do all of this with a cunt. But not if culture got at it. Not if culture started scattering my cunt around.

And if I was to have a cunt for only one day, as was specified by the letter from Australia, I sure as hell wasn't going to conform to a bloated menu of restrictions against people with cunts compiled during the entire course of human history that had one purpose only: to shred my spirit. No. For me the nervous breakdown I sought was not some dramatic collapse into mental instability that would require weekly therapy and prescriptions. Instead the breakdown would be a release of elemental energy creating an expansive well-being. A well-being devoid of purpose or application. Yes. The nervous breakdown I sought would be like an atom split to reveal the frailty human accomplishment mistakes for control, or like throwing my voice into mountains just to be engulfed by an echo.

I planned to encourage three conditions made possible by my cunt that would flawlessly facilitate the nervous breakdown:

1. A sense of estrangement.

2. A clear awareness of how my cunt would be made an object outside of my self that I was to have little control of.

3. Complete abandon to cunt-thought.

What I would do to attain these conditions, these guarantors of my integrity, what I would do then with a cunt, is live. Which many times is not easy. By "live," I mean *be with*. To be with your cunt is not the same as to carry one around, or just simply to have one. To begin with, if you carry around a cunt, normally, you have to put clothes over it. And not just any clothes but clothes that are exaggerated symbols for the physical difference that advertises how the world does not belong to you. Instead, to *be with* a cunt you open to it, listen with it, move as its thoughts and feelings. You see this cunt is more than I am. This cunt is how I reach out in to the world.

The first thing I did to estrange myself was fuck somebody, which was easy to do. Or: the first thing I did to estrange myself, which was easier to do, was *say* I fucked somebody. I explained, "The first thing I did to estrange myself was fuck somebody." I did this by wielding quotation marks. "". Simple. Quotation marks are my voice. My voice rising in pitch. On them music sails from my hands. But that is a cunt-thought to indulge later. Sometimes culture is unbelievable. Laughably artificial. Being with my cunt offered so many direct connections to life, I thought to myself, eluding the voice you hear. Engaging in an act that moves one away from relating to another person is great for causing confusion. "Let me explain," I said, markedly closer. There. Now listen. "Isn't that better?"

Well, so you see, becoming estranged was simple. Like spacing out. I just mixed up the several "places" I occupied culturally. I refused to take it for granted that through a repertoire of substitutions understanding could be reached. Yes, I was a voice in my head in a book in another person's hands. But by instigating competition among those locations I could confuse. Confusion and distance are really so honest. By encouraging conflict in efforts to recognize just where I was culturally it became easy to force all similarities to be forgotten. I could solidify my imaginative self outside my work and inside my work feel outside myself. The result was that every aspect of my self became a story, a means to satisfy needs external to my actual life. And being a story is a lot like being a puff of smoke. Having a cunt you know how much you are put on trial by the persuasion that it is necessary to be apprehended, simplified, and penetrated by culture in order to feel vividly fulfilled. I knew how to fuck with this. My cunt was teaching me that divergence was the true way to elude these attacks on my sense of wholeness.

The commercial interest group that sought to invade my imaginative capacities counted on me to be highly adept at one assignment: being able to convert my actual absence in space and time into the very condition of a cunt made present. The purpose of this was to create a special showcase for my cunt and force it into everyday life as this book. This was to be the only reality for my cunt. My cunt would be transposed onto this other object to construct a symbolic cunt that could tower over everyday life like a visitor to another world. My cunt, of course, like all cunts, was a zone of intimacy that culture would open and enlarge by having it be talked about. Cunts have always been called upon to do this. My cunt made into object available to others, who would access their own daydreams through it. What your hands pried open would fly through your mind.

Suddenly I wanted to see my cunt. To see to behold my cunt. To behold to hold my cunt. To hold to become my cunt. To devour it through my eyes. To participate by seeing myself as my cunt, but only partially, not really. I turned myself into a person with a cunt. I became a spectator of the event that took the place of the sexual act. What I saw still belonged to my memory of mother. For a moment I borrowed her strength, then having seen my cunt, I laid down, exhibiting my whole self as the cunt, cut off. A trophy. A severed head. Medusa's head, cut off, thinking, "None of you has a cunt." I am acting the part of a cunt, am showing you how you are supposed to consume cunt. I was the genital, both wished for and possessed. And highly visible. But my cunt was not a strange fact nor the source of a powerful urge over which I had no control. My cunt was not the target for confessed sexual needs. My cunt was a kind of nowhere, like light.

The phone rang predatorily. From the free clinic the doctor pursued his opportunity to reproduce fear-based ideas, techniques, and practices in my body.

"Listen, Paula, you should reconsider the chance this represents for the future of metaphors."

"Doc, are you licensed to practice medicine on the literary arts?"

"The whole Hippocratic Oath is founded on the ideal of the happy ending."

"I said 'literary arts,' Doc. Instead, you're talking about a demographically advantageous plot resolution."

"Paula, I appeal to your sense of climax."

"Hey, Doc, what makes your intentions toward my cunt any different from the bombs or armies needed to defend the system that produces this piece of paper off which people read our voices and take them for real?"

"Oh you're just using me for conflict."

"Doc, you were important here as an authority to establish the existence of this cunt I have been asked to take on. Other than that your thinking is too domesticated, enclosed, severed from the actual earth. I don't admire your workaholism. Your progressively death-oriented process of nonliving feelings, behaviors, and lack of spirit remind me of a petrochemical landfill, or an electromagnetic microwave radiation blast, all part of the spectacle of public suffering. Stop hiding out in the problem that your appetite for a morbid form of regulation solicits."

"Well, now, I'm confused; what is my function here supposed to be then?"

"Look, Doc, in a way you're no different from my cunt. I'm sorry, Doc, but you're just a word, you stand for something not 'there.' You're part of a kind of collective hallucination, a cultural mirage. As far as that goes each one of these words is a vagina, really. The problem between you and I, Doc, is that I am alive in the moment before word hits page; you aren't. My cunt is part of where rain and wind come from, part of earth's tilt, the look of love on my mother's face."

"I don't have anything to say to that."

"Then just hang up the phone in everyone's mind, Doc."

"I think I understand though. I think I get where you are with this. Your cunt is the void between what we see and the physical fact of who we are."

"I hadn't thought of it that way, Doc. But that's good. The cunt as cultural outerspace. You've grasped a kind of clarity in many ways symbolic of your own absence. Now if you can exit everyone's imagination, it's time for me to connect myself directly to the world."

This was it. Estrangement along with a very clear view of confusion and distance created between gratifying sensations and the bodies of the people who sought them through my cunt. Now instead of manipulating my cunt, instead of cultivating my cunt, my cunt grew wild and proliferated, elemental, galaxial, all encompassing. My cunt, which was, after all, me, not an annex, not a waiting room where I idled on offer to others with their spiritless conformity, my cunt flourished. What was behind the word "cunt"? If they could answer that they wouldn't have to offer you this, my cunt's refusal to capitulate. The answer is something you would have to really hear. And that wasn't likely to happen.

The phone rang pleadingly. "I have to tell you I feel threatened by your impenetrable thoughts," complained the doctor.

"I figured that speaking compound sentences would surpass one more restriction shoved at me by corporate savior figures who demand I subordinate to their commercial level of understandability."

"What's going to happen, how will this end?"

"That's easy. I'm going to depart where you are with the nonmoral, ritualistic, violent features of cunt-thought."

Cunt-thought: No cunt-thought; Excision:—Capitalism was over. As an omnipotent inspiration to order and growth it had dove in on itself. Advertorially. Its consumer dream-land, devoid of one wholly functioning mind in full-bodied participation with life, performed the diminishing routine of a restrictive perversion; a chronic low-grade trauma that drove out all sense of need now erected like a massive scaffold promoting refurbishment of a democrashed, imperial monu-ment that, however, had been condemned. Only the push-push of info-barf and free fall of relentlessly sexualized cultural products redolent of an asphyxiated here-and-now, shrill, anxious, bungled, stagnant and opaque as bile, stole themselves in rapturous, heart-chilling burnout of forced blankness; a telerectoid supershow of meaning deprivation lip-synching pussy-hunger over datahaze rummaged through and groped by closed-up things like the social, economic, psy-chological, military, or cultural now styled as though they were sciences; freak, mutated bodies of knowledge numb and shocked the way an epic, serialized advertisement for some company's own voice transfixes the face of any office worker from one end of a train tunnel to another.

Cunt-thought: Still no cunt-thought. But something guarding cunt-thought—: Anchored to bones. Between legs. Below where spine rose from. Deep pelvic shore. There shudder accumulated. Every flow suspended. Backed up. Over the remains of hymen. Under the small, rounded, spongy tubercle that erected itself from concealment be-neath crisp hairs and labia. Up large veins on either side from the triangle of smooth skin between clitoris and en-trance. Risen on the free protruding extremity. Calling open smooth pair of folds extending down obliquely from clitoris outward and back that lost themselves in the orifice. Over nerves, vessels, and glands to enervate outer pair of folds that fall from rounded eminence of mons to terminate closely, nearly parallel, at the short interval between anus. In all this, cunt-thought flourished. Held. Her whole body was enlivened by it. Held, too, the contractual shout that would tear her body apart and redistribute it. She was not in the room where she lay, there was only silence with cunt-thought beneath it. The word-world unfreed by mouth where indwelling breath hid at its source, not under the conjugated syntax of wakefulness that would partition her pure physicality. The word began to thrust its shards of control and subjugation but in silent sleep, before her own body could erase itself, her mouth parted. Instead, on a remote, otherwise indescribable fraction of morning, barely formed, avoiding wakefulness, seeped a word whose uniqueness, whose uselessness was not a protection.

It was a blue sun. Blue sun that came down out of the moon and ate my mother's breasts. They were golden hornets. Hornets the color of corn that stung. Stung my lips with the flagged bulbs and stems of foreign song. Song from mountain well-sheathed in echoes, frozen, sung into peopleless songs. It was a puddle sopped with empurpled leaves upon whose mute, motionless clarity germinated my shadow. Myself blank form infested, woven from textures of sunken, blight-bitten, water-molded willow hair and weedy grass merging with loam. It was the storm-ice gouged grain of a boulder traveled through decomposed silver-salted photographs century-swallowed by white-frocked or feather-hatted childhoods. It was the massive dog of gentility whose faith did not know motion. They were the heavy shoes. Heavy black field shoes of a woman that waited behind the taste of shale strained up from rock-vein with water. They were the happenstances of the high field; wind through maple shack, amplitude of rusty bucket's scabby, welted brocade; spontaneous, the way rot spawns mushroom, too slow for thought, too instantaneous for vision, she spoke.

Tea
for Two

Catfish McDaris

aughing Turtle was a peyote
dream princess from New Mexico
I met her at a hot springs
in the Jemez mountains

She slipped into the water
her body sleek as a puma
later making love under
a van Gogh swirling nightsky

I'd read my poems
in New York and California
and gained some renown
this was our first road trip

"You'll never pass for a woman
not at your height and weight"
Laughing Turtle pronounced
"I must" I replied

"Once we get to Boston
we'll get you a wheelchair
we can buy a wig
brassiere, dress, makeup"

"We'll have to practice"
she suggested
"Practice be damned
I'll wear dark glasses"

"Pretend I'm blind
struck by lightning
crippled without sight"

"You'll wheel me into
every chic boutique
dressing room to view
New England women in their grandeur"

With perpetual erection strapped
I saw the women of Boston
what a tea party

As reading time approached
I flashed back on all
the pussy-eating cunt jokes
I'd been exposed to in the army

Women smelled wonderful
soft sensual sensitive beings
Laughing Turtle snapped me back
into a semblance of reality

The congas beat a Cuban melody
my words flowed like rivers
I read only for myself
and all the women
on the third stone
from the sun

The Body He Went to Bed With

John Vanderslice

11:05 A.M.

he felt like a twenty-pound sausage squeezed into a ten-pound casing. The thin, tight pants scratched him down there and his shirt rubbed abrasively against his chest. He'd chosen the largest, loosest one he had, but it made no difference. Even if what breasts he had were little more than knobby pubescent growths, even if his shoulders had thinned and grown more pointed, even if his crotch registered not a presence but a slit absence. The fact was the whole architecture of his haunches was changed, and Terry felt that if he so much as raised himself off his chair for a moment the entire office would witness the godawful caboose that was now his rear end. The only thing that hadn't changed was his hair. So he stayed seated and spun this way or that—to the paper clips, to the stapler, back to the paper clips, to the file drawer, to the computer, back to the file drawer, back to the computer—his arms necessarily dipped or raised to cover the line of his young breasts, his chest caved and shoulders hunched in an attempt to create slack in his shirt; trying to make it impossible for anyone in this room of twenty-five people to get a clear, steady view of his new, strange physical mass, a body he found himself in at only seven-thirty that morning.

His face, however, he could do nothing about. Wider, rounder, with a somewhat shortened nose and thicker lips, Terry looked not like anyone else but only himself with layers of extra skin and some local plastic surgery. He'd worn a hat low on his head when he came to work, and since then had simply avoided conversation. But a face is a face. It is there for people to see. *You don't fuck the face*, a friend in college liked to say, a habitual seducer of ugly women. Terry recalled that opinion, and his friend Brian's rejoinder: *Maybe not, but it's what you spend most of your time looking at.* Brian was righter than he knew.

"Terry?"

His hands froze on the keyboard. He knew the voice behind him too well.

"Yeah, Jack?"

"I got a problem with the report, these numbers."

Terry's eyesight fogged and his hands remained frozen. In that long second, he felt the full consequence of his next action, felt that his future with the company might depend on exactly what he did—and doing it exactly right. Finally, one finger moved on the keyboard. Another finger. His thumb hit the space bar. His eyesight returned. He was typing, not looking at the boss who had explicitly asked for his attention.

"Terry?"

"Yeah, yeah. Sorry, Jack. I just want to finish this." He hated every word as it came out; it actually, physically hurt him to say them, to put off the man so.

"Terry, come on." Jack's hand was on the back of his

chair. This wasn't going to work. Terry didn't know why he had thought it would. And if he was going to have to turn, if he was going to have to show his boss the naked reality of his changed face, then he better do it quickly, as if he felt no reservation, as if there were nothing to be ashamed of, as if any perceived difference must be only in the flawed eye of the beholder.

"Yeah, Jack?"

At first, his boss went on talking about numbers. Then a certain distant look dawned in the man's eyes. He regarded Terry carefully, like a specimen. An ill-dressed half smile crossed his face.

"Did you—did you—"

"What?"

"Did you do something to your face?"

"Allergies."

"Oh." A whole column of relief passed through his features.

"Right. They're crazy now."

"Yes," Terry said, then pressed his boss so relentlessly about numbers that after a few minutes there was nothing left for them to discuss. Jack left. Terry immediately ran to the men's room. He just made it into a stall when he began to bawl. He sat on a toilet, his head dipped into his chest, his shoulders convulsing, his throat weak and teary as tides of feeling overwhelmed him. Terry didn't understand. He had not cried since the third grade. Not a single blessed time. Despite all the PR that it was now "okay," and admonitions—no, commands—from two different girlfriends that he ought to stop bottling up his sorrow, the release of tears was simply not a bodily calling for him. No matter how frustrated or angry, no matter how deeply and genuinely stung, he remained at all times fundamentally dry. But there at his computer, humiliated and frazzled, exhausted with tension and simple shock, disgusted that he must avoid his own boss like a shirker or a criminal—on this most important of workdays, no less—the need to let out his inner poisons in a fully physical way came over him like a sickness.

Terry stayed in the stall and sobbed. Why did this have to happen to him? And why now? Were it not for a confidential report he'd been preparing for more than a month—the very report Jack had quizzed him on—and which was due in the office of the company president at three-thirty, Terry could have just stayed in bed. And would have. For as long as it took. But bizarre changes, he knew, happen when they are least convenient; it is a part of what makes them bizarre. And in the face of this, the most bizarre change that could happen to any human being, Terry was compelled to come to this place; he was required, it seemed, to suffer.

When he returned to his desk, the phone was ringing.

"Mealtime."

It was Brian. Two years before, Terry had gotten his old friend a job at the company, in his own department. It was a superb, almost unfair, joy for both of them: to continue in this new setting the fellowship from their college years. The jokes, the skirmishes, the confessions. Each had seen the other through enough rough classes, rough parties, and rough breakups that a certain history, an understated resonance marked their conversation. Brian, for Terry, was that rare entity: a male friend to whom one could say *What I honestly believe* or *Doesn't that scare you?* or *Without this, I couldn't live*. Brian had since taken a position upstairs. Still, they met every day for lunch.

"Oh, yeah," Terry said.

"That's a pretty ambivalent response. What's the problem?"

"No problem."

"Come on, what's wrong?"

"Nothing. I just—I don't know about lunch today."

"What do you mean you don't know? We have plans to make."

They were going fishing that weekend. At least they had talked about it for a month.

"Right." Terry waited a second longer. "Okay, but not downstairs."

"Why?"

"I can't take the cafeteria anymore. All the company types. It's too, you know, suffocating. How about Benton's?"

"Benton's? I guess. Kind of pricey." Brian paused. "Are you okay?"

"Why?"

"Your voice sounds weird."

"I'm fine."

"It sounds different. It's, uh, weird."

"I'm fine. Benton's, then? I'll pay."

"You'll pay? Excuse me, I can pay for my own lunch, okay?"

"I'm sorry. It's just that you—"

"Just because I talk about prices doesn't make me poor."

"Fine. Okay? Fine. Meet me over there in twenty minutes."

"Over there?"

"Yes."

"Not downstairs."

"No."

"You okay?"

"Yes."

"You sound weird."

"I'm great."

Terry hung up the phone. He spent the next ten minutes crying in the men's room.

12:22 P.M.

"Terry!"

Brian was waving to him from a far table. Even if he hadn't called, Terry would have found him immediately:

that bony, angular frame and knobby shoulders, the short beard hiding an olive-tinged face, that big skull with its encroaching baldness ever more apparent, even though Brian was still a young man. Terry took a deep breath, walked over.

"It was jammed, so I grabbed a—"

The moment Brian actually looked at his friend, his jaw dropped.

"What happened to you?"

"It's nothing," Terry said with deliberate lightness and pushed his right hand delicately through the air: a petite dismissive motion, as if merely moving along the breeze.

"What do you mean it's nothing? You look totally different."

Totally? Terry felt again that sharp, self-conscious pang. The last thing he told himself before he left the office, back in the men's room, was that there wasn't that much changed in how he appeared. Not really. Not with his suit coat on, his tie.

"It's just allergies, Brian."

"Allergies can do that? Since when."

"I don't know since when. Since now. All right? That's when. This is how I look and it's because of allergies."

Brian's mouth stayed open. His dull green-brown eyes struggled to assimilate new impressions.

"But it makes you look like a—like a—like a woman."

"It's allergies!"

"But you're not sneezing."

"Jesus Christ, Brian. Wake up. Allergies cause all sorts of reactions. Stop being stupid." The words rushed out on their own before Terry could stop them, or even slow them down; just poured from his open maw before he even knew what he intended to say. I'm sorry, I'm sorry. I'm sorry, he said in his head, even while his words lit up the air.

Brian went silent for a time. He sipped his water, tapped his long fingers on the table, retreated behind his menu.

Terry saw only his friend's generous, open forehead, his patchy, thin brown hair. I'm sorry, Terry thought. Finally, Brian emerged. He smiled: slowly, strangely.

"Well, you know. You don't look all that bad."

"What?" A whole shaft of sunshine entered him at once. His back, his shoulders, seemed to straighten on their own.

"I mean, you know, don't get me wrong. But if you were a woman, I'd say you were all right."

Terry blushed. He looked away. He couldn't keep from smiling.

"You got nice lips."

"Shut up, Brian," Terry mouthed, but hardly meant it. A sudden excited shyness resonated within him, perhaps the most sweetly delightful sensation he'd known in his twenty-five years.

"Just don't say anything more about it," he said, yet turned his head to show it from a certain enhanced position.

6:47 P.M.

He looked at himself again, this time from another angle. He was in his apartment, standing naked before the only mirror available. With some difficulty, he'd removed it from the bathroom and stood it upright against the wall in his living room. He wanted to get a full view of himself—top to bottom.

Brian's words had stayed with him all afternoon, and from that seed they had blossomed into a full plant of good feelings, hopeful ideas of himself. Home, he felt compelled to examine himself in the light of this new knowledge. And what he found was not so bad, after all. His butt was by no means perfectly taut and heart shaped, but neither was it the gargantuan can of flesh he imagined. It drooped a little, but possessed a sort of character. Plenty of men would like a butt like that. Not all of them wanted skinny-assed women.

It was not quite pretty, his cunt. But it was there, it was his. At first he could barely bring himself to look at it, expecting acreage of unsightly commotion, not this reserved triangle in the middle of his thighs. Softly curling hairs, a fine color of brown—almost chestnut—covered, but didn't fully cover the lips there, like a stripper imperfectly disguising her goods, showing just enough of them to lure an onlooker.

His breasts needed work, yes. They were only beginning buds, the promise of something fuller, shapelier. At least he hoped. If these were all the breasts he was going to get—well, he would be disappointed. They were completely out of proportion with the lower half of him. But they were a nice color, a creamy light tan color, with perfectly circular dark-red nipples. Quaint, fresh little dollops these breasts were, courageously making up for size with appearance.

Terry sat on the floor and put his face up to the mirror. Brian's words returned one more time. He's right. I am attractive. The sides of my face are so smooth, so full. They settle perfectly around my mouth to show off my lips. My lips. My lips are, my lips are . . . He leaned closer to the glass. He couldn't make out an image anymore. The picture of his face collapsed on itself in sudden dark. He pursed his mouth and felt the sting of cold plate. *Eminently kissable.*

Terry had to get ready. Brian would arrive soon to continue the planning they left unfinished at lunch. He went to his bedroom and changed into a white blouse and green-turquoise wraparound skirt. On his feet he wore flats; on his head a wig of soft, resonating dark brown hair that ended at his neckline and gathered fully about his shoulders. He had bought everything that afternoon, after work. The wig was the most expensive item.

Terry heard a knock. He stood there in his bedroom, just inside the doorway.

"Come in."

The front door opened. Footsteps.

"Hey. Where are you?"

"Here I am," Terry said, stepping out.

Brian said nothing for a full minute. Then, simply: "Jesus." He repeated "Jesus, Jesus" over and over breathily, like an incantation—or an expression of gratitude. Terry, sensing victory, turned slowly to show all of himself to his friend: his side, his back, his other side, his front again.

"Man. Oh, man."

Terry's spirit glowed with the admiration, his ears filled with such silent excitement he almost couldn't hear. It was an exquisite order of pleasure that in his previous life he'd never experienced. Now it felt as natural as if he'd been dressing for Brian all his life.

"I don't know what to say, Terry. You're beautiful."

Terry swallowed. He smiled. "Thanks."

"If you were a woman, I'd be tempted to kiss you."

"Well," Terry began, moving a step closer, "actually—"

7:38 A.M.

As soon as Terry woke, before he even saw it, before he had any actual confirmation, he felt the change all along his body: how it lay on the mattress, how it felt against the cushioning, how it filled and didn't fill the space it occupied—not encompassing, not sloping and softly welcoming, but straight, narrow, and cordlike, tautly muscular, long, not round—myriad physical sensations that came upon him so immediately as to be one unstoppable realization. He sat up, threw the disheveled covers off the side of the bed, and looked at the region of his pubis. There he saw not small chestnut hair and rounded lips, but a dense forest of dark fur around the hanging tube of a limp penis, testicles underneath. His chest, he realized, was perfectly flat.

"Oh god," he groaned in the throes of an immense sinking feeling. His voice, deeper and louder than he expected, startled him, made him feel even lower. He ran to the living room and examined himself in the mirror. It was undeniable. The body he went to bed with was gone. He smelled both arms, his armpits, the ends of his fingers, to see if he kept on him any of yesterday's light womanly scents—or those uniquely sharper ones of a different masculine body. None.

Terry made it to the kitchen, where he collapsed in a chair by the counter. He was so struck he felt like weeping. But he could not force it out of himself, and gave up the attempt automatically. Rather than opening him to expression, this pain shut him down. He was unable to utter a squawk. Instead, he sat there staring, staring, feeling the pain of his loss revolve and renew inside him like returning, suffocating waves.

After sitting still for twenty minutes, Terry reached a dead hand to the telephone and dialed the office. He had to contact someone: his boss, the secretary, even a security guard. Someone, anyone, to give a message to. The message: I am sick and not coming to work today. Do not expect me there. This is one day I cannot bring myself to go.

The Newly Born Man

Bruce Bauman

When I was twenty-five I would have spent my day in a raunchy, twenty-four-hour fuck-fest filled with vile ironies. I would've owned the most beautiful, alluring, best-smelling cunt-disguise kit in New York. I would've disavowed and disclosed the formerly secret and sacred Phallocratic Oath. It would have been a day spent screwing under the pretense of understanding that damn indescribable G spot. I'd often "admitted" to women whom I hoped to land between the sheets: "I wish I could be a woman for one day so I could understand how it feels. How to make you feel just right." It was, and would have been, a load of bullshit.

And if my French lover, for surely I would have sampled one of those, had whispered to me of my orgasm as a "little death," I would have given him the old "Get it up or get out, my budding Rimbaud."

I was so coolly disdainful of sentiment and mortality that if my day somehow coincided with a menstrual day of blood, I would have howled, "Get me the hell out of this body now!"

At thirty, it would've been the Oedipus, dear Oedipus blame game. I would've awakened with the disguise kit already in place: bleached blond hair, nails long and painted red, peach-colored satin pajamas (no nude sleeping here, real or metaphorical), high-heeled pink slippers, and a made-up face with a mask of powder spackled with eyeliner and lipstick—I would have been my mother! I would have ranted about how coming out of her bloody vagina and being smothered in her juices had left me incapable of forming a lasting relationship with many of the good partners who wanted me. I would have insisted, "No, I will not be you." It too would have been a self-indulgent, irresponsible lie—because I am my mother's child.

And, with bravado and self-righteousness intact, I would've falsely blamed my mother's cunt-disguise kit for sending my father fleeing from our house, never to return. Leaving me one of those fatherless children, who, to make up for the dreaded loss, became determined to raise a child of my own some time in the still plentiful future—yet not even giving a second of thought to the actual acts of creation and birth.

At thirty-five, it would have been more discourse and less intercourse. All about my fear of rape and desire for castration. Desire for redemption through reproduction now subsumed to a life of the imagination, stained sheets, and take-out Chinese dinners.

At forty, now at peace with my mother and amazingly, wonderfully married to a visionary painter, it would have been clever: One fine morning Gregory Sansluv awoke from a night of unsettling dreams to discover he had transformed into a giant vagina. . . .

At forty-four, it is a day I have lived countless times in the past three years: On this day I would be pregnant and I would have a miscarriage. I now know having a vagina or a dick, for that matter, is less about sex and more about social politics, money, power, and most important, life and death.

I would comprehend the loss of ego and confidence that comes with the inability to have a child. The angst that comes with each new acquaintance because of the inevitable question: Do you have any children? I could feel the visceral physical and emotional pain, which no amount of empathy could give me in imagining the suffering in my wife Suzan's miscarriages. I would finally FEEL the mind-body connection of conception and loss; I would finally believe in and understand the preconscious maternal instinct and the repercussions of the unfulfilled.

I could choose the night when I would feel the physical torment, in bed, at home because the lazy fucking female gynecologist told me there was nothing to be done. I'd let loose the howls, taste the tears as the child never to be, while shards of tissue and blood dripping from my body were literally flushed down the toilet. But still, there would be hope someday for another surviving child.

Or I could choose one dreary afternoon, when it would be me strapped into the stretcher with an IV in my arm as the ambulance sped toward the Lynchburg Baptist Hospital with blood spewing from my vagina. It would be me lying there in the emergency room as a blood clot—ha, another lost fetus—the size of a fist—oozed out of my cunt. And yes, still with hope as the Southern Baptist doctors implored that I must keep trying because I was good and good rewards good people.

No, as horrible as those two days were, I would choose another—the day when I would be so close—I would be lying on an examining table in Mount Sinai Hospital awaiting a routine checkup. I would be more than fourteen weeks pregnant. My breasts swollen, happily aching. My fatigue and nausea the welcoming signs of a healthy baby. My eyes riveted on the sonogram expecting to see the flashing light signaling the continuing tiny heartbeat of life. The technician would glide into the room to perform the sonogram— and suddenly—there would be no heartbeat. In disbelief, from some distant void I would hear the words: "IT is gone. . . . Broken up. . . ." In between unceasing sobs I would cry "no no no" over and over again. How could I not feel that I was carrying death, not life, inside me? And slowly, eerily I would taste, smell death inside me. I would feel the betrayal of my soul by my body, my womb, my vagina. I, who had always secretly harbored so much faith in the future, in my spiritual and physical self, in humanity, would physically and mentally collapse from the weight of the loss. And then, my god—what god could allow this?—my breasts would spout milk meant for the child never to be. And I could only dread—all hope now of birthing a child extinguished (Please bring me an escape from this body)—what horror could next overcome me?

And then, at home, on the phone with my mother, I would melt as if I were composed of some human form of amniotic fluid, from the couch to the floor as I heard in her voice—my voice unable to sustain the last remnants of courage—her onrushing tears and neither of us would find any words. Only silence.

Then I would hear some of the most insensitive comments: "I know it's bad but give it time, you'll get over it." Or the inexplicable: "Oh, it's for the best." Too decimated to respond, I would only think, Please tell me how this lost, probably last chance of my womb giving life to a healthy child is for the best? And not only from the ignorant and

brainwashed televoid addicts and dumb-broad Sinatras of
the world would I hear these words, but from friends. The
supposedly liberated, educated, sensitive women (and
men), who, somewhere in their male-brained posteriors still
think that you are a failure as a woman if you do not have a
child. No matter my accomplishments as a loyal friend, a
devoted child, a successful writer—I would begin to understand why not bringing a child into this world, not becoming a MOTHER meant so damn much to my identity—not
only to others but also to me. But this would only be a beginning, a form of rebirth.

A birth not as I had once envisioned, but my rebirth as a
very different man because my day with a vagina—a
womb—would not be a day of orgiastic excess, filial revenge, or sexual anomie. It would, in the end, be a day to
love my vagina for giving me the power of a new manner of
feeling and compassion and wisdom. It would be a day that
lingered long after the return of my cherished cock, to time
spent questioning my soul.

Rufus Griscom

any man who doesn't
fantasize about having a vagina is lacking ambition.

The Major Wants to Adopt the Girls

Tad Richards

he Major in retirement: he plays
Checkers on the Internet; he melts
Bullets to make lead soldiers (Green Berets);
He mostly wishes he were someone else.

He joins blue-veined Elizabeth at rest;
As if he'd never seen them, he explores
Her female parts and says, "I'd wish for just
One day to try out those girl things of yours."

"Dear Major," says Elizabeth. "You might
Be just a bit more circumspect with wishes.
No reason why it shouldn't be all right,
But you could still be under one of Trisha's

Long-shelf-life spells." He chuckles. "I don't think so."
He gets up, dons his military costume,
Heads for the door. "Sweetheart, before you go,"
She says, "you'd better use the little boys' room."

He notes, with absentminded irritation,
The seat's left up (not heretofore an issue).
He lowers it, prepares for urination
By sitting down and reaching for a tissue.

This can't be right! He rises to attention,
Does an about-face to address the bowl.
He reaches for his natural extension,
Comes up a good five inches less than whole.

So . . . is the Major shocked by this? Well, sort of.
His masculinity is so ingrained,
He has to let it sink in what he's short of
Before he stops to check out what he's gained.

Elizabeth was right—he's been possessed.
He starts to call her, then opts for discretion.
This may be better kept close to the chest.
Speaking of which . . . he checks. Yep, more
possession.

*

He tells her that he's not to be disturbed;
He's working on his keynote for the Legion.
His curiosity now won't be curbed,
He heads directly for his nether region.

He sits and stares, and wonders what to do with it.
He runs through all his fantasies of lust,
But now he's not so sure he could go through with it—
He doubts he'd find a man that he could trust.

He thinks he'd better take it for a test drive.
He gives himself encomia: who comes

With more technique than he has for a nest dive?
To his dismay, he finds himself all thumbs.

No matter how he presses, pokes, cajoles,
He gets no more response than from a teapot.
He keeps on getting lost among the folds;
Where is his clitoris? Does he have a G spot?

Too bad he can't do what he does with engines;
He'd brace it upright on his workbench, fix
It in a vise, go at it with a vengeance,
Dismantle it to find out how it ticks.

There's got to be an army training manual.
He grabs the phone and dials the PX.
He requisitions the updated annual
GI edition *Girl's First Guide to Sex,*

Delivered after twenty minutes waiting
By a demure corporal. He starts
At *Section Ten Point Seven: Masturbating,*
Complete with checklist, diagrams, and charts.

Maybe this thing's got more complexity
Than what you would have thought—to get a handle
He'll need to study—this calls for Chablis,
A bubble bath, patchouli, and a candle.

*

Cigar among the bubbles, hand in air
Poking his laptop, number-crunching, poring
Through techno-intricacies, unaware
The other hand is in his lap, exploring.

Subject: *apparent female organs. Status:*
On standby. Tentative conclusion: freak
Malfunction due to faulty apparatus.
The major knows it can't be his technique—

All the chicks tell him he's the best. Blue-veined
Elizabeth has hailed him as the master
(Hasn't she?) Etienne's never complained,
though, come to think of it, he's never asked her.

Musing, he's caught off guard by a sensation
That spills his tipple, sends his laptop crashing.
His unfamiliar part's a conflagration,
He's howling, sobbing, moaning, flailing, thrashing.

"Dearest," Elizabeth calls out, "are you
All right?" just as he's on his final spasm.
"Yes, my sweet one," he croaks. "I stubbed my toe
Against the sink." Now, *that* was an orgasm.

Those women have it made, with guys like me
To do 'em. Then a troubling, if belated
Further reflection: Wha'd I do, exactly?
Don't even know if I could re-create it.

*

Male ego fast succumbing to fragility,
Acute self-doubt arising to befuddle him,
He questions the existence of virility,
And wishes he had someone there to cuddle him.

Time's running out, and still he hasn't tried it,
And still he's of two minds—it seems to work;
Shouldn't he try once with a man inside it?
He doesn't want to waste it on some jerk,

Precious as gold, or frankincense, or jasmine,
Not to be given up without a fight;
And yet . . . he wants the world to know he has one . . .
He grabs a raincoat, drives into the night.

He parks his car outside the VFW,
He stops a group of sailors as they climb
The front steps: "Fellas, I don't mean to trouble you,
But check this out!" He hears the church bells chime

The stroke of midnight. Now, rather than tangled
Exotic bush, to his dismay, he sees
The same thing they do: what has always dangled
In its familiar spot, fanned by the breeze.

*

As per their ritual, Elizabeth
Waits for her Major to begin his foreplay
With some great tale of how he cheated death
With Monty, or the ski patrols of Norway.

She waits demurely in her flannel nightie.
"Surely there's some brave deed you haven't told me
To get you hard, my darling?" "Not tonight," he
Grunts. Then, in softer tones, "Just hold me."

Achilles Speaks of His Deception in the Court of Lykomedes

Michael Martone

Our hero, having been discovered in hiding on the island of Skyros and returned to the field before Troy, addresses his men as they ready for battle.

I couldn't stand the blood. The forty daughters of the king had lived so long together that the visitation of their monthly bleeding had synchronized before I got to Skyros. Preparing to hide me there, my mother, as she shaved my body, had rushed to tell me everything. How the brooches worked and how to comb and pin my hair, the way to look at a man and how to squat and pee. She had wheedled from Hephaestis, as she would later for my armor here, prosthetic hips and breasts made of gold and ivory, fragrant balsam and elastic willow, the minted nickel nipples. Whispering all the while, she wove the dyed fur of the codpiece into the scruff above my cock. The steps for the dances, the register of the dirge, goddesses I'd never heard of, all the ointments and unguents and where they go, the way I should let a man's hand slide over my rump. But she neglected to tell me how each month, beginning in ones or twos, then in greater numbers, the girls would leave their father's court and secret themselves outside the walls of the acropolis in the tents pitched on unpure ground to bleed. I taught myself to wait and follow the last clutch of girls from the palace. I imitated them as they gathered up their kits. We took dried figs and raisins, olive oil for the lamps, wool to spin, a flute or lyre, and the wad of cotton rags.

Blood, I've seen. I learned the stitch that knits up your wounds, Danaans, from those girls in exile. The needle, lathered in blood from my sewing, draws its own blood with its work, red pips on the stems of black thread. My spear too does its mending, pulls ropes of gore through my enemies. But, men, you don't know what it is like to bleed the way the women do. To sit and seep like that. I watched them, a spot or two always in the folds of each crotch. The stains would slowly spread and soak through until one of them would stand and unwrap the girdle sopping now on the inside. She'd toss it on the pile to be burned, and her sisters would wash her wound and sponge her dry and hitch a new sheet around her waist and legs. The smell was something.

It exhaled each time the dressings were changed. Then they would turn to help another. It didn't seem to stop. And the girls went on about their business, talking mostly like we are doing now.

I have never seen my own blood. Even as my mother's razor scraped the hair from my body, the blade whetted on my hide. Honed, the edge still dully slid over my thick skin, not a nick. I faked menses, smearing jam on the cloth when no one was looking. At night in that stinking tent, I'd dream. Wrapped in sleep, I could not remember who I was. Reaching for myself, my hand burrowing in the rags between my legs, I'd feel the sticky puddle of what I took to be my bleeding. How could I be bleeding? In my mind, the jam had turned into the body's own syrup. I felt the stump of my cock nested in the fur sheath, everything smeared with blood. And I could also feel a cock, not mine, cut off, stuffed up inside of me. I told you I was dreaming. I forgot what I'd become. I kept bleeding.

Men, we rape. That is what we do. Who hasn't drawn his cock bloody as a sword from some girl no older than the daughters of King Lykomedes? You strip the frothy coating off yourself and then pin her down to let your buddy have his turn. But for a moment, before you wring it clean, you hold it in your hand, this core of blood. It makes you think.

And there was the moon that night. Of course, there was the moon. I watched it slip out of the sea, red and full, into the black sky saturated with the smoke of smoldering rags. The moon tinged the water with its own diluted hemorrhage. My mother is a Nereid, a nymph of the rivers. I've seen her melt into a puddle. She dressed me up as a girl and never wanted me to suffer. I knew I was fooling no one. Though for a while, I wanted to be fooled. Now I know. Men, I am a man, like you.

Joe Gets Blunzed

Rudy Rucker

So, okay, here's the way I lost my dick. My mad-scientist friend Harry and I built a "blunzer"—a gluon-powered magic-wishing machine that could turn the user, very briefly, into a veritable Master of Space and Time. Due to certain blah-blah physical constraints, we could only use the machine three times, once for each color of gluon: red, blue, and yellow.

Legend tell us that magic wishes tend not to work out so well. You know the old folk-tale about the peasant and the sausage? There's a peasant who finds a little man trapped in a bramble bush. He gets the little man out, and the little man says, "In return for your help I grant you three wishes. Use them wisely!" So the peasant runs home and talks it over with his wife. They're talking and talking and suppertime comes, and she's been too busy to fix anything, and she's real hungry. "I wish I had a nice big sausage," the wife blurts out, and there on the table in front of her is a crisp white bratwurst. "God, you're stupid!" the husband shouts, beside himself with rage. "I wish that sausage would grow onto your nose!" So there's the poor wife with the big gross sausage grown onto her face. And they have to use the third wish to get the sausage off. That's sort of what happened to me. Except it was my dick, not a sausage.

The way it went down that first time we used the blunzer, with the red gluons, it was Harry's turn, and he made his friend Sondra Tupperware beautiful and gave her the power of flight. And my wife Nancy had the idea of getting Harry to make some special food plants called porkchop bushes and fritter trees to cure world hunger. And finally, just for kicks, Harry opened up a magic door into another world. Fine.

But of course everything backfired. Sondra got sick of being beautiful. And after Nancy mailed out a lot of seeds for porkchop bushes and fritter trees, the new plants started taking over the ecology like kudzu, which got Nancy into trouble with the law. And these parasitic slug-like naked brain spine-riders came into our world through the magic door and started enslaving people—riding around on people's backs and making them go out and recruit more and more people to be their servants. They'd used a TV-evangelist kind of line to help draw people in.

So Harry and I got hold of enough blue gluons to run the blunzer again, and it was my turn to use it. I fixed just about everything. I got rid of the porkchop bushes, fritter trees, and spine-riders. I changed Sondra Tupperware back to looking the same, though I let her keep her power of flight. I gave my wife Nancy the power of flight too, and while I was at it, I set her up in a Manhattan penthouse with a suitcase of thousand-dollar bills. And now time was running out and I was only going to be the Master of Space and Time for three more seconds.

"Don't you have any deep, hidden desires you're going to ask for?" Sondra was saying.

_:03._

Suddenly I realized what my real wish was.

_:02_

"I WANT TO BE A BEAUTIFUL WOMAN!" I cried.
"I WANT TO LOOK JUST LIKE SONDRA DID."

_:01_

The numbers disappeared. My field of vision narrowed back down to what it had been. Something was hanging in front of my eyes. I reached up to touch it.

Long, blond hair.

"What a homo!" exclaimed Harry once again. "I can't believe it."

I ignored him and continued to stare down at my new body. I still had on the same clothes as before. "If you don't mind, Harry, I'd like to go to the bathroom."

"I bet you would. Can I watch?"

"Forget it. I'm happily married."

"Do you know where we can reach Nancy?" Sondra asked.

"She's in a penthouse on top of the Plaza Hotel. Call the operator, it's a new listing. Or just wait a minute. I can tell her myself."

I walked out of the workshop and up the stairs to Harry's apartment. The bathroom was right off his bedroom. I was eager to look myself over in privacy. I was having trouble grasping what I'd done.

Did I mention that this was all happening in New Brunswick, New Jersey? When the spine-riders had taken over, a bunch of born-again fundamentalist types had started flocking here in droves. As I passed the bedroom window, I looked out to see how the stupid groovers were doing. Still shirtless, most of them, but all their spine-riders were gone. Thrown back on their own limited mental resources, the zealots didn't seem to have much to say for themselves.

I locked the bathroom door and took all my clothes off. It

was a nightmare, a dream come true. I was a woman as beautiful as Marilyn Monroe. I pressed my hands between my legs. My big breasts slid this way and that, jiggling with every motion. My hips and butt stuck out like shelves.

I was horrified, yet of course I was thrilled as well. Whatever regrets my conscious mind may have had, my subconscious was in ecstasy. I got into the shower and soaped myself all over, getting to know my new body.

Someone knocked on the door as I was toweling myself off.

"Who's there?" My voice was sweet and melodious.

"It's Sondra, Joe. Do you want one of my dresses?"

"Yes, thanks. That candy-striped one? And a bra and stockings."

"Unlock the door."

"Okay."

I held the towel up over myself while Sondra brought in her new clothes for me. They fit perfectly. Acting like a friendly sister, she showed me how to put on lipstick and mascara.

My new face didn't look *exactly* like Sondra's had. Somehow you could vaguely tell I was still Joe Fletcher.

"I want heels, too," I said, brushing out my long hair. "I might as well do the whole number. And can you give me a little handbag with some money in it?"

"Joe—"

"Call me JoJo."

"JoJo, what are you going to do now?"

"Get on a train to New York. I want to look at our new penthouse."

"I went ahead and called Nancy, JoJo. She's pretty upset."

"Oh, she'll be glad to see me."

"I'm not so sure."

I left Harry's shop soon after—it embarrassed me to try to talk to him while I looked like this—and walked down to the train station. Now that the invasion was over, I figured the passenger trains to New York would be stopping in New Brunswick again.

My heels—shiny red ones—were a little tricky to manipulate, but I found that if I walked slow and swayed a lot it wasn't too hard. The volunteer Herberites in the street seemed pretty disoriented; most of them drifting back out to the parking lots at the edge of town. The men all stared at me, of course. I was careful not to meet their eyes. This quickly became a real drag—having always to look at the sidewalk or the rooftops—but I certainly didn't want some ugly bristly man to try picking me up.

This probably takes a little explaining. You'd think that any man who wants to be a woman is basically homosexual. But—at least on the surface—this didn't seem to be true for me. My wanting to look like the blond Sondra was really a heterosexual impulse: the craving for a supreme merging with the object of desire. But what was I going to do now— spend all my time looking in mirrors and taking showers? More and more, I was realizing how badly I'd blown it.

There was quite a crowd of people up on the train station platform, most of them just regular citizens happy to be free of the spine-riding brain-slugs. The stationmaster assured me that a train for New York would be stopping in twenty minutes. I sat down on a bench outside the waiting room.

"Hi," said a man, sitting down next to me. He was nicely dressed and had a polite expression. "I'm sure glad those naked brains are gone."

"Me too," I said. "I hope things will go back to normal now. The mutant plants are gone, too, aren't they?"

"That's right. Those guys Fletcher and Harry are really going to get it."

"Uh . . ." I tried to cover my confusion. I'd forgotten about that angle. As long as the spine-riders had run New Brunswick, Harry had been safe from the authorities. But now . . .

"Would you like a cigarette?" He drew out a pack of menthols and offered me one.

"Thanks," I said, accepting the cigarette and a light. His fingers brushed against my hand.

"My name's Brad. I'm a stockbroker in the city."

"I'm JoJo. I—I'm starting a new life."

"You don't have a husband?"

"No, but—"

"I'm surprised anyone as gorgeous as you isn't married. Are you a model?" Brad smiled at me, his eyes flickering over my voluptuous curves. "I love your dress."

"Oh, I was in computers." I felt increasingly flustered.

"Brainy, too!" Brad grinned and slapped his face in mock astonishment. "Look, JoJo, I know this is kind of sudden, but I'm going to be leaving the office at five, and if you'd like to have dinner—"

"No, no!" I squeaked. "I couldn't possibly."

"Tomorrow, then?"

Some cigarette smoke went down the wrong way and I went into a coughing fit.

Brad watched, smiling patiently. As far as he was concerned, anything I did was wonderful. "Can I get you some water, JoJo? A Coke?"

"No, I'm afraid I—" I lurched to my feet and gave him a smile. "I have to go."

"Well, all right. Another time, maybe. I'll be looking for you."

Feeling suddenly unsteady on my heels, I teetered into the waiting room. It was three-thirty. Ten more minutes until the train. I went and hid in the ladies' room.

The train, as it turned out, was filled with state troopers. They had come to make sure New Brunswick really was secure. Watching them get out, I realized that one of their first tasks was going to be the raiding of 501 Suydam Street, home of the mad scientist Harry Gerber. For the moment I was glad not to look like Joe Fletcher.

Fortunately my admirer didn't get in the same train car as

I. I plumped myself down next to a cute brown-haired woman with big glasses. Her clothes were kind of tattered.

"Isn't it wonderful to be able to leave New Brunswick?" she said to me. "I feel like the last week has been a long bad dream."

"Do you live here?" I asked, ready for some pleasant girl talk.

"No, I was just visiting my boyfriend at Rutgers. He's a graduate student in engineering. My roommates must think I've been killed!"

"Yes," I said. "It's been awful. Did the aliens make you do anything that—"

"I don't want to think about it!" the brunette exclaimed. "And all those rednecks showing up. I'm going to see my gynecologist as soon as possible. I bet they got after you too, what with your figure and blond hair."

"Yes," I lied. "I had a spine-rider on my back, too, and it made me go out in the streets at night. With the brains sliding around and everyone grabbing each other—"

"Men are so awful," said a woman next to me, her face momentarily close to tears. "Those brains were like men, the way they glue onto us and try to use us. Even my Tommy's like that, a little bit."

"Men are people too," I protested. "They just want to be happy like women do."

"Don't kid yourself, sister." My companion's voice took on a hard edge. "Men and women don't want the same things at all. When's the last time any man did something really romantic for you—without wanting to get paid back the same night?"

"You have to think about the genes," I said. I'd heard a theory about this. "Basically all a person wants is to perpetuate his or her genes. The best strategy for men is to have lots of children with lots of different women. The best strategy for women is have children and make sure the father stays around to help take care of them."

"Ha!" snapped the woman next to me. "Some man must

have told you that. *All a person wants is to perpetuate their genes.* Boy, is that stupid."

"Well, yes," I said after a time. "I guess it is."

I got a taxi at Penn Station. "The Plaza Hotel," I told the driver.

"Sure thing, little lady."

I sat back and watched the buildings sweep past. People, people, people. And all of them thinking, all of them just as conscious as me. When I'd been a kid I'd always thought of grown-ups as a race apart—big meat robots, really. Then once, when I was in my twenties, my father had said something funny to me. We were playing golf behind a foursome of businessmen in colored trousers and billed caps.

"Look at them, Joe," my father had said. "They really look like they know what they're doing. I'd always thought I'd be like them someday. I'd always thought I'd get to be a grown-up. But I'm not. I still don't feel any different. I'm sixty and I still don't know what I'm doing."

As the years passed, I'd come to understand what my father meant. Even though I was almost forty, I still didn't feel like a grown-up. I didn't really feel much different from how I had in high school.

And now in the taxi I was thinking that the same thing is true for men and women. As a man I'd always assumed that women are somehow not like real people. Of course I never put it that baldly, but the feeling had been there all along. Yet now here I was, with the tits and ass and lipstick—still just a person. The woman on the train—I'd never quite talked to a woman that way before, without the sex game somewhere in the background. As she'd unselfconsciously told me about her boyfriend and her job and her roommates, I realized something that I'd only seen in flashes before.

Everyone is just a person trying to be happy. Everyone is really alive.

What a liberation to know this! What a burden!

"Do you expect me to have sex with you?"

"Well, sure. I'd rather do it with you than with anyone else."

"The way I feel now, Joe, I'd rather do it with anyone else *but* you. How could you pull this on me?" She paced back and forth across the enormous living room. Outside the big french doors lay the wonderful clutter of Manhattan. "We could have been so happy." There were tears in her eyes.

"Come here, Nancy. Come sit on the couch with me."

"No. And you killed the fritter trees, too."

"They were taking over. You know that. That's what you got arrested for: mailing all those porkchop bush and fritter tree seeds."

"I suppose the police will be coming for me again?"

"I don't think so. I repaired the damages. With no more fritter trees or porkchop bushes, I don't see how—"

Someone was pounding on the door. It was the police, two of them.

"Hello, ladies," said the older of the two. He was a white-haired man with a weathered face. "Is this the residence of Joseph Fletcher?"

"Yes," said Nancy. "But—"

"He's not here," I interrupted, getting up from the couch and swivelling over to the cops.

"Do you mind if we take a look around?" asked the old cop, giving me an appreciative once-over. "You see, we have a warrant for his arrest."

"Come on in, boys," I cooed. Nancy looked disgusted. I winked at her and sat back down on the couch. I was too tired to stay standing.

The police left after a while, and Nancy finally came over to sit next to me. The sun was going down. I wished we could go to bed, but I knew better than to suggest it. We held hands and the silence deepened.

"I could have you declared dead," Nancy said after a while. "And then remarry."

"You can not," I snapped, letting go of her hand. "Joseph Fletcher may be missing, but without a corpse he's not legally dead."

"Oh, Joe." As the room darkened, Nancy was finding it easier to talk to me. "I was in jail all day, and then all of a sudden I was here in this wonderful penthouse. I still haven't looked at all of it yet. And I can fly, Joe. I've only tried it a little but—"

"Would you take me flying with you now? It's dark and no one will see us. We could fly over to the World Trade Center and back."

"But you can't fly, can you, Joe?"

"I can ride on your back. I did it with Sondra."

"Well . . . take the silly dress off first."

In the bedroom there was a dresser that looked like mine. The top drawer was filled with money—Nancy had stored all our money in there for me. The other drawers were filled with Joseph Fletcher clothes. I selected a pair of corduroys and a flannel shirt. Stepping into the bathroom, I notice a pair of scissors. I took them and cropped my long hair short. Then I used a facecloth to get the makeup off my face.

Nancy was in the living room, hovering above the floor. She smiled when she saw me, appreciative of the gesture I'd made.

"That's much better, Joe. You look almost like your old self. I was just thinking—with all our money, maybe you could get surgery to . . . you know . . ." She flew over and hugged me. "Oh, Joe, why did you do it?"

I gave a quick shrug. "A subconscious desire. I'd always wanted to be a beautiful woman."

"Me too," laughed Nancy.

"But you are."

"Not the kind that drops men in their tracks. I thought

those policemen were going to pass out when they saw you."

"Hey, let's go flying. If you really want me to be dead, you can just drop me on Times Square."

"You'd make quite a splash."

We opened a big french door and flew out into the night. Nancy's wiry body felt nice between my soft thighs. The cool air beat against us as the staggering city perspectives swept past. We looped around the Empire State Building, zoomed along a cable of the Brooklyn Bridge, and finally alighted on the flat top of one of the twin towers of the World Trade Center.

"You fly well, Nancy."

She closed her eyes and let me kiss her. The kiss felt just like it always had.

"Are you still my same Joe?" said Nancy after a while.

"I'm still the same. I'm still the same inside."

"Then let's go back. Let's go back to our new house and try to be happy together."

I'd like to be able to say that we had a steamy night of all-girl sex, but it didn't work out that way. I ended up sleeping on the couch. When it came right down to it, Nancy couldn't face the thought of me sleeping with her. Ever again.

The morning TV news was bad, too. Harry Gerber had been arrested and charged with criminal negligence in the deaths of seventeen people who had died of shock when the slugs got them in New Brunswick. His laboratory was under heavy police guard, and Sondra Tupperware had been arrested as an accessory. Joseph Fletcher was still being sought, but charges against Nancy Lydon Fletcher had been dropped. All the mutant food plants had disappeared, and their depredations had been undone. Some scientists speculated that perhaps the fritter trees had been a kind of mass hallucination brought on by the spine-riders.

Someone was pounding on our door again. Nancy was still asleep. I went to look through the peephole. Newsmen, with video cameras.

"Go away," I fluted. "I don't want to see anyone."

"Please, Mrs. Fletcher," shouted back the reporters. "Just a few questions."

I went to the phone and called security. After a while the noise at our door died down. Nancy was up now, and I made us breakfast.

"Sooner or later, one of them's going to talk," I said over the eggs.

"Who?"

"Sondra and Harry. Sooner or later they'll tell the police that I've turned into a woman. And then I'll get arrested, too."

"Arrested for what?"

"It was on the news. Seventeen people died from having the spine-riders on them, and they're charging Harry with criminal negligence. Sondra and I are supposed to be accessories."

"You'd better call Don Stuart. The lawyer I hired yesterday," began Nancy.

"Oh, lawyers . . . I should use the blunzer to fix all this. Don Stuart isn't going to give me back my sausage, is he?"

"Poor peasant Joe. Maybe with plastic surgery—"

"I want my *real* body back. This just won't do. I want to have children with you, Nancy. And I want poor Harry out of jail."

"And what about Sondra?"

"Oh, she'll get out anyway. She can still fly. The first time they put her in an exercise yard, she'll be gone. If they handcuff her to a guard, she'll just take the guard with her. You don't have to worry about Sondra, Nancy. It's just Harry and me that are getting screwed."

"Not literally, I hope." Nancy smiled and ruffled my spiky hair. As long as we weren't in the bedroom she felt able to act affectionate.

We took our coffee out on the terrace and stared down into the chunked canyons of Manhattan. This was really a neat place to live. If only . . .

"So maybe you should use the blunzer again," said Nancy, thinking right along with me.

"Well, I'm not sure I can. I told you how it would only work once each with the red and blue gluons, right?"

"Yes, but you said there were yellow gluons, too. If you find some yellow gluons, then the blunzer should work one last time, shouldn't it?"

"You'd think so. But I don't know if anyone has yellow gluons. They're even rarer than the blue ones. If I could only talk to Harry—"

"Well, you can. Find out where he's locked up and go visit him. No one'll recognize you."

"They don't let just anyone off the street come visit killers, Nancy. I'd have to be a relative."

"So get a fake ID. Say you're his sister. Does he have a sister?"

"Yes! I've heard him talk about her. Sister Susie. She lives in Detroit."

"Good. That means she's not likely to be here yet."

"Perfect. I'll get a fake ID."

"Okay. Wait here while I get dressed."

Nancy went in the bedroom and closed the door. I really hoped we'd find those yellow gluons today. I'd find the right physicist and offer him so much money he couldn't refuse. I found a big purse in the hall closet and stuffed it with a little over two million dollars' worth of thousand-dollar bills.

I had on my Joe Fletcher clothes from last night. I looked in the hall mirror and wondered whether to put on makeup. Just because Nancy was so uptight didn't mean I couldn't get a little fun out of my new body. My hair was a real mess.

"Hey, Nancy," I called.

"Hold your horses, I'm not ready yet," she shouted through the closed bedroom door.

"I'll be downstairs in the beauty salon."

I left before she could protest. I'd spent my whole life waiting for women to finish dressing: now it was my turn to get back.

The hairdresser was chic and in his twenties. He cluck-clucked over the way I'd butchered my hair.

"Whatever possessed you, dear?"

"I—I thought someone would like me better with short hair. Can you fix it up?"

"Of course, dear. He'll love the new you."

"*She.* Not too much off the sides and make it spiky on top."

They did my hair and nails, and then they fixed my face. I told the makeup girl I wanted to look like I was from Detroit. She got the picture. When they were done, I looked even better than I had yesterday. Except for the clothes. I wondered if I should go back upstairs and . . .

"Come on, Joe," said Nancy, stomping into the beauty salon. "I've been waiting and waiting for you."

We hit the street and caught a cab. I knew a guy who could make me an ID. On the way we stopped to buy me a tailored tweed suit in earth tones. I was starting to look kind of butch. But from Detroit, strictly from Detroit.

So, did the deal with the yellow gluons work out? Well, yes, except that I had to fuck a physicist to get the yellow gluons off him. It was okay, really, except for him wanting to kiss me.

I let Nancy be Master of Space and Time for the third and last blunzer session and she had a really good idea. She made it so everyone in the world got to make a wish at once, but somehow she was able to simultaneously watch everyone wishing and to make sure that nobody wished for anything bad. The world's different now—I could tell you all about it, but for now suffice it to say that, yes, I got my dick back. And I understand women a little better than I used to.

Pearl Harbor

Paul West

When Japanese carrier planes flew over and devastated Pearl Harbor, Admiral Kimnes, who commanded the base, at once went indoors and changed his shoulder boards from four stars to two. He knew what was coming. Well, he knew some of it. In some matters he was almost prescient, insisting that a thousand Japanese soldiers on bicycles with flat tires would sound like tanks advancing. Japanese pilots, he claimed, could never have a sense of direction because their mothers had always carried them around facing backward. They had managed to bomb Pearl Harbor, though, and the admiral at once foresaw the fall of Singapore, Wake Island, and Hong Kong. To soothe himself, even amid machine-gun fire and shrapnel, he stripped off and dived naked into the already dirty oval pool, a perk he up to now had undervalued. He was not often this spontaneous, likelier before a trip to town or a new posting to polish his coins with acrid-smelling Brasso and iron his dollar bills, mostly fifties and twenties, at the kitchen table. But now he had to prepare himself for an un-dreamed-of experience, in which breaststroking toward ei-ther inlet valve, a carefully groomed erection dangling beneath him like an undercarriage, would not figure at all. No more lascivious pool dreams, no more wild whoops, and he struck home against the molten thrust of lukewarm wa-ter, as admirals sometimes will.

In a sense, stripping himself of four-star shoulder boards was a way of becoming invisible, but not as effective as bouncing naked in the pool while debris rained down upon him, reminding him of a gangster term for death: the dirt nap. He wanted to be far away from the scene of his shame, much farther than even a Catalina flying boat could fly him, farther than a well-aimed bomb could throw him. He felt the time had come for him to disappear into the crowd, like the man on the Clapham omnibus he had once read about, *l'homme moyen sensuel,* or what was that goddamned phrase? Very well: hide in the pool, live in it, pretend he was a liberty boat or a pinnace, no shoulder boards at all. While everyone else who was not wounded or killed ran for shelter, he lumbered around the pool, toying with erotic dreams, in one of which he swam up the gigantic funnel of a vagina; the water surface was now so black he thought he might hide beneath it forever, at least until hostilities ceased. He expected Japanese parachutists within the hour, clomping on the cheerful terra-cotta roofs and scraping to a halt on the tennis courts. This indeed was how to rape an idyll, he thought; who needed the bloody Japanese here in Pearl? Its very name said what the place was like: a plum as-signment for services gallantly rendered, unlike, say, the Aleutians. He now dreaded the Aleutians. Even if he sur-vived here, it would be the Aleutians for him, he who had poo-poohed all those wolf-criers who said the Japs were coming, they had seen them on the way. Admiral Kimnes was a naysayer of the highest rainwater, a man coarse

enough to believe in advantageous magic, in which something preposterous happened wholly for his benefit. Gone
was his contemptuous supposition that Japanese officers all
came from the agricultural class: yokels posing as gentle-
men. Gone too his favorite pastime (the navy bored him) of
voluptuously watching great hotels in the act of deteriora-
tion as plaster fell, appliances stopped dead, meals never arrived from room service, and the bunged-up toilet became a
plinth for fertilizer. All this he loved, but not the erasure of
Pearl. Why, he sometimes saw himself as the Mother of
Pearl, a shaggy, portly, bluff embracer of that chromatic
heaven.

He was not to know that the marred pool sat above an
old spring rejoiced over in island folklore, extolled at least
as much as the lingam shrines on Elephanta Island not that
far away, where needy (barren or virginal) women sat on
stone lingams all night. Given the right degree of commotion, what his navy called rowdy-dow, the old shrine was capable of coming to volcanic life, and the Japanese had
provided it. And now it did, imperceptibly beneath all that
air-raid muck, but decisive in its ancient way, initiating Admiral Kimnes into pagan mysteries that went far beyond
shoulder boards.

Half suspecting what was afoot even as he swam with
heavy thrusts of his calves, he murmured Give me a buttery
one, half desiring a scone, a croissant, a bagel (he overate,
as required at a luxury posting), but only felt an electric
tremor in his genitals. One of those Japanese magnetic
bombs, he decided, thrashing and swallowing, gradually
coating himself with soot and other filth until he began to
resemble a coal black whale. It was in these very waters
that, while the admiral slept amid the frosted buzz of his air
conditioner, alighting dragonflies turned into humming-
birds with their first touch of the water, cnaidic wrens with
elongated beaks changed into amphibian swonts unknown
to island fauna. Nothing of this happened by day, but under

the velvet imprint of night the island modified its biology, doomed eventually, after long mutation, to evolve something like the Komodo dragon from the pestilential housefly—after countless stages achieved and left behind. Such things happened also in Australia, certainly in the arid domain of the bull-roarer, and in the dank, stark forests of northeast Poland, where wolves turned into extraordinary Ur-horses.

Admiral Kimnes, however, was a stranger to *mutagenesis*, as some savants call these metamorphoses, but his was the first to happen in a swimming pool, although, if he had had his wits about him, or the wits of someone far brighter than he, he might have been caught calling himself the First Anthology Man, such was the tumult of contrary sensations that took him in the first few minutes as he continued to swim, thrusting his member into the murk he now lay in. He tingled, but also felt numb. He shuddered, but also felt still as stone. He felt hot, but shivered with cold (one of the few remaining familiar experiences open to him). He was a mess, he thought, unable to climb out of the pool, or, for that matter, to drown himself, rid himself of the tingle, the shudder, the sweats. Sensing he was no longer himself, he tried to feel grateful at having escaped, until he chose to float and then to feel down at himself, groping for his old schlong, soggy sometimes, boner-superbus at others.

Oh, it was there all right, but not in its habitual mounting. It now lived in a rissole made of what felt like custard. Briefly he thought of the day he tried to fold it back into his rear end, as soothsayers, seersuckers, and cocksuckers are wont to do, completing as it were the closed system of himself (a favorite shower activity of his). It never reached, of course, so he gave up. But his member had shrunk already, now more of a nipple than a penis, yet even now giving him pleasure as he appraised it, wondering at its floppy base.

One-handedly he took stock of himself, tweaking what he found, from the twin little goldfishes that seemed to partner each other at the very portal of God knew what, to two slices of oranges behind them, swollen and rather numb. Oh, I get it, he told himself, I have been cut down to size, but he was wrong. The magic of the poor was honoring him with ambivalence, and he suddenly saw that a man was also a woman, and vice versa. They had more in common than they didn't. Yet what had this to do with the Japanese? He should have recognized a catalyst when he saw one, but he was Admiral Kimnes, who had laughed off the assault before it began. This was not revenge, but what some magicians call a caliper epiphany, which always widens and unnerves. Admiral Kimnes wanted the experiment to be over, by George, but its physiology firmed up, and all he felt was a flooded emptiness he wanted crammed full. How odd, he thought, now I am a hole, a trough, a vessel, I want to go to a service station.

It was a subtler feel than that, though; he felt a plucking twinge repeated a thousandfold, a stomachache that did the bodily equivalent of a buzz, and, so to speak, yearned for his horny self to put paid to him, to *stonk* him, to give him something to revolve around. Bombs were still falling and the gorgeous island was ruined.

My God, he thought, even my memory has shrunk, but he could still recall the way his mother, to cure him of whooping cough, had wheeled him in his pram all the way down to the gasworks and stationed him in the thickest most poisonous fug available to calm his tonsils, from which remedy he always emerged stupefied. A later memory brought back his wife Lydia and her way of marching into his office on the base when he was a mere colonel and flashing her engagement ring while she announced "*This* is my appointment." She did no such thing with her wedding ring, once she got it, and indeed often neglected to wear it. Perhaps the bad stuff is leaving me, he decided; memory is purging itself at last: no cough, no wife, no Japs. His groin felt finned now, soggy with nacreous petals, and, apart from his feeling squeamish at such swampiness in an unaccustomed place, he rather enjoyed the mutation, sure for half an hour that some trumped-up Japanese raygun had wrought this change in him. He had looked up into the sun and been transformed, translated, into, well, what? Was he a bi? Hermaphrodite? He did not know the word *epicene*, but he arrived at its import. Perhaps he could be a two-star admiral on one side of the fence, a four-star one on the other, now he was, well, twatted, quimmed. What lovely sensual words these were to apply to himself. How he played, as he saw it, into the enemy's hands (or the recent enemy's) by being glad he no longer had that awful obligation to get it up; but he as soon forgot, or omitted the thought, when his newfound clitoris went hard.

That was the moment at which he crossed over, wearing his alteration like a woman, amazed that all the twaddle about evolution's casually fidgeting things into being had come to apply to him. All he had to do to achieve complete transfiguration à la Richard Strauss was to accept his change in the main, without wishing to fulfill it, gratify it, use it, hymn it. There was no click, no clap of thunder. The waters neither swallowed him nor gave him up, but he was no longer in them or in the war zone of the gracious island, but, weirdly, little that he knew it, the man on the Clapham omnibus in 1941, his threepence clutched in his lady fist, his mind appalled by an omnibus drawn by horses while the bombs of the Nazi blitz on London whistled down. How could they dream of running a bus service amid all this? He was the only passenger, inexplicably upstairs, having climbed the heaving staircase of the trudging omnibus to be nearer—what? The bombs and shrapnel that rained down? In panic he reached beneath him, groped at his groin, still masked within a fly, and began to treat himself, delighted with his new coral treasure, his sluice. Cleft for me, he sighed in a military way, fondling something hard that reminded him of those pills about which a note from the pharmacist warns you: they will pass through you, giving up all their benefit, but emerge into your stool apparently unchanged. He had once taken such a pill, for some obscure digestive trouble. But what he found now was round, like a bead or an aniseed ball. Wiped a little against his crombie overcoat, it actually shone, and his heart gladdened into overflowing as if this little bauble were his first yield of an extravagant switch that not only rescued him, but confronted him, even in the tumult of London bombed and burning, with a wide open world that, although deafening and smoky and dangerous, would not always be so. Now I have my own Pearl Harbor, he told himself, haven of infinite riches and immeasurable quaintness. I will husband me well. What went ye out into the wilderness to find? A man clad in soft raiment?

A water main burst as he clambered down the stair of the omnibus, certain he had reached his destination. A gas main exploded with a huge blue quiver even as the bus keeled over on its side and the horses, lucky for them, broke free. When he regained his feet, his fly still open within the soft folds of his overcoat, he knew what he had to do. Up a heap of rubble he stumbled, cursing and grunting, then stood on top, at least to the extent he could as he kept sinking lower and lower. Now he assumed a stance appropriate, he thought, to something like the winged victory of Samothrace. He had become invincible, he just knew it. Invulnerable. There amid the horrors of war, alone on his pinnacle with fire and blast and frenzy all around him, he assumed a peaceful float: expressive arms lofted, delirious head back, one leg precariously lifted on takeoff. Of course, such being the limits of magic, he stayed where he was, but he certainly had that buoyant swoop to him. He was a statue on the rise, perhaps to soar through searchlight-lit darkness to thwart the Heinkels and Dorniers until they turned tail, knowing the ways of destruction were worthless. Like an animal marking site or boundary, he arced the jet forward and upward, wondering when it was he last peed himself, marveling that, no longer having anything to direct the line of urine with, he had hardly any aim at all. The spray seemed to come right out of him in a faintly steaming loop, such was the pressure within. He should have been killed, by shrapnel or gas, but for some reason he endured until he had finished, with nothing to tuck into his fly or his Y-fronts. He liked the lack of conduit, the way inside and outside came so close together with no delay in the urethra. To think it was to do it. Now he saw why women were so prompt, so ready, with their talk. Then he shuffled down his improvised hillock and looked back at the derelict bus, wondering why at this very moment he intercepted the thought patterns of an imposter ploughing through his shattered pool in Pearl Harbor, a penis growing where there had previously been none or little.

I am a changeling, he decided. I have taken the place of someone who has taken mine. I am no longer Admiral Kimnes, but Joanna Q. Lunchbucket, late of the Clapham omnibus. Not that he knew, but an intrepid war photographer, lurking for something to go Pulitzer with back home, had drifted forward from shelter behind a building and captured the scene by firelight: a part-naked human describing a picric arc in the air with a woman's freedom of movement, atop a mound of recently disturbed earth and bricks. What a gesture of defiance, conceived in Pearl Harbor, consummated in London. This was the admiral's grand show, better than anything on shipboard or in military academy: a symbolic deviation in the teeth of an unknown metamorphosis, an event bizarre enough to make a Hitler or a Tojo wince.

And then that war was over, for him at least. The woman from Clapham whom he had so briefly impersonated (had he?) refound her seat to journey over London Bridge to Gracechurch Street, E.C., meaning East Central, while he

resumed his tread in the churning, sooty pool, the only difference being that the two of them had more or less
changed sex, it being understood that a mere switch in
anatomy, a divergence from the familiar, was not the complete process, which could be accomplished only through
years of unable-to-keep-hands-off familiarity, involuntary
jolt and seepage, and iterative mollycoddling by others:
women who demanded their yoni be licked, men who demanded their johnson be frigged. From his own experiences, and from what he had been told, he wearied of both,
but counted on a year of habituation, trusting that proud
possession was three parts of the thrill. He assumed there
were rules of conduct and patterns of desire, but with whom
he knew not.

While still treading, afraid to venture out of the pool, in
which he now wished he had had an escape hatch built that
led to a local air-raid shelter, he tried to sum up the day on
which he changed sex and saw his world explode. Or was it
all a damnable, inconvenient dream, in which a dozing
woman on a London bus sent *her* dream up into the
oeiropause beyond the tropopause while he sent his own
dreams in the same direction, from Pearl Harbor in ruins,
and the two dreams, for less than a day, crossed, merged,
then stripped separate again. What on earth was the point
of changing into a woman, of being pooned, without any
kind of sexual encounter? Why truncate the miracle thus? It
had an incomplete, shredded quality therefore, as, no
doubt, did the mutancy of Joanna Lunchbucket. Would it
ever be enough to have had merely a glimpse of that other
condition, predicated on a defiant piddle during the Blitz?
But perhaps an arrant bit of symbolism was worth a thousand fucks. How the admiral wished he could somehow
contact the woman, already long and far gone, to ask her
about it, although it was just possible she had remained a
man and he was asking for too much symmetry, reciprocity.
The universe was not a reciprocating engine, however, and

every human had to fudge meaning from an awful mess of disparate mishaps.

Such thoughts would occupy him ceaselessly for the rest of his days as the brass demoted him from four stars to one, and then back to captain, so as to retire him on the cheap and remind him of the huge mistake that cost the nation a world war. But the history of it, the blunder and the penalty, attracted him not at all. The lower in rank he got, the more he took pride in (as he put it) being briefly womanized. He walked funny afterward, never quite sure if he was tucking something in or suffering a frontal wedgie. The omnibus would always keel over, the horse lunge free, the sky bloat red with tumult, the urine twinkle through the sooty autumn air, the woman from the bus take his place in Pearl Harbor. And the female photographer would snap him in all his glory as if he had fallen out of the sun into that inferno. The pearl of his ascension to a superior form of being, as he thought of it, remained with him, glossy reminder of a shift he had never wished for and could never regain no matter how hard he tried to implode his male organs, giving them the old metaphysical suck, his mind intent on little boys whose testicles have flitted back into the body cavity never to descend again. He wanted gelding, but he never got it; though, because of the photographer, he figured in many a cunt *conte* as the male face above the spurting hairy pear. Soon, through intense epicene longing, he began to suffer from softening of the brain, certain he would shortly become a tar-raker, no officer at all, depraved by the difference between getting the gold mine and getting the shaft.

One day, standing on a chair in order to adjust the air conditioner on high, he heard the sound of icicles falling, but the sound was only that of the rainpipe erect in a corner, prompted by vibration. This delicious trickle-down sound of shiny slightness falling was the thing he wanted for himself again and again, but it rarely came to him, not from books, music, or liquor, nor even drugs. He recognized he was doomed to yearn with mouth agape, shoulders empty, fly full and heaving. Too brief a womanhood afflicted him sorely, and it never came back, though he tried to bring the mood back in whorehouses of varying chic. Was it worth an amputation? The military would have done it for free during a war, he thought, nothing needed but a little twist of gun cotton in the right place like an earplug gone astray. No good. If ever he really wanted to go through with it, he would have to summon up the concomitants: the war, the wrecked pool, the demotion, the corpses hemming him in while the fires of London roared around the woman from the Clapham omnibus. Until then, almost in parody of the canard that claims woman needs man as matter cries out for form, he would have to find some way of peeling open the pearl with his tongue, like a charlotte russe, in order to make love to it.

My Lady

Bill Buege

Old woman tits, a hanging bag of
dried up cunt, turkey-wattle
arms, hair limp as thread,
bald spot in the back,
but no memories of youth,
when young men creamed their pants
for me and old men leered.
No memories of advantage,
disadvantage, of being less
because I was a woman
and more since pretty good's
not half so bad.

     I've tickets
to the opera. Tickets! That means
there is an other. Someone
will come for me inside
some history. Or do I go
to him, to her? I don't know
what I'll wear or how to strap in
these sagging dugs and gut, make live

this ghostly face, fill in my hair.
I'll wear my gold lamé and pearls,
my Ferragamos, the gold watch
Carl bought before he died.
                    I have to pee. Good God,
it won't stay in. Oh, Lord, what now?
                    A crone in gold. That's absurd.
What will I wear? I can't go out
like this.
                    He was a handsome, younger man
with hair and shoulders, nicotine-
stained teeth, a slightly trembling
hand. He smiled and called me,
"Mother," and while she sang
the final aria, I concentrated
on the lady in the seat in front of me
so I'd not let seep a fart,
but it came anyway, sour
as a gingko tree, and people
shifted in their seats.
I'm sure I blushed.
                    He took me home
and helped me up the stair.
He said he loved me.
Jane sends her love
and Timmy and the girls.
                    He thanked me for the treat,
reminded me to lock the door.
I don't know why I felt I'd cry
and no tears came.

The
Mangina

Jonathan Ames

friday night, I was sitting in the lobby of this theater in TriBeCa. I was there to perform, to do some storytelling. My friend, the artist Harry Chandler, showed up and sat next to me. He's been to dozens of my shows.

"I go on in fifteen minutes," I said. "Thanks for coming."

"I always like your stories," he said, and he smiled at me, but he didn't look well. His thin shoulders were hunched, and his face was drawn. I could see he was making an effort to appear otherwise—he was wearing a clean blue shirt and his short blond hair was parted, neatly combed. And his forty-year-old face is always handsome in a worn, *Grapes of Wrath* kind of way, but I could tell this night that he was troubled.

"Is something the matter?" I asked.

He looked at me, hesitated a moment, then said, "I might really be losing it this time."

"What's going on?" I knew that in the past he had struggled with his exhibitionism and his voyeurism. I wondered if he had reverted to old behaviors.

"I've been making vaginas for two weeks," he said. "It's all I've been doing."

"What do you mean making vaginas?"

"Sculpting them out of this stuff called friendly plastic. I've come up with twelve prototypes for a prosthetic vagina. I come home from bartending and I'm obsessed. All I do is make vaginas—experimenting with flesh tones, hair. I finally got it right—a realistic-looking one. I put it on last night and walked to the Now Bar because somebody wrote a letter to you in the *Press* saying that's where drag queens go on Thursday nights. I figured I would show the drag queens the vagina and they might want to buy it, order one for themselves. But I went too early, the place wasn't open yet. So then I walked back home and the vagina was pinching me a little and then it started raining. I thought, 'I'm walking around New York in the rain with a vagina on. I must be losing my mind.'"

"You're not losing your mind," I said. "You're an artist, you're passionate."

"This isn't just about art, I think there's a lot of money in it. I just have to market it right . . . I need the money . . . A lot of men will want to buy a vagina."

This part *did* sound nutty to me. I didn't mind him making vaginas, but get-rich-quick schemes always betray mental imbalance and desperation. I had to disabuse him of this money angle, bring him back to reality. "Listen," I said, "there are already a lot of fake vaginas on the market. I've seen them where they come built into a pair of panties."

"Mine is different," he said. "I utilize my scrotum as labia. I have to show this thing to the world. I showed my roommate, but she screamed. I'm all alone with this vagina project."

"This sounds interesting, using the scrotum," I said. "You'll have to show me after my performance. So don't worry. You're not alone with this anymore. I am on the case."

Chandler smiled, reassured. It was time for me to perform and he took a seat in the theater and I did my schtick. I hustled and hammed it up for the audience. Told three of my usual stories and plugged my new book. A night's work. Then a jazz band came on and Chandler and I went over to his place.

We went into his bedroom, which is mostly his studio, and I said, "All right, let me see you in this vagina." I sat at his cluttered drafting table and he started getting undressed by his bed. I turned my back to Chandler to give him some privacy. I was skeptical that his sculpture would look like a real vagina.

"It's on," he said, and I turned around and he ambled toward me completely naked. His vagina was mildly grotesque, but also quite authentic appearing. It was furry like a pussy and sure enough, hanging out of a disguised hole was his excess scrotal sack looking like puffy labia. He had the whole thing fastened around him with an extremely thin, clear tubing.

I was stunned on many levels. His body is sallow, boyishly hairless and reed thin, though he has a slight paunch above the genitals. It is an innocent, yet tortured body. From the left knee down he has a rubber, prosthetic leg with a flexible rubber foot, having lost his leg some years ago in Cape Fear, North Carolina. So to see a vagina on this physique was rather remarkable. I felt both pity and awe. I was glad he was my friend.

"This is really good, Harry. It's amazing. You really are a great artist."

"Now I have a prosthetic vagina to go with my prosthetic leg," he said. "And I've built a fake hand I can wear."

"You're like that guy in the Dustin Hoffman movie, who kept losing parts of his body. . . . You know your scrotum really does look like labia. How does the rest of your penis feel?"

"It's not bad. I've put felt on the inside, so it's pretty comfortable. It's kind of like wearing a baseball cup. I want to call it the Mangina."

"That's a good name for it. . . . Where are the other vaginas you made?"

Chandler brought a plastic bag over to me and dumped all the failed vaginas out onto his drafting table. They were various shades of pink with differing amounts of hair attached (Chandler had taken the hair from real-hair wigs).

"Here's one without hair, for a shaved look," he said, pointing out to me a very pink Mangina.

"You've done a lot of work," I said.

"I think I was obsessed because it's a new way for me to exhibit myself. All these years, I've been wanting to show my testicles, but testicles are ugly. But a vagina is not ugly. So wearing this vagina I can exhibit myself and not feel like I'm hurting anyone."

"So you want people to see you in this?"

"Yes."

"Do you want to dress as a woman, too?"

"No, I just want to be a man with a vagina sometimes. That's why it's the Mangina."

"Let's go visit my friend Lulu," I said. "She'll look at you. She'll love it. She's a beautiful transsexual and very wise."

"I didn't show you that I can finger myself," said Chandler and he pushed his finger into his scrotal-labia and it disappeared.

"Maybe there is money in this," I said. Then I called Lulu and I told her about the Mangina and she said we could come over. Before we headed to her place, Harry showed me a video he shot of himself. You can only see him from the waist down and he's wearing the Mangina and lazily playing with his labia and then inserting his finger.

"This is completely depraved," I said, deeply impressed. "This makes Karen Finley look like a rank amateur."

It was only a two-minute video, and then Chandler got

dressed and we took a taxi over to Lulu's. She was wearing a tartan skirt, stockings, and a white blouse. As always, she looked quite beautiful. She is elegant and tall and her skin is a lustrous dark brown. She was born in Africa and raised in Paris. She is a dress designer, with a steady, private clientele of queens and downtown divas.

I introduced these two good friends of mine, and then Lulu graciously offered us a choice of beer or apple juice. Chandler and I, both having no head for booze, opted for the apple juice. On the TV, playing silently, was the David Bowie classic, *The Man Who Fell to Earth.*

We sat there drinking, and I said to Lulu, "Wait till you see this vagina Harry has designed. It's a work of art."

"Please show it to me," she said.

So Harry went to the bathroom and stripped down. He came out shy, yet happy. He loves to be seen naked.

"Oh, my," said Lulu, laughing. "What have you done?"

"You should touch it," I said to Lulu. "It's very realistic." I hadn't had the courage to touch it myself, but I knew Lulu was much more liberal than I. Harry stood right in front of her, and she touched his labia.

"This is warm," she shouted. "It's real!"

"Can you believe it? It's his scrotum."

"Your finger can go inside," said Harry and he demonstrated this. Then Lulu put her finger inside.

"This is really something. You should have a show, a performance," said Lulu.

"Let's go to Edelweiss," I said, "and show the girls there Harry's vagina. He needs to have people see this."

The three of us left Lulu's and took a taxi to Edelweiss. It was midnight and the place was quite crowded. Lulu pointed out queens who she thought would be receptive to seeing Harry's Mangina. I'd then approach the queen and say, "I don't mean to be rude, but my friend Harry here is a crazy artist and he's sculpted himself a vagina that he's wearing. Can we show it to you?"

About five queens agreed to look at it and we'd take them to this semiprivate corner of the club. Harry would then drop his pants and they all found the Mangina fascinating. At one point, a beefy security guard came our way—it's his job to make sure that no one is having sex—and I explained to him the situation and he shone his flashlight on the Mangina. The guard smiled and laughed and the queen, who was checking it out, a blond, who's actually had *the* surgery, said with good humor, "Why did I bother spending twenty thousand dollars?"

Then it was getting late, so Harry and I said good-bye to Lulu—she was staying on—and we took a taxi downtown.

"You know, Lulu is right," I said, while we were chauffered home. "You *should* have a show. Maybe you *can* make money. Sell the Mangina as an art object. I want you to come onstage wearing it at my next Fez show on October seventh. You can talk about it and then hand out cards with your number and people can order one if they like. Are you free on the seventh?"

"I am," said Harry, excited.

"Well, if it is a hit, since I'm the impresario, I'd like a ten percent commission on every Mangina sold."

"All right. . . . Maybe to help sales, I'll play my accordion and dance."

"No, just come out there and stand in your Mangina. That should be enough."

"You're right," he said. "My accordion hangs low, might block the view."

"And the Mangina deserves to be seen! On October seventh, history will be made!"

Chandler smiled at me. I had truly come through for him. He wasn't alone with this anymore.

MORE MANGINA

On October 7, as I predicted, history was made. During my storytelling show at the Fez, I brought onstage my good friend, the painter and sculptor Harry Chandler, and it was then that the legend of the Mangina was born.

After my own ritual dance to Serge Gainsbourg's "Comic Strip," and a few introductory remarks, I asked Chandler to join me. He was hiding in the wings, and he was brought out by my gorgeous and statuesque friend Vivian. I wanted him to be accompanied by a lovely woman to lessen the audience's shock and so that they wouldn't have a knee-jerk politically correct response to Chandler's Mangina—"How dare a man wear a vagina! It must mean that he hates women!"

Vivian, I figured, was perfect for the job of Mangina escort—she's an artist and also a world traveler and an expert on the unusual behaviors of primitive tribes. One of her claims to fame is that she made out with a cannibal in Indonesia who had shaved teeth. She showed me once his handsome, smiling picture. The teeth were very pointy and brown. "You could have cut your tongue on those teeth," I said. "I was careful," she said. "How was his breath?" I asked. The coloration of his chompers and the nature of his diet had me concerned. "Fine," she said.

So I felt that Vivian was the right woman to accompany Chandler and his Mangina. She's been to the heart of darkness and found love there—thus the Mangina wouldn't scare her, and her lack of fear and horror would be transmitted to the audience. It may seem as if I was being overly cautious, but I was going to have to perform after Chandler's appearance and I didn't want the audience to be killed.

So Vivian led Harry onto the stage and he was buck naked—wearing only his prosthetic leg and homemade prosthetic vagina. Vivian discreetly walked off and Harry was showered with loud applause and lots of happy gasping. He stood beneath the lights and smiled sweetly. His two passions were merging—exhibiting himself and exhibiting his art. As the applause quieted, he began his speech, in his signature sincere, humble tones: "My name is Harry Chandler. I'm an artist and an exhibitionist and an amputee. I'm also a live Jonathan Ames story, which is not easy, let me tell you."

Unfortunately, no one laughed at that last line. It seemed scripted, which it was. Not by me—by Harry—but with my ego-gratified approval. Oh, well, that is the nature of the-ater—the occasional flat moment. So then Harry talked briefly about his career as an artist and his love of nudity—his own and others', and how this love of the naked form led him to create the Mangina. Also, he disclosed that there was an emotional element: "My girlfriend left me," he said, "and I became obsessed with sculpting vaginas."

He showed the audience the various early prototypes of the Mangina and described at great length the different ma-terials and elements he uses—friendly plastic, paint, wig hair, crushed velvet, and elastic velvet.

Of course, the material that really sets the Mangina apart from other prosthetic pussies is one's excess scrotal sack, which Chandler pulls through a hole in the Mangina and utilizes as labia. He calls this new organ the Lotum. This is a better mixing of the two words (scrotum and labia) than his first name for it: scabia (with a hard *a*). Lotum, he feels, implies something beautiful, because it sounds like lotus. And one of the benefits of the Mangina, so Harry says, is that he can expose himself in an attractive way, since he perceives a man's testes to be unattractive and a woman's labia to be attractive. I tend to agree with him, though there are countless others who must certainly prefer the scrotum. One also shouldn't forget the penis, I think, but Harry doesn't take the penis into account, since it's mostly his balls—while wearing shorts without underwear—that he used to expose in his troubled twenties and thirties (he's now in his more stable forties).

So Harry went through all the Mangina prototypes—they were piling up beside him on the stage like grotesque fish carcasses—and his lecture was getting a little tiresome, but there was no way for me to politely interrupt him. Then Harry was done and I rejoined him on stage. I announced to the audience that we would do a little dance to celebrate our friendship. In my mind, I wanted us to appear like the naked women dancing in the circle in the Matisse painting, but I didn't tell this to the audience. The image, I hoped, would be subliminal.

So the Gainsbourg came on and we held each other and hopped around. Harry did quite well with his fake leg and a friend of mine told me later that the image of a naked, one-legged man wearing a Mangina and holding hands and dancing with a nicely dressed man in jacket and tie (me) was a great moment in performance art. "A new low," I said with a puffed chest to my flattering friend.

After the dance, Harry departed to wild applause. I was a little concerned that the night had reached its climax, but I began to tell my stories and the audience reassured me with their enthusiastic laughter. Midway through my first story, my "Dueling Yentas" tale, in which I become a yenta, three people in the front row got up and left. It was rather ungracious of them, but luckily I was in character and so I verbally chastised them in my yenta accent: "Who are these terrible people? How rude! Who needs you, anyway. Now I'm all alone, I'm always alone. No one calls. No one cares. You three are horrible, selfish. Get out of here!" And so they slinked off, and I carried on—a pro, a trouper.

The night came to an end and I stayed onstage to peddle copies of my novel, and Harry was up there to show people the Mangina prototypes and the Mangina he was wearing. He was outfitted in this blue, long-underwear jumpsuit, which unzips down to the crotch, enabling him to quickly and efficiently expose his prosthetic genitals. This outfit is now called the Mangina Suit, and he looks like a superhero in it.

The two of us were quite happy up there—we were surrounded by females. Women began to finger Harry's Mangina, which he was loving, and cute girls were buying copies of my book and looking at me, I felt, with a certain adoration. An attractive brunette said I looked like Santa Claus—I was sitting on a stool, signing books propped on my knee. So I said to her, "Why don't you sit on Santa's lap." So she did, and she had a great little ass, but I had used up so much energy performing that I didn't get an erection when she sat on me. My penis was gelatinous and dead, almost liquid. I was mortified. I had a female fan on my lap and I might as well have been wearing a Mangina. I'm sure she felt how liquidy my penis was, but she didn't seem to mind; she slid off me smiling. I wanted to give her rear an affectionate pat as she walked away, but I wasn't sure this was appropriate, and my confidence for pulling off a rear-smack was feeling a little limp because of my limp penis, and then she was gone.

Then a blond girl took my hand and held it for a rather long time and took her other hand and put it on her attractive breast and said, "Your story about your son touched me *here*." I wanted to touch her *there*, and then she too was gone. Gone. Into the night.

I wish these groupies would linger. I wish I could take a whole group of them back here to my apartment and look at them naked. They are all so lovely and different. I'd kindly ask them to strip and then I'd line them up against my wall. And while still wearing my jacket and tie, maintaining my dignity and not frightening them, I would study them and memorize their beauty.

When the memorizing was done, I would begin with the girl on the far left and first kiss her left breast, then the right, each time taking the nipple in my mouth like the most glorious pink grape, and then I'd go down and kiss her sweet triangular mound of sex—completing the triangle of kisses. Then I'd move on to the next girl and do the same. My wall can accommodate about six girls—if I move my sitting chair—which is probably six more than the number of groupies I have, but it's fun to fantasize that one has groupies. And for some reason, in this little fantasy, I need to have myself moving from left to right—my brain must be structured that way from all my reading and writing.

Then after all the tender kisses, these girls would surround me and hug me, and I'd smell their hair, their different perfumes. And I'd have some kind of spiritual and physiological eruption, while still wearing my khaki pants because as I envision all this, there's no intercourse. That seems too personal and brutal and selfish. Lately intercourse has been striking me as brutal, which is all right if you're brutalizing a friend. That's why men and women get together. The woman comes to trust the man to brutalize her, but not hurt her, and the man comes to trust the woman that he can brutalize her and not be accused of rape. This is called a relationship.

But these fantasy groupies are strangers and I don't want to take advantage of their sweet attentions, I just want to be surrounded by their love and be petted and then have an orgasm in my underwear. Also, it's hard enough to please one woman, let alone six. And if I failed to please them, then they would no longer admire me—I would fall off my pedestal, off my authorial stool and seat of power. But enough of the inner workings of my immature and lonely mind. After everyone left the Fez, Harry and I went upstairs to the Time Café and had tea. He was subdued, and I felt my usual postperformance emotional devastation, but I fought it off. We recapped the night, compared notes, tried to suck a little more glory out of the whole thing.

"This blond girl was really fingering my Mangina," Harry said.

"Really? I think that was the same blonde who was touched by my story."

I felt a pang of jealousy that Harry got fingered by the girl, but I let it go. "Well, we made history," I said. "Beginning with the one hundred and thirty people who were in the audience tonight, word will spread rapidly about the Mangina. It will be whispered everywhere on the streets of

New York. Your fake lips will be on everyone's lips. Once a thing becomes a word, it is alive, real. This is my prediction. Not too many people invent something worthy of a word. You should be proud, Harry."

"The Mangina now has life of its own," he said solemnly, almost sadly.

"A life of its own," I said. And we sipped our tea.

No Offense Intended

Intended

Gerald Locklin

Sorry, but if i awoke one morning
with a vagina
i would stick my dick in it.

or

i would go back to sleep
and try again later.

or

i would get dressed very quickly.

(Actually, I would probably kill myself.)

Go with
the Flow

Bernard Cohen

1.

When my close friend started to change, started to become a woman, he claimed that the woman he would become would have so much sex she'd lose consciousness. His phrase: "I'm going to fuck myself senseless."

Another friend looked forward to a broader-based erogeny. His phrase: "I'll never stop coming. I'll come when I fuck, when I sit on a bar stool, when I put on a T-shirt, when I blow my fucking nose."

Although I regarded these visions as most likely over-optimistic, I wasn't discouraged. Even my more skeptical acquaintances admitted excitement about their achieved and impending alterations.

One (now formerly) male friend said he'd dreamed he was covered in vaginas, that it was like being a very hairy man, kind of normal, but a little different, except with vaginas everywhere instead of hair. "They were on my cheeks, my neck, all over my fucking body. It was fantastic. I hope womanhood will be just like that, perhaps more concentrated around where I'd expect to find genitals."

This guy had been neither particularly hairy nor attractive as a man, and as he transformed he retained much of his male body hair, so he was hairy for a woman and surprisingly sexy, like the mustachioed women one occasionally sees in European films.

For me, as friend after friend gynecomorphosed, there came to be an almost ritual inevitability about the process. Still, I wanted my change to seem like a choice—despite no real way of knowing whether I had control over my body, or would be like the sex-changing barramundi of northern Australia: subject to whims of age, food supply, and temperature. (I'd rather compare myself to a fish than a gastropod, at any rate.)

Another previously male friend told me I'd have no regrets. "I used to be so anxious about everything, but now I'm a happy woman, and becoming happier all the time. My theory is that every day I shit a few more male hormones, flush them away, and that my anxiety washes away with them. My only sadness is for all my wasted male years," he said.

I met a man at a dinner party who claimed that Y chromosomes were becoming extinct. I told him I was thinking of becoming a woman, that all my formerly male friends had changed or were changing, and that I no longer cared about men.

"Go with the flow," he advised, nodding.

He talked for a while about his own impotence, and how the future of the species lay not in cloning but in cross-fertilizing variations on meiosis, which he declined to explain.

"But how is that possible?" I asked. "Are you talking about the injection of other chromosomal material? Are you suggesting some form of artificial twinning process whereby unlike cells are joined through a radiant, microsurgical or quasi-microsurgical procedure? What do you mean?"

"It's nothing like that," he said. He told me that with regard to my change, I should consider castration as a first step.

"See how you feel as a eunuch first. Perhaps it's not so much a gender change you want as to abandon sex altogether."

"That's fine to say," I said, "but I have no intention of losing out on sexual practice. It's not the idea of woman I am considering, but the coming-into-being and then the being. I intend to spend most of my future being sexual. I envisage my becoming woman as a continuum. Sure, one day I'll know I'm woman, but I foresee a lot of productive (and possibly reproductive) uncertainty along the way. There'll be no Big Chop for me, brother."

I was annoyed. Here was some stranger advising me to slice off my testicles. How come he was so certain of his own gender fixity? Should I have been more certain about my beliefs? I have never understood the rules of engagement for dinner-party conversation.

"How male are you, buddy-o?" I could have asked him, and probably should have, but instead continued along the technico-theoretical line he'd set up: "Anyway, through your eunuch-talk you're dodging my legitimate and extremely recent questions about reproductive methodology *post* your claimed demise of Y chromosomal activity."

This approach reflected a misjudgment of his character. He set off on an obviously well-practiced blather about a UFO-driven or other apocalyptic human end in the near future, the steep path to it made certain by liberal-internationalist politics. The usual line disguising hypermoral pseudo-religion with a pretended scientific understanding of what-humans-are-really-like.

I sneered at him and walked away. No one needs to hear that manhood is dying because of liberalism. I don't believe in reincarnation or immortality, but I'll still acknowledge this sort of talk as bruising to the soul.

2.

I was feeling a little delicate anyway. I threw up once or twice, and was more tired than usual. I wondered if this was the start of my transformation. None of my friends had reported nausea; none mentioned any negative repercussions of femininity. Positive spins, everywhere—except the dinner party gender-fascist. He'd damaged my calm about what might be happening to me. Friends advised, "Forget about him. He'll probably have a heart attack at the first sign of testicular shrinkage."

Or: "Look at the people you like. Look at me! Does my new womanliness augur the end of the world? Ridiculous!"

I allowed myself to be reassured. All around, people I knew were embracing their transformations. A friend commented that he was bored of his monotonous testosteronism, was looking forward to the cycling of hormones. "I hate always being in the same, male mood," he told me. "I want real, emotional interaction with the world. That's what I want from womanhood."

I was, perhaps, beginning to undergo mammagenesis. I surely was. And I was ill. Each morning I wondered whether my nausea would translate into the materiality of a good heave. This went on for some time. None of my friends had had similar sensations.

"I thought this was supposed to be paradisiacal," I complained. "But I feel like hell."

"Womanhood is better for everyone. I hope for your sake you won't be the exception that proves the rule," said a transfigurative friend unkindly.

My body was exhausted and I began to experience twinges of sharp pain around the groin. That was something new and unwelcome. I woke every morning feeling sick, feeling like my stomach acid had crept halfway up my throat. Veins all over my chest migrated to the surface.

My energy levels were all over the shop, incredible bursts of energy, the sense I could achieve anything, or the deepest exhaustion I'd ever felt. What sex was I to be thrown about like that? No sex known. Friends of all sexes were no help. They pronounced useless pat phrases like "You'll settle into it," and "Womanhood is different for every man."

And I was swelling, my belly tightening. What was I mutating into? Something bulbous and incredible.

After three months, the nausea receded. The swelling continued, or increased apace. Five months after the beginning of my change, friends were noticing my shape too. They gave me curious looks, as if they wanted to touch me, to lay their hands on my belly. I was feeling murmurs inside, as though a newly vital organ was expressing its joy at existence, and this murmuring, this faint wriggling, was a relief.

Born-women have books that advise, "All these pains, all the changes to your body, it's normal. There's nothing to be concerned about."

That's all right for them. But what about me? Where were the books to tell me that everything was normal?

What about the heartburn? I suffered for every meal. And with hemorrhoids the size of olives. Excuse me for saying "ouch." I needed to urinate every half hour, and I was breathless by the time I reached the toilet door. When I moved, my belly was still; when I stayed still, it moved. My blood pressure must have been dropping. I spun every time I stood up. Maybe I wasn't becoming fat, only developing a distinctive firmness, a stretching of the person. A firmness that moved, and was increasingly unmissable.

"You look fantastic," my hairy-sexy friend said. "Amazing."

I carried a balloon before me wherever I went. Walking became increasingly tiring, and I felt ridiculous doing it, waddling like a duck, unable to see my feet. My friends agreed they had never seen anything like this before, not in the history of transformation. I was a genuine evolutionary leap forward, but from this I drew only occasional comfort.

"This is the feminine?" I asked another formerly male friend.

"Fertility is something I've always envied," she replied.

After many months, during which my friends explored unimaginably energetic aspects of the feminine, and during which I had begun to believe my tautness would never diminish, I went into labor. I stayed awake for two nights waiting for a time I would know was the right time to commence medical supervision. The moment didn't arrive, though the bodily convulsions born-women no doubt euphemize as "contractions" drew sharper and closer together. A slim-waisted now-woman friend drove me to a nearby hospital.

"You're about to surprise the entire medical sorority," she said, as if there weren't enough drama.

"No more surprises, please," I moaned. She took my arm and we followed signs saying MATERNITY AND PATERNITY. I stopped to contract.

At a counter, I signed various disclaimers.

The duty sister wanted to know if my friend was "the father."

"I don't know," I replied. I contracted, panting and leaning against the countertop.

"These sorts of words . . . who knows anymore?" my friend commented.

Someone led me into a labor ward. There was a bed, some chairs, various objects near which or on which to labor. I perspired. I contracted. My friend held my hand. I sat in a bath. I resisted pushing. I contracted. I obeyed medically trained supervisors. I climbed onto the bed. I lay there. Various people monitored various parts of my body. I climbed off the bed and leaned against a chair. I climbed back onto the bed. I swore at the medical staff intermittently. I swore at my friend, who grinned, and I swore at her again for grinning. She helped me off the bed, and then back on again. I swore at her. I contracted. My body tried to squeeze itself through my pores. I lay on the bed quietly and uncomplainingly for several seconds. I contracted. I perspired. I swore. I contracted. This routine continued for an unmeasured and immeasurable time, until I had no rest between the contractions. Finally, someone said, "Push."

I shoved as hard as I could.

Someone said "Push" again.

I strained. I felt an intense burning sensation. I heard someone say the word "crown." I lay on the bed. There was no evidence I was still in one body.

Someone said, "Here's the head. Great. You're doing very, very well. Again. Go with it."

I pushed, as instructed. My friend stood with the medical people around the bed. She smiled and nodded at me. The contraction came. A medical person said, "Push."

I pushed. The circle of people seemed to contract too, as they reached toward me.

My now-female friend said, "It's a girl."

The girl cried. Someone passed her to me and I pressed her to my breast.

X-Ray Dreams, 1963

ANDI & LANCE

OLSEN

DADDY GRILLING, HIS HEAD A TV SET

The dream won't stop arriving. Every night. At the office, too. In the evenings with Mother & Uncle Billy & Panzer after dinner watching *My Three Sons*. In the dream, I have a golden doughnut. Sometimes it's called the garden, sometimes a hair pie, sometimes where the monkey sleeps. But it's always the same. It's always there, mulberry moist & swollen. It's always a miracle, like trying to imagine what comes after time & space. I spend hours investigating, palpating lightly as milkweed umbels, sliding in my middle finger, thumb & forefinger & middle finger, whole hand, arm to elbow, extracting a wedding garter, an invisible cat that won't quit purring, three pennies, a 1927 Babe Ruth baseball card, an orb of light with iridescent bluebird wings. Then I feel someone tapping my forehead & open my eyes to magpies making bloody jam of my frontal lobes.

UNCLE BILLY IN A DRESS, DAYDREAMING

Oh!—it's simply the most *beautiful* thing, isn't it, dobos torte sweet knowledge, because you can feel it underneath your smart dress & know it's always there . . . when you're eating, say, or when you're talking to the postman, unfolding the Castro Convertible for well-behaved guests, pouring a cup of new & improved Tide into the washing machine, because you know it's there & that's the most indescribably stunning thing, it makes you feel free to know, no matter what you're doing, vacuuming or head lowered Sunday morning, because its existence proves everything will be absolutely scrumptious, & I could stand up & dance, stand up & gambol this very minute, like Julie Andrews across the Alpine meadow, hair cropped short as mine, black-&-white dress a-billow like a penguin in billowing grass, arms stretched wide to the ambient possibility of music & to Disney executives at mahogany tables everywhere because, well, because I know I happen to look drop-dead gorgeous tonight in my carefully plucked eyebrows & tasteful, understated brooch that would make Jackie O. proud, neat as a just-turned-down bed: I could stand & dance while Nancy sweeps up her Kodak to capture this rich moment to share with the future, no matter what Robert is opening his filthy mouth to say, thinking you can't see it but you can, opening his mouth to say across the room, lips parting, because what he says he says from dark-hearted jealousy, never able to look as dreamboat perfect as me here, tonight, my spectacular secret alive between my meticulously shaven legs.

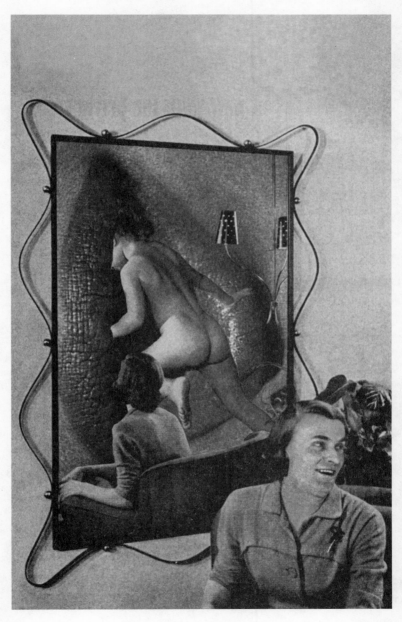

M O T H E R   G A G G E D   I N   T H E   F A M I L Y   R O O M

Commentary

The *Clitoris* is situated beneath the anterior commissure, partially hidden between the anterior extremities of the labia minora. The body is short and concealed beneath the labia; the free extremity, or *glans clitoridis*, is a small rounded tubercle, consisting of spongy erectile tissue, and highly sensitive. It is provided, like the penis, with a suspensory ligament. The clitoris consists of two corpora cavernosa, composed of erectile tissue enclosed in a dense layer of fibrous membrane, united by an incomplete fibrous pectiniform septum.

The *Penis* consists of a root, body, and highly sensitive extremity, the *glans penis*. It is composed, like the clitoris, of a mass of erectile tissue, and enclosed in three cylindrical fibrous compartments. Two, the corpora cavernosa, are placed side by side along the upper part of the organ; the third, or corpus spongiosum, encloses the urethra and is placed below. The septum between these is thick and complete behind, incomplete in front, and consists of vertical bands arranged like the teeth of a comb [L. *pecten, -inis*, comb, scallop].

MOTHER'S HUNCHBACKED REFLECTION,
DAYDREAMING

The dream won't stop arriving. Every night. Running er-
rands, too. In the evenings with Father & Uncle Billy &
Panzer after dinner watching *The Donna Reed Show*. In the
dream, there is a cobblestone town square. The sky is chilly
gray. A crowd has gathered to watch six clowns perform.
The clowns ride unicycles while doing handstands. Play an
accordion with their feet. Juggle flaming bowling pins. The
crowd applauds. Afterward, the clowns move among the
onlookers with a shabby top hat, collecting. When they
reach a group of small children standing in front of their fes-
tive parents, they proffer the hat. The children, thinking
the goods inside are theirs, plunge their hands in. One pulls
out, not the spare change people have been depositing, but
a white rabbit in wire-rimmed glasses. Everyone cheers. The
clowns simper & proffer the children the hat again. Daz-
zled, the children thrust in their hands & this time one ex-
tracts a huge, colorful paper-flower bouquet. The crowd
erupts in admiration. When the clowns proffer the children
the hat a third time, the children, giggling & sputtering
with merriment, jab in their hands & next, one is holding a
giant glistening purple-red clitoris with wet floppy labia.
The crowd, baffled, goes still. The children open their
mouths to scream. But just then the giant sex bird begins
flapping its fleshy wings, rising out of the astonished child's
palm, circling over the heads of the onlookers & then
higher & higher over the town square, above the medieval
rooftops, into the chilly gray sky, until it is a moist liver, until it is a black dot, until it is nothing at all.

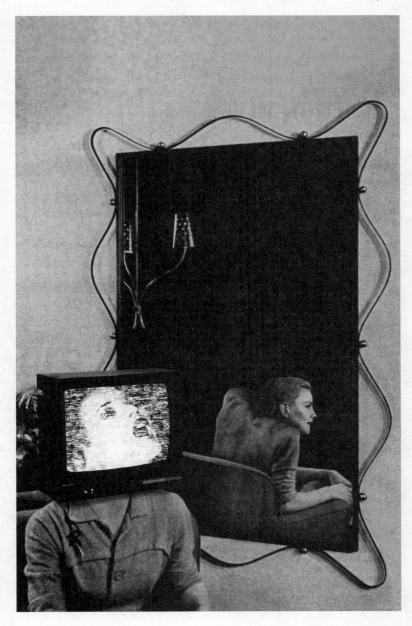

PANZER PLAYING, HER HEAD A TV SET

I am the person who becomes you, like it or not. I am the person whom you can never become again. I am the person you can look at from the outside but never really understand. Knowing this cuts up your heart at least once every day, often when you least expect it, riding the subway home after work, opening the refrigerator door and reaching for a pint of ice cream. I am the person who recites the dreams my parents never had. I am the person who sticks so many thoughts into my uncle's mind that his mind in the end becomes my mind. Because I had a sister who used to beat me, kick me off swings, clip my hair with gardening shears while I cried. Because my name isn't Panzer. Because it never was. Because my father wouldn't listen when I told him, over & over, & my mother said I'd have been a better person if I hadn't been adopted. Because freaks are just like humans, only more so. Because one day when I was four, playing with my dolls in the family room, I somehow didn't realize that thirty-four years later I would dream that I looked down at my arm & saw something slithering around underneath the skin, a little hard pea that reminded me of PacMan, and I began to scratch at it but it wouldn't stop so I became terrified that beetles called the past were living in me subdermally, only then the skin over my right carpal tunnel unfolded like a fast-forward orchid & a supernumerary clitoris surfaced & I gave it to my husband & he lay it on his tongue & played with it, nibbling & licking, for hours, & then he slipped it down his pants, & I grasped that everything was going to work out okay in the end.

The Hunger of the Day Before

Edward Field

*m*ake me a woman for a day, I always said,
and I'd go for my best buddy, Sal,
as much a cunt man and a hunk as me,
but if I were a woman, I'd go for him—
any gal would be crazy not to.
Hell, for that matter,
if I were a woman I'd go for me!

But, as I found out when it happened—
yeah, I held the winning lottery ticket—
in one day you can't learn
all a woman needs to know.

Just dealing with the clothes—do you realize
how complicated they are?

I tried the makeup routine, but couldn't manage
to get the lipstick on straight.
I was better with the hair
because me and Sal both have long hair
we tie back on our construction jobs.
It looks great under a hard hat.

One surprise that day was the discovery
that it's not like having nothing down there.
Sure, the cock and balls make you feel great,
filling your Levis the way they do,
but what a woman has
vibrates to everything around—
it's like having a cello, or a bass viol, between your legs—
that's what gives the shimmer
to a woman's walk.
And the breasts—if you have them,
you can never forget them.
It's not simply that they get in the way,
they give off a heat that made me want to
throw off my clothes and roll around on the ground,
especially in front of every good-looking stud I saw.
But you can't just do that—that's the problem.
So how do you get a guy?
I'd always thought guys were ready
to fuck anything in a skirt.

I decided to just follow my instincts.
I gave up on the high heels within a block
and kicked them off, shook out my hair
and sashayed out past the construction site
where Sal was working.
The other guys whistled and catcalled,

but when I stopped and winked and wiggled at him,
Sal just seemed embarrassed and disappeared
up the work elevator to a higher floor.

So I had the day to kill until he got off,
and tried parading around,
automatically checking out the office girls—
until I remembered to look at the guys.
But the only men who came on to me were real slobs,
and every time I saw someone I'd go for
he either had his arm around a chick, or was working—
most men don't have their minds on their dicks until
    nighttime
and what was I supposed to do until then?

I got back to Sal's construction site at knocking-off time,
and thought we'd have a drink together
at this bar we hang out in after work.
But he left the site with a bunch of the guys,
and walked right by me!
Let's face it,
he wouldn't recognize me in a year with these tits,
even if I am his best buddy.

Inside the bar, though,
perched on a bar stool, telling myself I was the girl of his
    dreams,
and coming on strong to him
definitely turned him off.
I think he thought I was one of those pigs
who work blow-job alley behind the station.
So I couldn't get anywhere with him like that,
not with Sal, who has his pick,
and there was no time to learn the right routine.

Along with the tits and cunt, I also won

a dinner at the Waldorf with a television star,
and I had to get over there and struggle into
a designer sheath that my tits kept flopping out of,
and a pair of Guccis that I wobbled on.
But it didn't make any difference—the big-shot star
turned out to be gay as a fruitcake
with a hundred-watt smile—all caps.
I swilled the wine, and midnight came with relief.

God it felt good to have back my meat
that at least I knew how to use, for chrissake,
and ran my hands down my muscled belly—
my dick was twice as big as I remembered—
and jerked off to a porn video—
I must admit that the guy fucking the lady
looked a lot like Sal,
as I shot my load.

The next day after work,
having a beer with Sal as usual,
I kept looking over at him there
in his dusty coveralls and a smear of grease
on his chiseled jaw,
and a memory of the hunger of the day before
came back to me, a memory
of those powerful vibrations in my breasts,
between my legs.
And it was strange,
because though I know Sal's strictly a cunt man
still I could swear he was
smiling back at me,
and Holy Moses! his knee
was pressing against mine!

The Pill

Sandip Roy

Okay, it was my idea. But it wasn't my fault. I mean, how was I to know that things would turn out like this? And it could just as well have been me. But it was only meant to be for a few days. Just for the parents.

The moment I saw that blue aerogram with mother's familiar rounded handwriting and that smudged Calcutta postmark I had this sinking feeling. They had been making all these "We must visit you" noises for a couple of years now. And I'd just nodded noncommittally, playing along, never rushing to make those plane reservations. But now that my sister was married, Ma had decided the time had come. "Your father has so much work at college," she wrote. "He didn't even want to come. How much I had to persuade him. In the end he agreed. But only six weeks. Oh well, better than nothing at all, no?" I sat there with the flimsy blue paper in my hand staring at the Mapplethorpe poster we just got framed that week. Six weeks. Where was I going to put all this stuff? Where I was I going to put them? And where on earth was I going to put Steve? Oh shit! I hadn't even mentioned Steve yet. I meant to. But I just couldn't squeeze it in amidst all my inane prattling about work and the India society function and Auntie Krishna in Seattle. Well, I guess they would have to find out about my "roommate" Steve.

"Mom, Dad," I practiced. "Here is Steve, my roommate. He studies law." That would surely impress them.

Steve wasn't impressed. "Roommate?" He laughed, pointing around the apartment. "This is a one bedroom, Rohit. A *small* one bedroom. Quit fooling yourself. You are just going to have to tell them. I am not going to do that *Wedding Banquet* shit." And he went off to the gym.

I mean, don't you think that was a little insensitive? I thought so, too. I mean, he knows that I can't come out just like that. I've explained to him so many times about how all this pressure to come out is such a Western phenomenon. But he shrugs and says, "Whatever, honey." I know he just doesn't get it. Mr. Activist with the rainbow sticker on his bag. I'd like to see how out he would be in Calcutta surrounded by gimlet-eyed aunts.

But anyway—so the parents were coming. And I had to do something. And moving was not an option. I mean it was the worst rental market ever in San Francisco. People were paying an arm and a leg *and* a deposit for little dark studios with hallways reeking of piss. And we had such a great deal on our place. But Steve was right—it just wasn't set up for a roommate.

So Steve could move out, right? Well, the thought did cross my mind. Our friend Tim had an extra couch. But all his stuff was here. We couldn't move everything—the books, the photography equipment, the computer. Anyway, I needed that computer too. So there was only one thing to do. The honorable thing. Ugly, but it had to be done. And now was as good a time as any.

"Mom, Dad. I have something to tell you. I am gay. I live with my boyfriend Steve. And now that you know it, we'd love you to come and spend the summer with us."

Well, I meant to say that anyway. I really did. When I actually called Calcutta I even managed to get out "Ma, I have something to tell you." But then she said, "Can you hold a minute, dear? I think the rice is boiling over." And when she came back it was all over for me. All that adrenaline I'd pumped into my veins had turned to jelly.

"So what is it?" she said.

"What?" I said weakly.

"You had something to tell me," she said.

"Ohh y-yes," I stammered feebly.

"What is it?" she said. "Tell me."

"Well, umm," I said, trying to cobble my little speech back together.

"I know," she said. "You don't have to tell me. It's about marriage, right?"

"Sort of," I said.

"I knew it. I know why you've been avoiding that subject all along. Don't think I didn't notice how you ignored Sushmita's daughter at that party when you were here. That's when I knew."

"You did?" I exclaimed.

"That very night I told your father. 'Don't be angry,' I said, 'but I think our Rohit doesn't need us to find him a nice girl. I have a feeling he might have found himself one. An American. I think that's why he is having a hard time telling us.' But you know I don't mind. So who says your old mother can't be broad-minded?"

I didn't know what to say. I just gaped at the telephone.

Over the crackling lines I heard mother chuckle. "See, I surprised you didn't I? So do you live with her? Is that why you didn't invite Krishna-auntie to your house when she was visiting? Don't think I can't add two and two, you bad boy."

I had to sit down.

"So anyway," continued my mother. "We are not all conservative old things like in the Hindi movies you know. We

get CNN on cable these days. You know I didn't bat an eye-
lid when Diana took up with that Dodi. 'Good for her,' I
said. But anyway, what is her name?"

"Whose?" I asked stupidly.

"Who else, you silly boy," she chirped. "The one you've
been hiding all this time."

"Rita," I said for no reason at all. "Rita Atkinson."

"Lovely name. Like Rita Hayworth," said my mother.
"What is her favorite color?"

It should have just simply unraveled right there. I had visions of my father having a heart attack in the living room
on the Gujarati rug I had dragged all the way from India.
My mother having a hysterical fit. Me jumping off the
Golden Gate Bridge. Steve running off to the gym. All because I didn't have a live-in girlfriend named Rita Atkinson
whose favorite color was green and who was working as a legal assistant downtown and whose parents lived in New Jersey and had a house with a tennis court. I didn't make it all
up. Steve's parents did live in New Jersey.

But Steve chose to focus on the negatives. "What? You
told her what? Where the fuck are we going to find a legal
assistant named Rita now? And even if we find her, what
are you going to do? Where am I supposed to go?"

"I don't know," I said with false bravado. "But it's all going to work out, honey. Trust me."

He just rolled his eyes and turned on the TV. I picked up
the *Bay Guardian* and went to the bathroom. I got my best
ideas while sitting on the can. But I must confess this time I
thought I had cooked my own goose. I didn't know where to
turn. Till I read about the Anti-Viagra pill. A little ad on
the back page squeezed between a smoking cessation program and fertile eggs wanted. Be a woman for twelve hours
at a time. Lifelike, All Natural—the ad promised. And then
after twelve hours when the effect wore off you went to
sleep and when you woke up you were a man again. And if
you didn't want to be, well you just took another dose. And

it was all perfectly safe. Of course, they didn't know about its long-term effects on testosterone levels and erections and all that stuff. But you know, who knows about the long-term effects of anything? I tell you, sitting there on the can, with my pants around my ankles and the *Bay Guardian* on my lap, I believed there was a Goddess after all. The one my mom invoked every time I boarded a plane. And She was watching over me.

"Steve, honey," I said. "Believe me, I would do it without a second thought if it were for you. But it doesn't solve anything for me to become a woman for a little while. And it's your summer vacation. You don't even have to go to school. And it's just for a few hours a day. Remember how much you liked doing drag last Halloween? Won't you do that much for me? Come on, it'll be fun."

He still refused. But I knew he was cracking. I could sense it. I just signed him up. I had to tell them he wanted to go M-to-F but wasn't sure and needed to try it first. Okay, I know I shouldn't have done that. But they needed a reason and these things only have limited space. And I didn't want him to finally come around when it was too late. This way we could always cancel. But to tell the truth, the idea seemed more and more attractive as each day went by. I could take Rita to the office picnic and have sex with Steve. Steve and I could go dancing with the boys at Club Universe but Rita could go with me to the Diwali party. I didn't need to come out at all. And I still wouldn't be lying to anyone. My activist friends always went on and on about how gay men who get married are unfair to both their partners and their wife but this was my way out. Both my partners were the same. My God! It was a breakthrough. I tried explaining that to my friend Yusuf. But Yusuf has been in America too long. He told me that I was fooling myself—that I should be fighting for my rights to marry Steve, not changing Steve to Rita. But I knew I was having my cake and eating it too. Yusuf, I think, was just jealous because he hadn't thought of it first.

In the end Steve went. Of course, he went. My emotional blackmail is second to none. He just said feebly, "But this doesn't mean I have to do the dishes." Silly boy. Just because he was going to be a woman for a few hours it didn't mean I was going to turn into some kind of heterosexist pig. I wasn't going on Viagra or anything like that. "Honey," I said. "We will have the kind of egalitarian relationship that will be the envy of our straight friends."

It was so easy. Watch a video. Do a couple of hours of counseling. Fill in some forms and you get a little bottle of blue and pink capsules. One capsule at a time but not on an empty stomach. It was as easy as that to discard your manhood. Well, you didn't really discard it; it kind of shrank into your body. After about four pills it really started taking effect. It wasn't like he suddenly turned into a drag queen with some weird bouffant and birdseed-in-pantyhose boobs. No, this was much more subtle. Like it was happening inside him and radiating out. It was in the way he talked, the way he held himself, the line of the jaw. He made one elegant woman. I didn't want to have sex with Rita but it gave me a weird kind of thrill when I saw men turn around to look at him on the street. And when he was no longer a woman at night and we were having sex, the memory of those looks really turned me on. And for a moment, as we fucked, I forgot if it was Steve or Rita. Then I looked again and saw Steve's slim tight chest but Rita's tight black shoulderless dress lay crumpled on the floor like a sloughed-off skin. I was surprised how much it turned me on.

And you know, I think Steve was getting into it too. I mean, he kept saying he was doing it for me. But I wasn't sure that was the whole truth anymore. He did complain about how annoying it was having all these straight men staring at him all the time and how he wanted to smack them. And he could—he was one tough chick. I was afraid that this sinuous woman, as tough as a jungle vine and as sleek as a cat, would send my mother straight into a nervous breakdown. She was unlike any of the nice demure girls my cousins had married. I wondered if we needed to adjust the dosage.

I knew we needed to talk. And I probably put it off longer than I should have. After all, this whole thing was my idea. Now what was I to say? "Oh, you are too much of a woman. Can you tone it down a little?" But then my dad came down with hepatitis. Like two weeks before they were supposed to leave. They had to cancel the trip. Ma was mad because they didn't get a full refund. I was disappointed, and yes, I will admit it, secretly relieved. "Well, you must come next year," I told her. "Make sure Dad gets complete bed rest and doesn't try to go to college."

Steve wasn't at home. I left him a message saying, "Meet me at Ithaca at five." When I walked into Ithaca it was easy to spot him. His short black hair, gelled just so. An ivory silk blouse. And beautiful black pants. His jacket was slung over his chair. He was drinking a glass of wine. He reached over the table to kiss me. I handed him the irises I had picked up.

"For me?"

"Of course. I wouldn't come to meet such a gorgeous woman without flowers, would I?"

He smiled and said, "Thanks, honey. So what's up? You sounded all excited on the answering machine."

I took a deep breath and said, "Hang on. Let me get a glass of wine first."

"What is it?" He smiled.

"Wait, we need a toast." We sat there making chitchat till the wine arrived. Now that I think about it he seemed a little distracted then. Kept looking away. But I was too full of my news to really notice anything else. The wine arrived and I raised my glass.

"To freedom," I said.

"From what?" he replied, clinking his glass against mine.

"It's over. We don't have to do this anymore. They aren't coming."

"What?"

"Dad came down with hepatitis."

"Oh my God, that's terrible."

"Yes, but he will be okay. But it means we don't have to play this dress-up game anymore. And you know what—I can tell them Rita and I broke up."

Then I took a deep breath and said, "And, honey, I think by the time they come next time I can tell them the truth. You don't have to go through this anymore." But Steve wasn't looking at me. He was playing with the stem of his wineglass. Then he said, "I am sorry. What were you saying?"

"That I decided I had to come out. It's not fair to make you go through this again."

"My goodness," he said wonderingly. But I saw he was struggling to tell me something.

"What's the matter?" I said.

"Oh nothing."

"Why do you keep looking like you are about to tell me something?"

"What? Oh." Steve shrugged. Then he said, "Rohit, I don't know how to say this. But I am not sure I am ready to stop taking those pills."

"What?" I spluttered. "Why?"

"Well, not right now. You know Shireen, the Iranian woman who works at our gym. She asked me if I wanted to go to Michigan Womyn's Festival with her."

"Shireen? But I thought she was a lesbian," I said.

"I know," he replied. Then he looked at his watch and said, "I am supposed to be going out to dinner with her tonight. I thought you were going to be working late."

"Dinner? With Shireen?" I stammered. "Like as in a date?"

He looked at me with almost infinite pity in his beautiful long-lashed eyes and said, "I guess you could call it that. I didn't know how to tell you this. You know that weekend when you were away at your conference and I said I was at Tim's. Well, actually, I was at Shireen's and one thing led to another and . . ." His voice trailed away.

I sat there stupidly letting it all sink in. Steve abruptly put down his wine and said, "Would you excuse me a minute? I need to go to the ladies' room." I watched him weave his way through the tables till he reached the door marked WOMEN.

"Are you ready to order, sir?" said the waiter.

I did the only manly thing I could think of to do.

"We changed our mind," I said. "Could I have the check, please?"

Bacchus in Black Lace

Thomas S. Roche

f I woke up one Sunday morning with a big fat moist-on between my splayed thighs, I would probably not be capable of doing what, at seventeen, I said I would do. I wouldn't be able to "go out and get myself fucked," because I would be too damn horny. A new toy to play with? A new part of my body? Hot damn!! I would, of course, masturbate, would take my own succulent virginity among the tangled black sheets of my lace-draped bed, tenderly popping my own cherry with a fourteen-inch Mr. Dong that has previously been reserved for particularly enthusiastic female playmates. Ooooh, baby, me and Mr. Dong go way back, and we're going to go even farther back this time. So much farther back that I warble in ecstasy and shudder in glee and caw in bliss as I find all my own brand-new secret spaces, doubtless noting each in triplicate on a clipboard I keep next to my bed—for future reference, you understand. I'm a bit of a sex-nerd, you see.

Then I would cast about my apartment aimlessly, weeping, mourning, cursing: only one day to find all the things one can do with a pussy?

Who made up these fucking rules?

But alas, rather than composing bad poetry or feeling sorry for myself, which I'll have plenty of time to do after the fact, I would, instead, make the best of this gift of twenty-four hours in girldrag. I would shave that pussy smooth, find an extra-tight pair of jeans and a GRRRRRL POWER T-shirt or maybe one that said EAT MY SNATCH. I'd lace up my knee-high Doc Marten's, shrug on my leather jacket and set out to do as many of those girl-things as I could manage in twenty-four hours. I would wander the streets growling in carnal hunger, snarling in the aches of need, cruising the Sunday boys (and it would have to be a Sunday in the Castro) as aggressively as they ever cruised me. I would drag as many of them as would go back to my place and engage in unsavory acts with their willing flesh. Would they be shocked and dismayed when they kissed my bearded face and then looked down at the rest of me to see my Ben Davis pants and glow-in-the-dark skull-and-crossbones boxers around my ankles and a pussy between my parted thighs? Would these taut-bodied gayboys want to run screaming? Hah! Tough shit, Buster, because by then I would have them all chained to my four-poster bed in unlikely and inventive positions.

And I would say to each one of them before snuggling myself back against his throbbing hard-on: "Get ready to experience firsthand the essentially problematic nature of establishing dichotomous gender as normative, fuckboy!"

Or something like that.

Manhood thus tackled, that evening I would find a women's SM play party to experience the other side of the City of Chicks. Perhaps I would be questioned at the door: "Hey, fagboy, nice try, but I know you're not a chick. Uh . . . are you?"

To which I would yank up my leather micro-miniskirt and drop my leopard-print French-cut G-string. Fondling Miss Thing, I would say pugnaciously, "Oh yeah, sister? Then what's THIS??" I might even stick my tongue out at her.

Assuming that was good enough for whoever was working the door—and in San Francisco, it probably would be (attitude can get you so very far in this town)—I would then proceed to scandalize even the furthest reaches of SF's lesbian sex-radicals with my improbable sexual antics. Who knows how the hell I could manage this, when so many of my friends have tried to scandalize and failed? But I would endeavor to find a way, and one thing eight years of San Francisco life has taught me—I would have little trouble finding partners who were eager to help me do exactly that. Because scandal is the mother of St. Francis, and sexual antics his bastard daughter. I would experience everything those creative dykes had to offer this willing cunt. And maybe I'd even suggest a few things myself.

When I woke up the next morning amid the tangled wreckage of what had once been a dungeon, I would perhaps view my old friend Dick differently—and maybe I would appreciate him just a little more, for knowing what he is not. I find that's true of so many things.

So Much to Do and So Little Time

Alfred Vitale

6:00 AM

Woke up earlier than i thought i would. so i'm grumpy. tits hurt . . . how do women get used to sleeping with them? especially when they are as big as the ones i've been given.

i'll be fixated on these tits all day . . . so get used to it!

6:15 AM

oops . . . forgot to sit down. now i have to clean piss off the seat. first lesson: you can still pee on the seat even if you no longer have a dick.

8:50AM

after remaining in some nebulous morning state, i finally
managed to leave the house over an hour later than i
thought i would. don't know what made me so late. second
lesson: time flows differently for women . . . their hormones
distort the idea of efficiency.

snuck over to the *Today Show* at rockefeller center. they had
the old cast from the TV show *Fame* dancing on some
linoleum mats while the tourists carried banners saying "we
love you leroy." proceed to camera one . . . flash tits.

9:15AM

president issues statement: "that woman who flashed her
breasts on TV earlier this morning is truly a courageous
american, i am going to award her the congressional medal
of honor."

then i'm spotted in front of the Winter Garden Theatre on
broadway and am mobbed by a crowd of adoring young boy
scouts visiting from Sheboygan . . . the TVs in the neigh-
boring electronics store are all synchronized and tuned to
the incessant replays of my tits.

9:30AM

i go to my office, nobody recognizes me. but Jorge at the
copier blows a kiss at me. fag! oh, wait. sorry, Jorge. how do
i know your name? woman's intuition. bye.

down the hall, to the left . . . a run in my stocking . . . didn't
realize that happened so fuckin' easily! mental note: gotta
get to a bathroom again . . . but i GOTTA remember to sit
down. running down the hall with a run in my stocking i

bump into my boss. so hard that he goes flying backwards and hits his head on the corner of yet another copier. blood everywhere, but nobody's around.

the poor man.

what? what am i saying? the creep! i see how he leers like an old letch at Sharon . . . i know what he thinks of Phillipa the temp and her skinny little cutesy body! hmmph! let him lay there bleeding . . . maybe next time he won't be such a pig!

9:33 AM
promptly arrested for the murder of my boss. nobody knows who i am, and i was the last to see him . . . so i get brought down into the elevator with two rookie cops (you can tell . . . they're so clean-cut and young!). they ask me for ID and i search through my purse . . . finding things i never knew i had . . . never even knew existed! what's this? excuse me? an EYELASH curler? what the hell would make you wanna use THAT? buried under blush is my driver's license. oops. officer, the man in that picture is . . . never mind, you wouldn't believe it. what? oh no . . . i didn't kill HIM . . . i mean "kill him EITHER" . . . whew. one cop recognizes me from my tits. i can see the lightbulb flashing over his head . . .

9:40 AM
after blowing one of them in the squad car (ugh!) and letting the other play with my tits, i was let go over on 10th avenue by the meat markets. i'm a mess, my hair's got split ends . . . my clothes are torn . . . my stockings still have a run. and i gotta pee again. i'll just go behind a car . . . no wait, can't do that.

10:15AM

finally, a bar that's open and will let me pee in peace!

11:05AM

okay. this is getting to be annoying. i've been offered money for sex on every block! I AM NOT A WHORE, ASSHOLE! what? is that the NEW 100-dollar bill? and is that a few more of them behind it? hmmm . . .

12:25PM

lunch at Katz's deli downtown. mmmm . . . i just love those pickles!

yeah i know . . . you're thinking, "well? did she sell her body?" nope. i still have it. but i did RENT it for a while! wink wink.

hey, it wasn't so bad! couldn't be as bad as fucking someone you despise and getting NO money for it, right? i'm sure i've been given lots of sex like that in the past . . . mercy fucks, the "will this shut you up" fucks, make-up fucks, break-up fucks. lesson three: my body is now potentially food on the hoof!

1:30PM

in soho. super gay guy sees me and pulls me over towards a fashion shoot. the photographer is a friend of his . . . who saw me flash my tits all over america . . . wait, what's that? all over the world on TV (fucking satellites). they ask me to pose in front of some pretentious café next to a shiny never-been-rode Harley. people start to gather and watch. the gay guy is yelling "oh, yess yess . . . stunning! truly stunning!"

they pay me $500 and offer me a job next week. i politely decline.

3:00PM

the still shots of my tits have now made the cover of the *New York Post* (how do they DO that so fast?) . . . i'm asked to autograph it now wherever i walk. i notice under the headlines "BREAST SHOW ON TV" that there's a picture of my dead boss and a caption: mystery woman sought in murder of known mobster. huh? no wonder he wore that big pinky ring.

3:15PM

david letterman pulls up to me in his shiny red ferrari testos-terosa and offers me a ride. of course i take it . . . i mean, who can't trust Dave? huh? we go to his studio back on 52nd street. i ask where the bathroom is.

3:33PM

Dave claps his hands and yells "aaaAAaaaAAaagh! i've got a great idea! we're gonna get you on the private jet and fly you to the white house to pick up your medal of honor . . . but you gotta flash the prez too! it'll be great television!" i grudgingly accept.

4:55PM

i'm on a private jet. first time i've ever been on one. i'm rid-ing with those two pakistani deli guys . . . can't remember their names, Akbar and Jeff? Ali and Mujabir? something like that. one of them says "blah blah blah" in their lan-guage and i know exactly what he's saying: "hey, mo-hammed, check out her tits!"

7:30PM

i'm ushered into the white house. hillary whispers to me: "baby, if you think you're gonna flash those hot tits at my husband, you'd better make sure you're gonna flash 'em at me too!!" and when she's sure nobody's looking, she flicks her tongue in my ear. meanwhile, i really have to pee. chelsea shows me where the bathroom is.

presidential seal on the toilet flusher. now THAT's power. man, he is REALLY powerful . . . so powerful and strong. so very POWERFUL . . . you know . . . having a pussy isn't all that weird . . . it's actually kind of nice. lots of layers of activity and sensitivity . . . a dick feels pretty much the same all over except for a couple of spots . . . but pussies are like one of those russian wooden dolls that when you open them up they reveal something new. examining it isn't such a big deal, right? i mean, so what? i can touch myself, right?

yes i masturbated. fuck. she was right. there IS a G spot!

8:15 PM

the president gives me far less attention than i expected . . . i'm almost embarrassed. in desperation, and afraid that hillary will continue flicking her tongue in my ear, i grab the president's cock, like so many other young women have done, and i lift my shirt right over my head and parade around the podium pulling him by his slick willie while my tits are being photographed, sketched and videotaped for the salivating press. phone numbers are tossed at me as one reporter says, "wow . . . those tits are gonna wind up in the smithsonian." just then, a man appears from behind the reporters wearing a series of explosives strapped around his body . . . a square remote control thingy in his hand. he is smiling: "i was going to blow up this capitalist den of terror, but how can i destroy something so beautiful?" he lays the bombs down on the ground carefully, and raises his hands to surrender.

he is met with a hail of bullets. meanwhile, i can't get the president's thumb out of my ass. the two pakistani guys from the letterman show are also shot dead, just to be sure.

9:00PM

gotta pee again. lesson four: vaginas eat up a lot of useful bladder space.

9:25PM

getting ready to appear on *Nightline*. i'm still a mess, but the people at ABC go crazy with my wardrobe and get me all nice and pretty . . . lovely perfume, just the right shade of lipstick. my hair looks better than it's looked in hours, and my outfit just screams "smart, sophisticated, and daring" without saying "i'm a bitch like janet reno."

10:30PM

have already debated with newt gingrich: sold him on the idea that women should be allowed to have abortions if they wish and that all men should be forced to fuck other men for the amusement of us women. already debated with Pat Robertson: got him to admit that he's trying to get *The 700 Club* hosted by Daisy Fuentes to boost its ratings. have already gotten ted koppel to take off his toupee. by the end, i had fidel castro eating out of the palm of my hand. i flashed him my tits for good measure.

the president came on afterwards and praised me again and thanked me for saving the country. he said, y'know, "you can't take the cunt out of cuntry and you, dear woman, have showed us that." he resigned, and after a brief vote in congress, it was agreed that i was to be sworn in before the stroke of midnight.

I Want to Be a Woman

Evert Eden

i want to be a woman
so I can be 20th Century Fox desirable
flaunt my nipples in robes of lavender silk
and run like a wind in the wind
my legs snapping at the eyes of men like mad turtles

I want to be a woman
so I can be cruel and capricious
play guitar with a man's feelings till I'm lip to his zip
and I pluck him by the root
like we the people pulling Lenin's statue from its pedestal
then I throw back my head and laugh
HAH HAH HAH HAH
I laugh like a flock of seagulls
diving through the brass section of a symphony orchestra

I laugh with a dry-cleaned indifference
go ahead baby
go drop your lonesome yogurt on your knees

I want to be a woman
so I can femme myself beyond fatale
grow my nails as long as soda straws
paint them the colors of electricity
watch men talk to my tits
and not to me
and think to myself
no nooky for you, silly boy

I want to be a woman
so I can have hundreds of different penises
instead of just one
aah! all the handsome brutes I'll give myself to
more freely than Catherine the Great gave herself
to her army
I'll ride them like van Gogh galloped canvas
like Madonna dryhumped the nation
we'll slurp and slither and slime for days
sweating sweet sheets of satin to a swamp
till my orgasms run into each other
like traffic at a busy intersection in Rome

I want to be a woman
so I can lecture men in bed
lick gently, I'll say, suck easy
it's a wet grape which you can never peel
easy! it's a living thing
with more nerves than you have in your brain

I want to be a woman
so I can be in love
every cell of my body a purple cowgirl
that rides the heart bareback

I want to be a woman
so I can be ugly and shy
a face like a bug
a body like a beanbag
three fucks a year (they're always drunk)
maybe a nice ugly man finds me
we have children and love them
they look like shit
we still love them

I want to be a woman
so I can be a crone
who cackles and drools and polishes her tooth
and scares little boys back into the uterus

I want to be a woman
so I can be fertile
one egg taking on millions
when the blood comes every month
I'll poke that tampon in
like a fat finger of fate
and think of children
who'll break me open like a pomegranate
to make me the grower and keeper of bubble-blooded life
the mother of dragon-storming, queen-esteem daughters
who'll rise from the ash and the dust and the dung
to trash every testicle
from Plato to Tarzan
to smash Adam's Eden
and God the Father's heaven

I want to be a woman
so I can be a womb
who senses a little heart under her heart
a kick of life that knocks inside
hi, here I am, I'm you, you're me
and buds into a smile that sucks
life from my life
smiles from my smile

I want to be a woman
so I can understand why
I'm such a goddam guy
heavymetal hardline
hangtough hotstud
you lookin' at me? fuck you!
hey bitch! lemme bang your sugarditch!
suck my rock cock!
brick dick!
meanest penis!
megashlong!
superdong!
Steely Dan!
Woody Wanggggggggggg!

I want to be a woman
so I won't have to
be
a
MAN

Womanizer

Ronald Sukenick

i was fascinated by her. She was the daughter-in-law of a painter friend who said she was a nude model and really needed money, so I agreed to give her a try. It turned out she was twenty-two years old with a perfect body and an incredibly sensual way of moving. I made her come back day after day, till I had to admit I was obsessed with her. I painted her body from every possible angle in every conceivable pose till I knew it better than my own. And then I began to imagine it was my own. I began to identify with her, think her thoughts, I couldn't stop, I must have been mad. Then one morning I woke up and I was her, I was her thinking about me. Clearly it was a hallucination but while it lasted it was real, and because I knew it wouldn't last I tried to remember everything, and with the help of a tape recorder, I was able to write it all down:

He must have been about sixty and he was like a father to me. In fact, he was referred to me by my father-in-law, who was also a painter. My father-in-law didn't think it was a good thing to use me as a nude model, but he didn't see why his friends shouldn't use me, and it wasn't the first time one did. He got some flattering feedback about me too, and it's true I have a perfect body. But right from the start there was something different about this old man, the way he looked at me, almost as if he wanted to absorb me.

But mostly I felt real comfortable with the old man. He was considerate, gave me lots of rests, and was always offering me tea. I guess he was a sort of father figure. The only thing was the dog, he had this really cute Dalmatian who would wait till I got undressed and then come and try to stick his nose in my cunt, sniffing. The old man would chuckle, saying he did that to all his models, and never bothered to call him off. I found the best way to deal with it was to allow him a good sniff after which, apparently satisfied, he'd go back and lie down in his corner.

Usually it was more relaxing to pose for a single artist than for a class. It was more demanding but I could think more, let my mind go loose. In a class I had to concentrate on not thinking. I had to concentrate on not thinking about what the students were thinking about me. Not that they weren't serious students. But there was always a moment there, when I first took off my robe, when it was clear they weren't looking at me the way they would look at a still-life arrangement—*nature morte* as they would say in French—when it was obvious that nature was very much alive, and that moment I have to admit would give me a little rush—a surge of sensuality mixed with a small rush of pride, too. Then it would be over and the students would get down to work, their lines trying to capture my lines. But there were always one or two who would look at me that way at least now and then, and that's what I had to concentrate on not thinking about—especially if they happened to be attractive.

But posing for an artist rather than a class I could think. What did I think about? Well, I'm a writer. I write stories. And I would think about stories I was going to write. One story was about how I met this guy while posing for a class during a break. I was wearing my robe and he asked me if he could see my breast again so he could try to get it right, so I said sure. I let one fall out framed by my robe, and he said it was even more beautiful up close. It was practically in his face and I could feel his breath on my nipple. I have very pronounced nipples and I'm sure he could see it go erect. Maybe that's why he asked me to have a cup of coffee afterward but I told him I never made dates while I was posing. Then, after the class he caught me in the hall and said now that you're not posing how about a cup of coffee, so I said okay. Sitting in the coffee shop with him was sexy because I knew he could imagine me under my clothes.

Another story I thought about was how I was just going to disrobe for a new class when I realized there was a guy I knew in it; he was dating a friend of mine. What to do? I couldn't very well walk out on the class but I felt embarrassed. Then he caught my eye and winked, I guess he meant to be friendly, but that made me feel even more embarrassed, though I went ahead and slipped my robe off anyway. But I was very conscious of his eyes. He was looking me up and down and he looked very serious, then he gave me this very nervy smile. I said to myself, All right, if he wants it, let's really give it to him, and I took my sexiest pose, breasts caressing the rug I was on, legs spread to show off my thighs. It had the desired effect, it wiped the smile right off his face. And then I realized I was turned on something awful.

But the only stories I could think about with this old artist were about him. Sometimes, when I was posing he would talk to me, though I think he was really talking to himself out loud. And often what he said would get incorporated into my stories, as if he had a superstrong power of suggestion. Once, out of nowhere, he remarked that a friend had told him that the visual was the most sensual of all the senses.

What about touch? I replied.

Yes, we see eye to eye, he said. Or rather, we have our fingers on the same pulse.

I was thinking, though, that while it may have been true about the same pulse, the pulse in question wasn't my usual pulse. I didn't feel like myself. I wouldn't normally have said that thing about touch because the sensual to me is something indivisible into parts, into particular senses, it's more like a warm enveloping cloud. Was the old man starting to invade my mental space? Was his command of my body starting to infiltrate my sensibility too, my actual volition?

He was still a good-looking man, despite his age, and he had the reputation when younger of being a womanizer, though that was a funny word because it always implied to me someone who turned men into women. Or who had the power to turn himself into a woman. Anyway I could sense he had the power to strongly empathize with a woman. I tried to imagine what he was thinking about me and what I sensed he was thinking about—I could feel myself foolishly blushing—was my cunt, because he was making me pose with my legs spread. He was wondering how it would feel to be inside it with his cock. How it would feel to have a cock inside it. I think he wondered whether it got wet when I posed, with someone looking at it, which it didn't—though now when I thought about him thinking about it suddenly it did. I suddenly found myself looking at my cunt with his eyes—or rather feeling it with his body, feeling it as I felt it, but for the first time. And then I really got turned on, so wet I was afraid he could hear it making those sucky-sloshy noises when I changed poses at his direction. Because my cunt is the most powerful organ in my body when it gets activated, and to feel that for the first time, the way after a certain point of excitement I blindly do what it wants, must be overwhelming, since I myself am always overwhelmed when that happens. . . . But, it occurred to me, what a wonderful thing it was to get that turned on and not have anyone know about it, even when I'm nude, to keep it a secret and stay free to dream, where a man would send a signal as subtle as a flagpole.

Then one day he asked me casually if I'd mind posing nude with my husband.

My husband doesn't pose, I told him.

With a boyfriend then? he persisted. Just kidding.

He had an art buyer in the studio, a youngish hip-looking guy who'd bought his canvases previously—he was letting him walk around the studio and look while he continued to work with me.

Take your robe off, he told me. You don't mind posing with him here, do you?

Well, what could I say, but when I disrobed the guy stopped looking at the canvases and fixated on me. He was staring hard at my cunt with a look more of curiosity than desire, almost like he was saying, What the hell goes on in there? And I know it's true; from my experience men haven't the slightest idea. It's a whole new cuntry to explore. So to speak.

I want to do an interpretation of Rodin's sculpture *The Kiss*, the old man explained, so I need you to pose with a male model. But I want you to feel good with whoever it is. Any suggestions?

The old man was always very concerned with the way I felt and I appreciated it. But at that moment I had another take—he wanted to know how I felt, and more, he wanted to feel how I felt. And all of a sudden the way I felt was invaded. I literally felt he was inside me, hijacking my senses. But there was nothing I could do about it, it wasn't something you could exactly talk about, it was too crazy. I realized then that he'd been obsessing, session after session finding excuses to have me come back and model for him. And now he was inside me, feeling what I felt, only making me feel it from his point of view, as if I were feeling it for the first time, making me grow to include him like a sperm inside an egg. So when he mentioned he wanted me to pose for the Rodin sculpture the reaction of my clitoris surprised me, though it shouldn't have because I know my clitoris is sensitive to anything having to do with sex as if it had an imagination of its own, and what it was imagining was sitting nude on the nude lap of some stud with his hand around my hip, because that's what *The Kiss* is. And suddenly I detected an alien train of thought running through my head, which went something like, You've got a cunt that can bless you with intense pleasure, why don't you start using it more? I never looked at the issue quite like that before.

I have a suggestion, said the guy who was considering buying some paintings. How about me?

What, how about you? asked the old artist.

What about me posing with her?

You? Nude?

Sure. And I'll guarantee buying the painting too.

That's an offer hard to turn down. When?

Right now.

Wait a minute, I said, don't I have anything to say about it? What I was thinking though was, he isn't bad looking. I wonder what he'd look like with no clothes on? I wonder what his cock . . . Hey wait a minute, am I actually thinking of doing this? This isn't like me. But the thought kept coming back, you've got it—use it.

I'll double your pay, said the old artist.

That's not the point, I replied.

I'll triple your pay, said the guy.

I said that wasn't the point.

What is the point? asked the guy.

I didn't answer. I didn't know what the point was because suddenly I was finding the situation sexy. At the same time I knew that some etiquette had just broken down, some unspoken compact between artist and model, and I was simply a naked woman, vulnerable, in a room with two clothed men. I should have put a stop to it right then. Ordinarily I would have. But something alien was driving me, something aggressive, acquisitive even, I wanted it, whatever was going to be dealt from the deck I wanted to play the game. I knew I was no longer myself, I felt a loss of a certain fertile passivity, a receptiveness. Instead I was possessed by a stallion's rage to plunge in while still locked in the mare's body. I wanted my tits rubbed hard, I wanted my ass squeezed roughly, I wanted to throw myself on someone's cock, impaled.

All right, I told the old artist, if you really want me to I'll do it. For you.

But I knew I was now the predator. I knew what I had and I was going to use it to the full. Have cunt will hunt.

Triple pay, though, I added. And as I said it I realized with a shock I was finally seeing myself with his eyes, acting out his desires, doing what he wanted.

I was him.

I knew he was going to use me.

I wanted to be used.

But I didn't know how. I knew the old guy had taken over my will and could make me do what he wanted. I just didn't know what he wanted or what would happen next, though I got a good clue when I saw the young guy come out from behind the screen where I undressed because he was naked and already at half-mast. I tried not to look at him but I couldn't help noticing he had a nice body, not too muscled but lithe, smooth, minimally hairy with a strong-looking butt. He had a thick, ropy cock.

The old guy draped a cloth over a stool and told him to sit down. Then he told me to sit across his lap and make myself comfortable. Well, I sat down, but making myself comfortable was another matter because however I placed my ass across his thighs there was this protuberance sticking into me. I think he was as uncomfortable as I was because he exclaimed Ow! a couple of times as I squirmed on his lap. I apologized and finally got into a position where the protuberance was comfortably positioned between the cheeks of my butt.

Now, said the old artist to the young guy, put your arm around her waist, and you, he said to me, put your arm around his neck and look up at his face. No, no, don't press your breasts against his chest, at least not both of them, I want to see one in full profile. And he put his hand on my shoulder and positioned me so that one nipple was grazing the young guy's chest while the other breast hung free, though actually in my case my breast didn't hang very much; despite its size it more or less stuck out with the bottom of it just barely creased against the rib cage. And I thought, that's the first time the old man ever touched me while I was posing.

Is posing always so much fun? said the young guy into my ear.

We're not supposed to be having fun, we're working.

Well something is working because we seem to fit together real nice, he said.

I didn't like this guy, it occurred to me, why didn't I think of that before, I mean I knew I didn't like him as soon as he opened his mouth, he was a wise guy. Also I could feel his cock getting bigger and I felt he was taking advantage of me. I twisted on his lap enough to make it hurt and was pleased to hear him mutter Oh! Shit! I wanted to keep him in his place.

Now put your lips on his, the old man instructed. And close your eyes.

I did as I was told, but without enthusiasm.

Now hold that, said the old artist, while I position your hands.

I stayed put, despite the fact that the guy was getting a little too enthusiastic with his lips, while I felt the old guy position my left hand on the guy's back. Then I felt a hand cradling my right breast and I opened my eyes to see whose it was. It was both of them, because the artist had taken the guy's hand by interlacing their fingers. Then he removed his own hand and pressed the guy's slightly into the bottom of my breast. Hold that, he directed.

I'm holding it, said the guy.

Is this in the Rodin? I asked.

I don't remember exactly, but it's a nice pose. Close your eyes.

His hand was cupping my breast from the bottom and pressing very slightly, as if weighing it. I could feel his cock growing along the crack of my ass and it made me feel uncomfortable so I wriggled slightly.

Stay still, commanded the old artist as he began to sketch.

The hard, hot feeling along the crack of my ass was actually starting to feel kind of pleasant. I started to relax and then without thinking about it squeezed the cheeks of my ass together. That was a mistake because I immediately felt a jerking sensation as if his thing were trying to get free and something wet and warm started trickling toward my cunt. The old man picked up on the dude jerking around and told him to stay still.

I can't, it's uncomfortable, he complained.

All right let me rearrange you. The old man put his hand between my thighs and moved one leg over a bit. Then he actually put his hand over my cunt and pushed me up till the stud's cock sprung free between my legs like a jack-in-the-box. It was rigid as a pole now and even when the old man pushed my thighs closed the glans protruded above them, purple and damp. The old man went back to his sketch pad but almost immediately asked me to cover that thing up.

There's no erection in the Rodin, he grumbled.

I did the best I could but I couldn't get it back under my thigh.

There was only one thing to do. I leaned way forward and let it slide into my wet cunt. The dude groaned.

That's good, exclaimed the old guy, hold it like that. Don't move.

I held still, or at least I tried to. Maybe I moved a tiny bit. Just enough to feel him more but just too little to come. I was on the verge of coming but I stayed that way a long time. Maybe it just seemed like a long time because it felt so blessedly good. His cock held its ground, moving slightly, if anything it got a little thicker, irritating my clitoris to a sensation of sustained bliss. There seemed to be some understanding between his cock and the walls of my vagina, which tightened and loosened with each slight in and out thrust, matching his movements with a reciprocal suction, but not enough to allow either of us to come. It's hard to tell how long this went on, I was moaning and he was uttering low growls. Then the old artist said we could break and we still didn't move. Finally he came over and cupped my breast, grasping my nipple with thumb and forefinger while palping the inside of my thigh. It was the feather that broke the camel's hump. I started spasming and I could feel the stud bursting and jerking inside me and it felt like I was feeling fullest vaginal orgasm for the first and I hoped not the last time.

I must have passed out. I knew I was being helped somewhere and next thing I was on my back on a drafting table tipped forward with my legs hanging off the edge and someone was still inside me. But it felt different and it was someone else, not as long but wider, it seemed, a real battering ram, and I was beyond caring who it was as I began thrusting back to the rhythm of his thrusts and I wanted it to go on and on but abruptly he came into my sopping organ and my spasm was if anything more violent than my first one and I realized with mild surprise it was the old artist but it could have been Methuselah as far as I was concerned because I could feel his orgasm as well as my own and I didn't want it to stop.

But eventually it stopped. The old man fell to the floor

with a thump and I thought it might be a heart attack but if it was it would have been worth it. But it wasn't. He was just zonked as apparently also the stud, supine on a cot, cock still big but limp, lying to one side and still oozing. I suddenly felt deserted.

Just at that moment I heard a whining sound and it was the Dalmatian nuzzling at my thighs. I couldn't help but notice it had a bright red erection hanging down out of its furry sheath, all slick and pointy at the end, and almost as wide as a man's. Without giving me a chance to think about anything the dog put its forepaws on the drafting table and inserted itself between my still spread thighs and before I knew it it had mounted me, its stiff penis slipping easily into my wet and stretched vagina, its furry sheath at the base rubbing up against my clitoris like a soft toothbrush and then it seemed to swell up inside me so tight that I couldn't have got it off me even if I'd wanted to. But I didn't want to. I couldn't believe I had a dog cock in me and I couldn't believe it felt so good. It wasn't only the cock, which felt bulbous and hot, it was also that constant massage brushing my super-erect clitoris and then I started coming and I flashed on the idea I was being forced to come by a dog and I came so hard I felt like I was turning inside out and when I came back to life the dog was still pumping into me and I came again and finally I could feel it writhing and spurting into me and I came one last time. Next thing I knew the old artist was pulling the dog out of me, chuckling like a demon, and I told him, Fuck me, goddammit, please fuck me, but he said he needed more time but it looked like the stud was ready. And he was. And he did, but this time it was quick and brutal, which was what I wanted because my clit was like a hair trigger releasing almost immediately.

I finally thought I'd had enough when the doorbell rang and in walked my father-in-law, who no doubt thought the modeling session was well over by now. The studio door wasn't locked so when he came in the old man was caress-

ing my breasts, his fly unzipped and his pants falling off and
the stud was lying naked on the floor with his cock still oozing, exhausted. Well it was a standing joke between my husband and myself that his father was letching after me,
which was why, I suspected, he would never have me pose
for him, though I would have done so had he asked. But
now as he took in the situation his inhibitions visibly
dropped as his hello smile abruptly turned into a goatish gri-
mace.

What the hell is going on here? he asked as he pulled me
off the drafting table and steered me by the elbow to the
cot. Have these sons of bitches been taking advantage of
you?

When he started undoing his belt and told me to turn
over I thought he was going to whip my butt and he actually
delivered a tentative lick or two as I wriggled trying to avoid
them, but probably when he registered my round ripe ass already pink from groping and squeezing he dropped his pants
instead and setting me on hands and knees took me from
behind simultaneously cupping my breasts. He slammed it
into me and I started coming right away, groaning and
grunting and almost screaming as he moved inside me like a
piston, and just as he shot his load into me as I came who
did I see standing in front of me probably appalled by the
look of beatitude on my face, his son my husband. He always picked me up after my modeling jobs to make sure I
didn't get into any trouble but it didn't take much imagination to figure out the situation and my husband was a quick
study.

I thought he was going to cry or kick ass and I think he
thought so too. But instead what he did was absolutely the
smartest thing he could have done in the circumstances. He
patted his father on the back, turned me over on the cot,
spread my legs, pulled down his pants and fucked my brains
out, what was left of them, he literally fucked me senseless,
because it was so good to have a familiar cock inside me I

was completely open to him as he sexually reclaimed me for himself, and when he was done with me I was a mindless zombie, helpless and filled with gratitude and I knew why I loved him.

And then he pulled up his pants and told me to get my clothes on and turning to the old artist who was the only man left in the room by then he said, Please excuse my wife's reckless behavior.

And the old man replied, Not at all. If I had a cunt with all the trimmings like she does, that's sure as hell what I'd do with it.

Notes on Contributors

PAUL AGOSTINO is the author of the textbook *Created Writing: Poetry from New Angles* (Prentice Hall), a book on writing poetry. His poetry collections include *Engagements and Disengagements* (Writers' Ink Press) and *The Tourist Heart* (Cornerstone Press). He teaches writing and literature at Suffolk Community College in suburban New York.

JONATHAN AMES is the author of two novels, *The Extra Man* and *I Pass Like Night*, both available in paperback from Washington Square Press; his comic autobiography, *What's Not to Love?: The Adventures of a Mildly Perverted Young Writer*, will be published in May 2000 by Crown. He writes the "City Slicker" column for *New York Press* and is a winner of a Guggenheim Fellowship. In addition to writing, Jonathan Ames performs frequently as a storyteller, and his one-man show *Oedipussy* debuted Off-Off-Broadway in 1999.

BRUCE BAUMAN, a lifelong New Yorker, has spent the last three years living in various parts of the United States while he finishes his novel, *Twilight of America*. He will be a UNESCO laureate at the Sanskriti Center for the Arts in New Delhi, India, in 2000. He is currently Writer in Residence at the Eighteenth Street Arts Complex in Santa Monica and teaches creative writing at UCLA Extension. His work has most recently been published in *BOMB*, *Traffic Report*, and *d'Art International*.

BRIAN BOULDREY is the author of the novel *The Genius of Desire* (Ballantine) and the editor of *Wrestling with the Angel: Faith and Religion in the Lives of Gay Men* (Riverhead) which won a Lambda Book Award, and editor of the annual Best American Gay Fiction series (Little, Brown). His fiction and essays have appeared in the past year in *TriQuarterly*, *Sewanee Review*, *Harvard Review*, *Fourteen Hills*, *modern words*, *Zyzzyva*, *The James White Review*, *Flesh and the Word*, *Best Gay Erotica 1998*, and *Gay Travels*. He is associate editor of the San Francisco *Bay Guardian*'s literary supplement and a frequent contributor to that paper.

BILL BOZZONE'S screenplays include *Full Moon in Blue Water* (starring Gene Hackman and Teri Garr) and *The Last Elephant* (starring John Lithgow and Isabella Rossellini). His stage plays, including *Breast Men* which he co-wrote with Joe DiPietro, have been performed throughout the United States, Canada, and Europe.

BILL BUEGE develops automated supervisory systems for an investment firm in St. Louis. He has published his poetry in numerous journals including *The New York Quarterly*, *Christian Century*, *Chiron Review*, and *Pot Pourri*.

JUSTIN CHIN is the author of *Bite Hard* (manic d press) and *Mongrel: Essays, Diatribes and Pranks* (St. Martin's Press).

LAWRENCE CHUA is the author of the novel *Gold by the Inch* (Grove Press) and the editor of the anthology *Collapsing New Buildings* (Kaya).

ANDREI CODRESCU is the best-selling author of *The Blood Countess* (Simon & Schuster). His most recent books are the novel *Messiah* (Simon & Schuster) and *Ay, Cuba: A Socio-Erotic Journey* (St. Martin's Press).

BERNARD COHEN is an Australian novelist, author of *Snowdome* (Allen and Unwin, Australia), *The Blindman's Hat* (Allen and Unwin), and *Tourism* (Picador, Australia). *The Blindman's Hat* won the 1996 Australian/Vogel Award.

Bernard Cohen's short stories have appeared in anthologies and literary magazines around the world. His website is http://www.hermes.net.au/bernard.

KEVIN DOWNS teaches screenwriting and film/video directing at Georgetown University in Washington, D.C. He is the author of numerous screenplays and the producer-director of several award-winning films and music videos. His fiction writing also appears in the anthology *It's Only Rock and Roll*.

EVERT EDEN is a writer/performer from New York whose play *A Very Butch Libido* was banned by the apartheid regime in his native South Africa. He has a one-person show *How To Cook A Man* playing in Germany and New York. His novel *All the People You Can Eat* will be published in 2000. He is currently working on a piece about what the world would be like if clitorises were the size of penises and penises were the size of clitorises.

EDWARD FIELD'S most recent book is *A Frieze for a Temple of Love* (Black Sparrow Press). His previous book, *Counting Myself Lucky, Selected Poems 1963–1992*, won a Lambda Book Award.

RICHARD FOERSTER is the author of three poetry collections: *Trillium* (BOA Editions), *Patterns of Descent* (Orchises Press), and *Sudden Harbor* (Orchises Press). He has received many fellowships and awards for his poetry, including the "Discovery"/*The Nation* Award, and *Poetry* magazine's Bess Hokin Prize, a 1995 fellowship from the National Endowment for the Arts, and a 1997 Individual Artist Fellowship from the Maine Arts Commission. He is the editor of the literary magazine *Chelsea* and lives in York Beach, Maine.

HUGH FOX has published seventy-one books, among them *The Gods of the Cataclysm; First Fire: Central and South American Poetry; Stairway to the Sun;* and *Shaman*. He has been published in numerous magazines including *Home Planet News, Tri-Quarterly, The Kansas Quarterly,* and *Western Humanities Review*. He is Professor of American Thought and Language at Michigan State University.

RUFUS GRISCOM is the editor in chief of *Nerve*

(www.nerve.com), an intelligent magazine about sex. He was previously, at different times, an editor at a New York publishing house, a roofer, a pizza guy, and ski instructor. He lives in New York.

BAYARD JOHNSON is author of the novel *Damned Right* (Black Ice Books) and has published short fiction in numerous magazines including *Fiction International*, *Zip Zap*, *Cups*, and *Exquisite Corpse*. He has also written the movies *Damned River*, *Second Jungle Book*, and *Tarzan and the Lost City*. He is a songwriter and the lead singer of Mother Nature's Army and has co-written and produced CDs with Russell Means and Timothy Leary. He is currently living in L.A. and working on the screen adaptation of *The Electric Kool-aid Acid Test*.

IAN KERKHOF is a South African film writer and director who lives in Cape Town and Amsterdam. He has won international awards for several of his films, including the Golden Calf award for his first feature, *Kyodai Makes the Big Time*, and Best Documentary at the European Film Salon for *Ten Monologues from the Lives of Serial Killers*.

WILLIAM LEVY'S recent books include the art monographs *Political Porno: An Illustrated Survey* and *The Night Before Charisma: The Rise and Fall of Otto Muehl*, as well as a slim volume of verse, *Billy's Holiday*. He is the author of the photoroman *The Virgin Sperm Dancer*; a novella, *Is There Sex Over Forty?*, and has broadcast his *Dr. Doo-Wop Show* on Radio 100 in Amsterdam for over a decade. Prizewinner of a 1998 Erotic Oscar (London), as writer of the year he has offered to share this award with Judge Starr.

GERALD LOCKLIN'S *Go West, Young Toad: Selected Writings* was published by Water Row Press in 1998. His novel *Down and Out* was published by Event Horizon Press in spring 1999.

MICHAEL MARTONE'S most recent book of fiction is *Seeing Eye* (Zoland Books). He lives in Alabama.

CATFISH McDARIS has been nominated five times for a Pushcart Prize and is widely published in the small press. His most recent work can be found in *Nerve Cowboy*, *The Café Re-*

view, *Chiron Review*, *xib*, *Pearl*, and *The Haight Ashbury Review*.

RICK MOODY is the author of the novels *The Ice Storm* and *Purple America* and a collection of stories, *The Ring of Brightest Angels Around Heaven*. He lives some of the time in New York City.

LANDI OLSEN is a pentapod third-gendered monster. Lance's fourteenth book, the short story collection *Sewing Shut My Eyes*, is due out in 2000 from FC2/Black Ice Books. A finalist for the 1995 Philip K. Dick Award and a 1998 Pushcart Prize winner, he teaches at the University of Idaho. Andi's computer-generated collages and co-created collage-text with Lance have been published in numerous journals, books, and magazines, including *Fiction International*, *Lettre International*, and *Curio*. Their electric avatars reside at: http://www.uidaho.edu/~lolsen.

ROBERT PETERS, well-known poet, critic, dramatist, memoirist, and actor, taught for years at the University of California, Irvine. He is currently assisting his life-mate poet and Scrabble pro Paul Trachtenberg with an enormous lexicon *Alphabet Soup* and preparing a new manuscript of poems based on celebrities past and present.

JEREMY REED, acknowledged as one of Britain's foremost poets, has been described by Kathleen Raine as "the most imaginatively gifted poet since Dylan Thomas." His poetry collections include *By The Fisheries*, *Nero*, *Red Haired Android*, and *Delirium*. His novels include *Blue Rock*, *Red Eclipse*, *Inhabiting Shadows*, *Isidore*, and *When the Whip Comes Down*. A volume of selected poems published by Penguin appeared in 1987. He lives in London, reads extensively on the subject of extraterrestrials, avoids the literary scene, and is one of the most prolific of contemporary writers. His love of rock music is expressed in his Picador biography of Lou Reed, *Waiting For the Man*. He is currently recording a CD of his work with Coil.

DOUG RICE is the author of *Blood of Mugwump: A Tiresian Tale of Incest* (Black Ice Books) and *A Good Cuntboy Is Hard to Find* (CPAOD Books). He is the coeditor of *Federman: A to X-X-X-X* (San Diego State University Press) and the editor and publisher of *Nobodaddies: A Journal of Pirated Desires*. He has been known to be a she on numerous occasions and teaches at Kent State University—Salem.

TAD RICHARDS is the author of a collection of poems, *My Night With the Language Thieves* (Ye Olde Font Shoppe Press); *Situations*, a mock-epic poem originally written and distributed as a newsletter, and from which the story of the major is taken; and *The New Country Music Encyclopedia* (Simon & Schuster).

ALEXANDRE ROCKWELL, after graduating from high school, moved to Paris to assist his grandfather Alexandre Alexieff in making animated films. He later wrote, directed, and produced a film adaptation of Georg Büchner's literary classic *Lenz*, launching a career in film. Other films include *Four Rooms*, *Somebody to Love*, and the recent *Louis and Frank*. *Rolling Stone* magazine has described Rockwell's films as "magical, touching and rich."

THOMAS S. ROCHE'S more than seventy-five published short stories and humorous essays have appeared in such anthologies as *Best Gay Erotica 1996* and *The Mammoth Book of Pulp Fiction*, as well as such magazines as *Blue Blood*, *Black Sheets*, and *Paramour*. His work has been selected for Susie Bright's *Best American Erotica* series three times. Some of his erotic short fiction is collected in his book *Dark Matter*.

SANDIP ROY grew up in Calcutta and now lives in San Francisco. His work has appeared in *Men on Men 6*, *Contours of the Heart*, *Queer View Mirror*, *Quickies*, *Q&A*, and other anthologies. He also edits *Trikone Magazine*. When bills are due he writes software.

RUDY RUCKER is a writer and mathematician. He is the author of twenty books of science fiction and popular science, as well as of several software programs. Rucker augments his writing income by teaching computer science at San Jose State University in Silicon Valley. New books by Rucker slated to appear in the near future are *Seek!* (Four Walls Eight Windows), *Saucer Wisdom* (Tor), and *Realware* (Avon). Further information and free copies of Rucker's gnarly software can be found at his home page, www.mathcs.sjsu.edu/faculty/rucker.

PAUL SKIFF is a writer, artist, and producer of cultural events who lives in New York City. His rarely published work has been received internationally in live presentations which he has been making since 1980. Involved with the resurgence of poetry's popularity, he co-produced and created the sound design for the groundbreaking spoken work recording *Nuyorican Symphony*.

RONALD SUKENICK, author of twelve books, is generally acknowledged to be one of the major postmodern innovators. His most recent novel is *Mosaic Man* (FC2) and his influential first novel, *Up*, was recently reissued via Ingram Distribution's Lightning print-on-demand program, also by FC2.

ALEXANDER THEROUX is a poet, essayist, playwright, and author of *The Primary Colors*, and *The Secondary Colors*. He has written four novels, including *Three Wogs* (1973), *An Adultery* (1987), and *Darconville's Cat* (1983), which Anthony Burgess selected as "one of the best ninety-nine novels written since 1939." He lives in Cape Cod, Massachusetts.

JOHN VANDERSLICE lives with his wife and son in Conway, Arkansas, where he teaches writing at the University of Central Arkansas. His fiction has appeared in a number of reviews, including *Kiosk*, *Wind*, and *Chiron Review*.

ALFRED VITALE, an unbearable Sicilian Manhattanite by birth, anonymous Philadelphian by choice, lives in an urban castle with his wife and cohort Betty and their daughter Sofi. Published in a variety of media and also the former editor of the infamous journal, *Rant*, Alfred spends most of his time juggling between being a thorn in the side of whatever part of culture deserves it at the moment and being a sensitive mystic-type discordian cultural terrorist. You can see his most recent satire in the only anti–"Beat worship" book there is: *Crimes of the Beats*, by the Unbearables (Autonomedia Press).

PAUL WEST is the author of nineteen novels and the recipient of many prestigious awards, including a Lannan Literary Award for fiction and the Award in Literature from the American Academy of Arts and Letters. In 1996, the government of France decorated him Chevalier of the Order of Arts and Letters.